T0195872

Other books by Lem Moyé

- *Statistical Reasoning in Medicine: The Intuitive P-Value Primer*
- *Difference Equations with Public Health Applications* (with Asha S. Kapadia)
- *Multiple Analyses in Clinical Trials: Fundamentals for Investigators*
- *Finding Your Way in Science. How to Combine Character, Compassion, and Productivity in Your Research Career*
- *Probability and Statistical Inference: Applications, Computations, and Solutions* (with Asha S. Kapadia and Wen Chan)
- *Statistical Monitoring of Clinical Trials: Fundamentals for Investigators*
- *Statistical Reasoning in Medicine: The Intuitive P-Value Primer Second Edition*
- *Face to Face with Katrina's Survivors: A First Responder's Tribute*
- *Elementary Bayesian Biostatistics*
- *Saving Grace—A Novel*
- *Weighing the Evidence: Duality, Set, and Measure Theory in Clinical Research*
- *Probability and Measure in Public Health*
- *Finding Your Way in Science: How to Combine Character, Compassion, and Productivity in Your Research Career Second Edition*
- *Catching Cold Series*
  - o *Volume 1: Breakthrough*

CatchingCold@principalevidence.com

# Catching Cold
## Vol 2 - Redemption

LEM MOYÉ

Order this book online at www.trafford.com
or email orders@trafford.com

Most Trafford titles are also available at major online book retailers.

Print information available on the last page.

ISBN: 978-1-6987-1339-7 (sc)
ISBN: 978-1-6987-1341-0 (hc)
ISBN: 978-1-6987-1340-3 (e)

Library of Congress Control Number: 2022921034

*Trafford rev. 11/11/2022*

www.trafford.com
**North America & international**
toll-free: 844-688-6899 (USA & Canada)
fax: 812 355 4082

# CONTENTS

*What would you trade yourself for?*

The world wants nothing of the bad, demanding instead the ultimate sacrifice from the good.

# MARKS ON HER MIND

" Twenty-seven million dollars?"

New thoughts from a spirit, now vibrant and prowling, compelled Meredith Doucette to action, pulling her with hungry ferocity to some unknown destination.

"This can't be right," she said.

"Yes, it is, Meredith," her chief financial officer said, standing before her tall boss, mentor, and friend. "Your annual compensation is $27,540,400.07, plus bonuses, which increase it another 40 percent."

Meredith's breath caught. The CEO of Triple S Pharmaceuticals understood that she made serious money. CEOs raked it in all the time. That was part of the expectation of the community, the American capitalism accelerant, leaving poorer America behind. She just hadn't seen it put so plainly before.

The CEO closed her eyes. This was all so much easier when she, wounded and disoriented, simply acceded to consensus.

Sure, she rose over the last fifteen years to be CEO.

*But at what cost?* she asked herself.

Fearless, but an emotional cripple. A corporate heart zombie.

And here she was, chased by an empowered spirit.

Chased by herself.

It pursued her for a year, not letting her sleep, leaving its mark on her mind.

And finally, it captured her.

Commanded her.

And this new powerful thing just didn't care about the rules.

# GET READY FOR DIFFERENT

"Take a look at this," Meredith said, handing a one-page document to Nita Laghari, her chief financial officer.

"You're the only one who's seen it."

Meredith watched Nita's hand jump to her mouth as she read it.

"Meredith, you can't." She collapsed onto the brown sofa across from the desk in the CEO's austere office.

The CEO turned away. "It's my money. Of course I can."

Meredith turned back in a moment, waiting as her CFO collected herself, then walked over to sit on the sofa next to her confused subordinate.

"Listen, what you want to do is not illegal," Nita said, adjusting her scarlet hijab. "But why send this?"

"To announce my intent."

"Why? Just take your salary and give it to your archdiocese, or distribute it across several charities."

Meredith sighed. "I have done that. People know what I do with my money. The point is to involve SSS in a positive way. By returning my salary to the company, I will invigorate our charity work, which right now is on financial life support."

Meredith leaned back on the sofa and rubbed her eyes. "I think that we will need a board of external advisers who'll direct our contributions." She shook her head, putting her hands down. "I'm afraid that our internal people don't have the right frame of mind to run this."

Nita looked at her. "What frame of mind is that?"

"A 'giving' one."

"Will you pay them?" the CFO asked, leaning back into the sofa.

Meredith's lips stiffened. "No."

"Uh-huh." Nita pursed her lips. "Meredith, you have over forty-three thousand employees working for you. They look to you for strength. For

2

direction. By sending this letter, aren't you telling them to alter tack to follow you? A 'go thou and do likewise' kind of thing?"

The CEO smiled. "Thanks for mixing the 'anchors aweigh' and 'New Testament' metaphors."

Nita laughed. "I've tried to learn some. I know you are fond of your time in the navy.

"And not to hit this too hard," Nita said, now in a softer voice, "you are by yourself, right? The death of your husband, Geoff, and your sons, has left you alone and independently wealthy."

"Nine one one's curse."

"My point is," Nita said, now leaning forward, "that you don't need your SSS salary, right?"

Meredith sat silent, her spirit helplessly watching the logical arguments detonate in her heart.

"Your employees here are not in the same position," Nita reminded her, placing a hand on Meredith's shoulder. "They have ill parents who need nursing facilities. Spouses with strokes. Children with cancer who want to go to college. All with house and car payments. They need their money, and for all you know, they already donate to charities. So what message are you sending them, 'give more'?

"And what happens," Nita added, leaning closer to her boss and friend, "to those who don't donate? This is a paranoid culture. Are you out to get them?"

"Nita," Meredith said, looking at her, "this letter does not transmit that."

"It's not what it transmits," the CFO said, softening her voice. "It's the message the reader receives."

Meredith stirred on the sofa. "I think it's fair to say that all of our employees are well compensated and therefore can deal with the concerns and difficulties they have with some financial discipline."

Nita shook her head. "That sounds like a stiff-necked press release, but OK." She leaned forward again. "We're dancing around the real point, aren't we? What you really want to do is to change people's hearts."

Meredith's voice rose. "I want to change the selfish culture here. Show our people a different way."

"Same thing. Look, you have a powerful moral compass. It wasn't always so obvious, but clearly you are in touch with your convictions now. In fact, you bristle when someone pushes against it these days, don't you?"

"Yes."

"You get defiant," Nita said, sitting up. "I get that. Well, might not your employees do the same thing? Who's to say your convictions best theirs? Are you omniscient now as well? They do different things with their money. Are they criminals because they look at life differently? They're not unethical. Make your own decision about your own money, Meredith, but leave them out of this."

The CEO stood, walked to her desk, then turned around, sighing.

"As always, Nita, your points are dead-on, and your logic is"—she put her hands up—"unassailable. Jan," she called into the intercom, "can you come in here please?"

The administrative assistant appeared at once. "Yes, Ms. Doucette?"

The CEO held out her hand with the note. "Please transmit this letter to all employees at once."

After Jan took the letter and left, Meredith walked over to her CFO, who she saw was sitting perfectly still, staring straight ahead.

"You are my best friend here, and I treasure your advice. But, Nita . . ."

The CFO looked up.

"Get ready for different."

# STEEL TO THE END

The clang of the leg irons ground guilt's sharp stones deep into Cassie's heart.

Yet the ex–vice president legal of SSS Pharmaceuticals held her head level, eyes straight ahead.

No blinking.

Barely breathing.

Statuesque and steel to the end.

The courtroom was identical to the hundreds of ones the tall woman with black eyes had inhabited before. Light streaming through the tall windows illuminated the floating dust where the defendant attorney sat.

*Please, God, just end this verdict day. To think—*

"All rise," barked the bailiff.

The judge entered as Cassie struggled to stand, her breath now ragged.

*Months ago, in the time of light and sweet life—there was no thought of life behind bars.*

*But now.*

For months, she'd inhabited the same small cell.

Same small bed.

Same filthy leering cellmate.

Same clogged toilet.

*Again and again and AGAIN.*

And there was likely more of that coming.

"Can we have the jury please?" the judge asked.

Time's ticks slowed as she studied each of the jurors like she had done each morning and afternoon throughout the monthlong trial.

But today was different.

Before, they came in laughing, talking, easy with themselves and each other.

Today, the jurors were mum.

Silent, stiff, moving statues.

Cassie at once broke out in a sweat, the leg chains a thousand pounds heavier. She wanted to cry ou—

"Let the record reflect that we have now been rejoined by all the members of our jury panel and our alternates," the judged intoned. "You may be seated." He motioned to the large audience before him. "Ms. Calthrone, do you have the envelope with the jury forms?"

"Yes," the plump brown sixtyish clerk said on cue. Cassie watched her lift the manila envelope for the judge to see.

"Would you please give those to Deputy McDaniel, and would you, Deputy, please return them to juror no. 1?"

The sweat rolled down Cassie's back. In just a few brief moments, her fate would be known to her.

And the world.

The deputy walked over to Ms. Calthrone who sat to the right of the judge. Cassie rocked a little, as the deputy took the forms from Ms. Calthrone and then walked over in front of the judge to the jury box on Cassie's left.

*This is taking forever.* Cassie bit her lip. *My life's being treated like it's a worthless thing,*

"Madam Foreperson, would you please open the envelope and check the condition of those juror forms."

*What?* Cassie's right knee began bouncing as she watched the young African American woman seated in the front of the jury carefully open the envelope. Extracting all twelve ballots, she inspected each page one at a time.

Cassie, now sweating, thought the plump juror was going to eat them.

"Are they in order?"

*Get on with it.*

"Yes, Your Honor."

*Just read the—*

"Have you signed and dated those verdict forms?"

*Damn.*

"Yes, Your Honor."

*Verdict.*

"Thank you very much. Please hand them back to Deputy McDaniel."

*This is intolerable.* A quick glance to the right revealed that her attorney was focused on the ballots, a look of solemn wisdom on his face.

Deputy McDaniel walked back to the judge, who took them and—

*What now?*

—inspected them himself, one at a time—

*I can't take this.*

—then closed the envelope and gave it to Ms. Calthrone.

"All right, Ms. Calthrone."

Her head pounded. *I'm going to scream.*

She watched as the judge turned to face her, Cassie's heartbeats falling on top of each other in a runaway fear cadence.

"Ms. Rhodes, would you please stand and face the jury."

Her counsel rose. Cassie, at once nauseous, stayed seated, leaning onto the left chair armrest. She coughed, holding back the bile load that ejected up into the back of her mouth. *Is this how the end of life feels?*

Cassie took a partial breath and, gripping the hand of the counsel, leaned on the cold wooden table to stand.

The judge looked up from her to the courtroom. "I would caution the audience, during the course of the reading of this verdict, to remain calm."

Vomit suddenly filled her mouth. Using what remained of her self-control, she swallowed it. She slumped but regained her unsteady bearing.

"All right, Ms. Calthrone?"

Each heartbeat was now a hammer blow pounding her chest as if it wanted to break out.

"Superior Court of Indiana, County of Marion. In the matter of the People of the State of Indiana vs. Cassandra Rhodes. Case number ZQ097121. We—"

*It's all over. Doomed.*

"—the jury in the above-entitled action find the defendant Cassandra Rhodes not guilty of the murder of Cristen—"

Cassie collapsed back in the chair. *Not guilty, not guilty. Jesus, Lord.* Suddenly she weighed nothing. She sat down on her own stool that coated the seat of her pants.

*Not guilty, not guilty, not guilty, not guilty . . .*

Muscles all relaxed, her porous skin completely was open to the lightest sweet-smelling air that entered and raced through her.

She was clean. She was free.

The chains were gone. Ruined clothes replaced.

Suddenly, CEO Meredith Doucette was with her.

Her SSS legal team was with her.

Breanna was with her.

The judge was gaveling. Such noise turned into fingernails on chalkboard. Louder and louder.

Gunshot.

Screaming throughout the room.

Cassie looked down.

Fresh brain on her blouse.

All over her clothes.

In her mouth.

The lawyer defendant screamed herself awake from the dream.

# THE WHAT AND WHEN OF THINGS

Cassie awoke from the nightmare in the small apartment drenched in sweat, her nightgown clinging like it owned her. The attorney's breaths came in huge gasps, and she flopped onto her stomach, hoping to stop the quaking.

Two months after Cristen's suicide, and no answer.

She'd not killed herself because of Cassie. Cassie knew that she hadn't even killed herself because of Jasper.

*That probably disappointed him*, she thought. Such an evil man.

She shivered in the dark room.

No, the Sanders woman killed herself because her department was being gutted, yet Cassie felt responsible for the death.

It didn't take a Froid to interpret these nightmare horrors.

She shuddered, tired after eleven hours of anguished restless sleep, all appetite banished.

*And what of Breanna?*

She swung her legs around, letting them touch the cold floor. Then a stagger to the toilet.

Vomited.

Cassie stood up, looking in the mirror, restless eyes seeing not herself, but reaching into the past.

*The what and when of things but not the why.*

Then to the shower.

Letting the water warm up, she screwed her eyes shut, refusing to relive both the night's dream and the horror of that day in March.

*But what of Breanna?* the voice persisted.

It had been two months since she'd seen Breanna.

She knew she needed Cassie, and Cassie was AWOL.

Cassie exhaled pressing the palm of her right hand hard against her chest.

She needed Breanna too.

That thought broke through to her like water tearing through a confining dam, and the attorney began to weep.

Cassie stomped her foot.

*Today is not the day for this.*

This was the day the pain ended.

She commanded it.

So it is written and so it is done.

The battle plan was laid out.

First things first. Reestablish contact.

After all, her reputation as a trial litigator was ironclad.

Heads turned and breaths held when she strode into a courtroom. The warrior lawyer.

Resources plus will are victory.

And there was no better place to start then with Meredith Doucette, her boss and whose protection Cassie knew she had shunned.

# HANGING A CAREER

"Have any peyote?"

"What?" Rayiko said, one foot in, the other out of his red Jeep Cherokee, twisting to face Jon as he was getting out. "You know, I don't do drugs. In fact, I also know that you don't either. What are you talking about?"

"Something I once heard that Billy the Kid did," Jon, CEO of CiliCold said to his program director, shutting the Jeep's door behind him. He stepped out onto the wide unmowed pasture, white sweater over faded blue jeans.

"When he needed to pull certainty from uncertainty, he did peyote."

"Well," she said, hoisting herself up onto the warm hood of the car, black slacks sliding all over the hood. "Your ideas are weird enough without drugs."

He laughed as he watched Rayiko in her gray turtleneck look around at the new green leaves on the hundreds of trees that surrounded them.

"So nice out here," she said, turning all the way around on the hood. "And no insects yet."

Jon studied the trees as they gently swayed in the fresh clean breeze that kept it cool but not cold. "The bugs haven't figured out that it's warm enough to wreak havoc on us."

"Perfect Indiana weather," she said.

The CEO watched her stretch out on the car. The oblique rays of the afternoon sun illuminated Rayiko's lithe figure. "Not as perfect as you, Rayiko. Even on this perfect day, nature is in awe of you. You ever been out here before?"

"Never," she said, shaking her head. "It's gorgeous. Where are we?"

He playfully scowled. "That's a military secret."

She sat up on her elbows and looked at him, black hair falling away from her face and down her back.

Jon swallowed. "We're on Connor Drive, way out on old State Road 25. Maybe thirty miles from West Lafayette."

"And why did you bring your program director all the way out here, Jon?"

"I come out here whenever I have to think things through. Was out here once or twice in February when we were struggling to get the partial antibody idea to work. Freezing then. This place straightens me out whenever I get turned around."

"And I'm here because?"

"You have the same effect on me, and I could use your help today."

He opened his mouth to ask if Richard minded her being out here with him, but stopped. If her husband expressed any concern, she simply would have refused the trip to this park. He sensed growing trouble at her home where Richard's ambition and rapid rise in the data mining field was becoming an issue.

*The storm that you knew was coming approaches*, he thought, *and you can only watch from afar.*

Leaning against the front of his car, elbows on the hood behind him, looking ahead, he stopped tempting himself with her, letting his head clear. He needed his program director's help today.

"What's on your mind?" she asked from just behind him on the hood to his right.

"Everything, and all at once." He paused then turned to look back at her. "I don't know where to take CiliCold."

"We're moving?" she said. He felt the hood pop down then up as she slid forward.

"Aren't we? We've pretty much tapped out in West Lafayette. Landlord's on to us with our animal experiments and water use. Plus, I don't know what we've done to piss off Triple S, but they've been doggin' CiliCold unmercifully."

"Of course they have, Jon. They want your idea."

"Well, there may be a better one."

"What?" She was standing straight now, looking up at him.

Jon moved his head left then right in tiny figure eights, eyes searching to make out an invisible path. "The partial antibody project of ours was a fine theoretical first step." He took a deep breath. "Luiz and Dale broke the barrier by getting the immune cells to make only part of the antibody, allowing the extracellular fluid to make the rest, but it was—"

"Incomplete."

He turned to face her, smiling again. "How do you get to complete my sentences?"

She nudged him. "Go on."

Suddenly, his eyes narrowed. "We can . . . I can . . . do better."

"Like what?"

He exhaled. "Can't see it yet, but SSS needs to be thrown off our scent."

"To what?"

"Not 'to what,'" he said, looking directly at her, letting himself stroke her hair. "To where."

"Jon—"

He smiled at her. "Just playing with some ideas."

"Which is what you always do," she said, now up again on the hood on her back, looking at the cotton ball clouds in the blue sky.

He watched her lying there, so small, so delicate, her hair down to midback. He ached at the thought that Richard, the database corporate climber, was ignoring her.

"If we leave the state," she said, turning toward him, "where could we go?"

"Dunno yet, but I'd like to take as much of our team as we can. We've all had enough of the cold Midwest so that cuts the north out. But"—he shook his head—"it's not just a question of getting away. We need to go underground. Get some breathing room from SSS."

"Who would agree to go with us?" Jon sighed. "Breanna?"

"I don't know, Jon. Our accountant's been, well, untethered since March."

"My fault?" Jon pushed off the car. "I thought I was clear with her that she wasn't to blame for the back-channel communication to—who was that lawyer again?" He snapped his fingers. "Catherine."

"Cassie Rhodes. No, I think Breanna's OK with you, but I hear things. Can't make any sense out of any of it. There was a suicide at SSS. In some way, Cassie was caught up in it. Apparently, some real psychological wreckage."

"You think she and Breanna are an item?"

Rayiko shook her head.

Jon looked down, quiet for a moment. Then he said, "Let's put Breanna in the 'maybe' column. WB's out though."

"Yep."

He gaped at her. Wild Bill had sworn Jon to secrecy just yesterday about him and Emma. Yet Rayiko knew. *Oh well.*

"They're moving back to Monetta, South Carolina. Wedding will be here in about three weeks," he said.

"Did you ever meet her?"

Jon laughed, nodding. "Crazy love. Couldn't keep their hands off each other in the car last winter."

"So maybe we have an accountant but—"

"Right. Breanna."

"We are down a regulator. How about our biology guys?"

"I think Luiz will be open to a move," Jon said. "Dale?"

They were both quiet for a minute.

"Was yesterday's fight the last one?" Rayiko asked, looking down at the hood.

"Yeah. He's had it with me." Jon picked up a small rock and threw it into the wide green pasture in front of them. "Dale's a practical guy with no imagination. And I—"

"You're all imagination." He felt her hand brush across his low back. "Do you miss Robbie, Jon?"

Jon closed his eyes, his head now full of his admin assistant of earlier this year, now in Texas. Who both needed him and who grew beyond him. He licked his lips. "You know I do. Not every day, but yes, I do think of her."

"She needed you. More than anyone. I never told you this, but I thought you handled her leaving well."

"Barely," he said. "I've never known a woman so open. So vulnerable. Well"—he cleared his throat—"she's finally got a family. In Texas of all places. I think her life is now stuffed full of the things she loves."

"So if we move, we will be hiring some folks." Rayiko jumped off the car.

"Yep. Any sense where we stand with money?"

"$410,000 in the bank after June payroll and bills."

"Well, that's enough for an escape."

"And to the next miracle, eh?"

He shrugged his shoulders, then remembering, took a deep breath. With a thick tongue, he said, "But . . . but . . ." He looked down at her. "What about my program director?"

He watched her flip the switch into practical mode. "Richard is angling for a position in the west. Riverside? Somewhere near LA?" She shook her head. "I'm not sure. He's out there now. Plus, Gary's not yet in preschool. Of course, he'll love a move."

"And your brother is in California as well. How is he doing?"

"In another drug program. My parents hope, but . . ." She shook her head. "Well, every day is new."

"And what about you? Will you hang your career on an uncertain future?"

He watched her look up at him, brushing hair from her unreadable face.

"You are my iceberg, you know," he said with a smile, pointing at her. She cocked her head. "Cold?"

"No. Hidden."

They were in each other's arms in an instant.

Her face turned up to him, and he covered her mouth with his own. The softest of skin on him, in him. She yielded to his urgency, kissing back, letting him chase her tongue until she surrendered it to him.

Connected. He rejoiced, heart wild and out of control.

When they separated, he saw that her eyes were wet.

"I'll let you know," was all she said. Then she added, "We'd better head back."

She dried her eyes as she got back in the truck for the quiet half-hour drive under the benevolent Hoosier sun to West Lafayette.

At her house, he let her get out without saying a word. Then as she put her hand on the car door to close it, she turned around and said, "Pick a good place."

"Already have."

She smiled. "I know."

Then she was gone.

# REGIME CHANGE

"Jasper. Enough of your nonsense. Open the damn door."

Claude Stennis put his ear to the two-inch-thick door of the (acting) VP legal's office.

*Was that metal that was moving on the door's other side?* he thought.

The tall director of infectious diseases for SSS Pharmaceuticals pulled his head back to check the office number again: 29-2003.

*Of course, it was the right room.* The senior scientist had been tramping up here to "Officer Country," the top floors of the Sovereign building of Dover, Maryland, for weeks now.

Planning with Jasper for the CEO's replacement.

With prejudice.

Time was critical now. Half of 2016 was almost gone, and Stennis didn't see progress in getting rid of the chief operating officer. All those complicit were at risk, each planning meeting providing a new opening for exposure.

Every time the door opened, the guillotine could fall.

And now Jasper, de facto head of legal, de jure head of the coup, was locked behind his own office door.

*Avoiding me?*

The director savagely kicked the door, making the wienies across the narrow corridor jump.

Nothing.

"Hey, kid," Stennis called out to the security guard who had just stepped from the elevator. "I think we need to break into 2003."

"Why is that?" the burly black guard asked, now hurrying down the corridor.

"I have reason to believe that there may be an injury in there."

The director watched the guard put his ear to the door. "There's noise in there, all right." Stennis watched the guard whisper something into his shoulder mike then took out his universal keycard and swiped.

Nothing.

Again.

Again.

"What the hell," the director said, slapping his wrinkled right hand against his thin thigh. "Can't you call somebody with the right car—"

Green light.

Door opened.

The guard walked in first. Hand on his baton. Two steps, then stopped.

"What the—"

Stennis pushed past him into Jasper's spacious office.

Papers were in one big heap on the floor to the left side of the massive brown desk, itself a debris field of scatted yellow pads.

On the floor, behind the desk, was Jasper, still in the seat of the wheelchair that had itself fallen onto its side.

"Somebody get me up," Stennis heard Jasper whisper.

Stennis turned to the guard. "I can take care of this, Officer. I don't think we need you now."

Stennis watched the guard stare down at Jasper. "No ambulance call?"

Stennis chose to be more revealing than he needed to be in order to lose the guard. "Happens three times a month. Thanks for the offer, but I'm a physician and have helped him before. I'll be sure to mention your help to your supervisor. May I also ask you to please close the door on the way out?"

"As you say." The burly guard nodded then turned and walked out, hand still on his baton, talking into his shoulder.

When Stennis saw the that door was closed, he turned back to the attorney.

Jasper was starting to gasp for breath now. The director realized that in his twisted, awkward position, Jasper's chest wall fat had shifted, adding a burden to his already overworked lungs, making it difficult for them to move air.

Stennis stepped back, hands on his hips, watching the man struggle to breathe.

*A wounded animal. Pathetic.*

The room was now full of the attorney's gasps. To the director, Jasper resembled a fat goldfish thrown from its bowl onto the floor, its orange mouth stuck in an oval as it tried to move absent water through its empty gills.

The attorney was beyond words now, choking on his saliva, desperate for air.

Stennis found a chair as Jasper's neck muscles began to contract spasmodically, the attorney involuntarily trying to recruit additional muscles to help his flagging breathing efforts.

*How must it feel?* Stennis asked himself. This fat man on the floor, who makes a living ripping the guts out of witnesses and opponents, now approached death himself.

*Well,* the director thought, leaning forward to watch the attorney's sweat drip-drip-drip onto the lush carpet, *the hell with you.*

*Insulting my department.*

*Making fun of my family.*

Stennis knew that the attorney's nervous system, recognizing the threat to life, was kicking catecholamines and powerful stimulants into his system. His heart must be racing wildly, Stennis thought, as liver and gland pushed sugar and stimulants to his respiratory muscles, coaxing them to just please, please move air.

The department head knew that in just a few moments, the fat man's bowels would break loose. *Ugh, what a mess that would be.*

Still, he watched the death show, letting the fight continue, relishing the power of life and death.

Then with a sigh, the director bent over and, with a deep groan, righted the Jasper-wheelchair combination.

•

After five minutes, Jasper had left most of his gasping heaves behind him. Stennis noted with a twisted smile that the attorney was soaked in stinking sweat.

"I almost died," the attorney sputtered. "And you, you son of a bitch, you just watched it. I ought to bring you up on—"

"Stop whining, Jasper," Stennis said, sneering at the acting head attorney. "You didn't die. In fact, if I hadn't come by your office, you definitely would have." He continued, leaning into Jasper's ugly, wet face. "By inhaling your own nasty vomit."

He stared at the fat powerful lawyer then leaned back, unbuttoning the top button of his own wrinkled blue shirt. "I came up here to see why that damn Meredith is still running this company. You were supposed to drive her out by now."

"She and her board friends are not making it easy," Jasper said. Stennis saw that the attorney still moved air in ragged breaths.

"So what?" the infectious disease director said, tapping a stiff finger against the desktop. "You own half of the board of directors. The other half fears you." The department chief shook his head. "Good thing they weren't here today."

"I'll have SSS in my pocket in short order." Jasper coughed.

"Really?" Stennis said, standing then walking around the desk. "With the exception of the suicide, the Tanner absorption went well. We are integrating their products. That's growing the company, and that only helps Meredith's position." Turning his back to Jasper, he studied the diplomas and certificates nailed to the wall.

"Doucette's a Girl Scout," Jasper said.

"Yeah, sure she is. One who's kicking your fat ass."

The director whirled. "You need to control this company, and it just is not happening fast enough!" he yelled, spittle flying out of his mouth with each word.

"CiliCold is the key," Jasper said, sitting up while waving his hand at the invective. "They have the immunology breakthrough of the century. Meredith's not interested for some jackass reason. But when we take it over, the board, the shareholders, and the banks will stampede over her to invest in it. With me as her replacement. And," the attorney said, "you were supposed to get the status of CiliCold's advance on this . . . soon to be our . . . project."

Stennis raised his eyebrows. "I'm supposed t—"

"Don't dare equivocate," Giles said, slamming his huge arm on the empty part of his desk.

Stennis jumped.

"Cassie's stupidity got in her way!" Jasper shouted. "You accepted her assignment after she tanked. What are you telling me—that you have doubts about your ability now?"

"It's just not out there."

"What does not mean?" Jasper waved his right hand in the air. "They're not writing about their progress? Not bragging about it on the lecture circuit?

"I have people scanning all the virology and immunology journals. Nothing, and it's already May," he finished, putting his dirty shoes on the desk, then sitting up as Jasper knocked them off.

"Also looking at all the late breaking schedules for major immunology meetings."

"Whatever the fuck. We need it, Stennis. Find out how far along they are."

"Well, even if I learn what is it, how will you take it from them?" Stennis stared hard at the attorney.

"That's my business and my job. Get your damn head out of your petri dishes and Dora's short skirts and get me the answer."

Stennis set his jaw at the mention of his admin assistant. *This legal clod couldn't fit his fat head between a cow's legs, much less those of a woman.*

"What's the word on your boss?" Stennis asked. He sighed. "Everyone knows that she supports Meredith."

"Last I heard, Cassie's not so good. A couple of jagged wounds have left some obvious scars. Plus, she's mental."

"Well, I hear that she's coming in tomorrow. Meeting with the sister."

Jasper sat up. "With Meredith?"

"Yeah. It's on the books. That means—"

"I know what that means," Jasper said, sweeping some of the legal pads off his desk. "Meredith put Rhodes over me, but now she's out and I'm in charge of legal again. If she's coming back in, then I should know. In fact, I should be there."

Stennis stared at the sloppy desk. "Seems to me that you have a problem with Meredith—communications."

"That should make you happy," Giles said.

Stennis heard him fart.

"Just get me CiliCold's technology," the attorney said.

"I heard it was Cassie's idea to acquire it. Not yours."

Stennis returned Giles's hard stare.

"Just get what I need and stay out of my way, Stennis."

The infectious disease chief shifted in his chair, a forgotten obligation welling up. "Need to see Edgar today."

"Ah yes," Jasper said. "The secessionist. You are as lousy a father as you are a doctor."

The scientist stood, eyes full of the hardness of hate, and turned to the door. "I saved your damn life today."

"Now just get me the location information I need."

The infectious disease chief walked out.

*Jasper might not be so lucky next time*, Stennis thought, closing the door. Putting Jasper and Edgar behind him now, he let his thoughts drift to Dora and what outfit she might be wearing.

# A LIFE YOU DON'T HATE

Meredith stared over her desk across the large austere office, searching for the doubt in her heart.

Nowhere to be found.

She had the words she needed when her protégé entered the office. *Now, there is only strength and po—*

"Ms. Doucette," Jan, her administrative assistant, said, stepping just inside the office door. "Ms. Rhodes is here."

To Meredith, it seemed as though Cassie strode the fifteen feet to her desk in a second. Her appearance took Meredith's breath away.

The CEO had expected a brittle projection of false calm, balance, and competence.

The person standing above her looked like she had just been nominated for governor.

Dark brown hair neatly trimmed to her collar. Perfect makeup, the minimum her exquisite face required. The scar on her chin, still pink, would likely always be there, but the cheek lesion was barely noticeable and the forehead cut had vanished.

Meredith watched as Cassie, beaming down at the CEO just a few feet away, extended her right hand, the attorney's face adorned with a smile that would raise sea levels.

"Good morning, Ms. Doucette. I am so pleased to have an opportunity to meet with you again."

Ignoring her hand, the CEO stood and faced the taller attorney, taking two steps toward her, holding her arms out.

Cassie fell into them.

They both cried, holding each other close, sharing the anguish of the past sixty painful days.

The senseless disobedience.

The senseless annihilation of life.

These could be ignored no longer.

Meredith pulled away at the scratch of her intercom.

"Ms. Doucette, Mr. Giles is demanding to join your meeting with Ms. Rhodes. He is insistent that—"

"Under no circumstances is he or anyone else to be permitted to enter my office until I say otherwise," the CEO said, voice tight and clear.

She motioned Cassie over to the sofa in the far corner of the office where the sunlight streamed bright and warm this morning.

"In fact," Meredith added, leaning low over the beige intercom, "please post a security guard at my office door. Anyone who does not follow my instructions is to be arrested."

After a pause. "As you wish, Ms. Doucette."

Meredith joined Cassie on the couch. *She looks so good. How do I begin?*

"Well," Cassie said, turning to look at the CEO with a smile. "Nice to know that you and Jasper have patched things up since I've been gone."

They both fell out laughing, Meredith holding her right side the laughter hurt so much. "Part of me hopes he shows up. I'd love to see the mug shot."

Softer laughter, then moments in silence.

"He's not doing well," the CEO said.

"Health?"

"In a wheelchair now. Plus the usual—"

"Hates?"

She paused. Then in a low voice, "Appetites."

"For you? Your position?"

"For all of it."

"But you're the most delicious meat on his plate, Ms. Doucette, right?" The CEO heard her sigh. "Jasper wants you exited from SSS. Always has."

Meredith dismissed him with a wave. "Cassie, we have so much ground to cover. But let me first ask you if you have any questions for me?"

Cassie, all vestiges of a smile now gone, asked, "Does Jasper have my job?"

The CEO pursed her lips, nodding while hoping to hide the anxiety that seized her. "Yes. After that young woman's suicide and your disappearance, I was compelled to make him senior VP legal."

Ms. Doucette noticed the new rapid blinking of Cassie's eyes. "Is that permanent?"

Meredith shook her head. "I hope not. Listen, to ask you how you are is too complicated. Your health records are your own business, but—"

"I am ready to work with you again, Meredith," Cassie said, leaning forward on the sofa. "To defend you."

Ms. Doucette held her hand out.

"Cassie, I have studied the attendees, police, and medic reports." She almost mentioned that she had also read Jasper's repugnant summary, but let that go.

"Fagen said that it was the hottest meeting he'd ever attended," the CEO continued. "You, Jasper, and the safety team traded insults. The result was that Cristen Sanders used a gun to blow the top of her head off, with most of the skull and brains of that young woman landing on your face and chest."

Cassie crossed her ankles, dropping her head.

"You screamed yourself into a stupor that lasted three days. When finally released from the hospital, you disappeared for weeks. You never showed up for anything. For debriefing, for counseling, for your things. Neither I nor anyone else heard from you until three days ago.

"So no, Cassie," Meredith said, leaning back on the couch. "I do not believe you are OK. A normal person commonly takes months to recover from watching a suicide. It inhabits them. And you were much more physically involved than the usual. Should I tell how long it took you to pick all the brain matter from your hair?"

The attorney leaned forward over her knees, shaking her head. "OK, OK. That was horrendous. I know. I was there. But why won't you accept that I am better?"

Meredith leaned closer.

"Look at me, Cassie."

The CEO watched the attorney turn to face her, blinking rapidly, mouth set.

"Because you never let yourself hurt. You keep it in. Maybe you gorge on it. I don't know. This ability of yours to absorb pain is not a strength. It's a weakness. Its why you exploded at the suicide meeting."

Meredith took both of Cassie's hands in hers. Her own pulse was pounding. She was derailing her own prodigy's career, and she knew it. "I don't think you started to feel pain until you walked into this office just a

CATCHING COLD VOL 2 - REDEMPTION

few minutes ago. And until you hurt, you can never heal. Even worse, you are eroding your inner strength. Little supports you anymore.

"And, Cassie"—she let go of her hands—"you ignored my instructions."

"Meredith, I—"

The CEO raised her hand. "Perhaps I did not make myself clear that morning. Before the final meeting where that lady committed suicide, I gave you specific instructions that you just set aside. From what I have heard and read, you went on the attack."

"They came after Jasper and I. The safety department wanted a fig—"

"Which is precisely why I wanted you to back off and listen," the CEO said, enunciating each syllable, eyes closed. "But rather than follow my specific directive, you insulted those people when they were most vulnerable.

"And," Meredith said, "look at the result. Look at you." The CEO waved her hand up and down then again. "So elegantly put together, yet falling to pieces."

"When I come back, I can . . . I can try counseling."

Meredith's stomach revolted at the suggestion of SSS counseling. Their tact was "treat 'em and street 'em."

*No.*

"I'm going to need your resignation, Cassie."

"What?" Cassie leaped up, staring at the CEO, mouth open in astonishment. "Ms. Doucette, I want to protect you from Jasper."

"I am not asking for your resignation because of disloyalty or even your disobedience in March," Meredith said, motioning with her hands for Cassie to sit.

"There is a serious fight that's coming for control of SSS," the CEO continued. "Jasper is leading it. It may start over CiliCold or some other flashpoint. But like tomorrow's sunrise, it's on the way and—"

"I know CiliCold. You know that I do."

"Sure, I could use your help. It's going to be hard and bloody. Bu—"

"Then you will need friends like me." The attorney was weeping now. "Please, Meredith."

"Cassie. If you stay, you will be sucked into the corporate sickness that has already chewed up your heart." Meredith shook her head. "I can live without leading SSS. I cannot live with finishing your destruction, and that is exactly what will happen."

The CEO stood. "This is not your fight. Your fight is for yourself. And you are nowhere near winning it. You need time. Time to look at facts. Time to ask good questions. Time to think. You need to be expelled from this place to have a chance for a life that you don't hate."

Cassie cried in a room thick with emotion. Quiet. Then . . .

"What will I do?"

"Whatever you need to."

The attorney picked her head up. "Is there anything else?"

"We will likely not see each other again, Cassie. I'd like your letter tomorrow."

•

Walking out, Cassie had no thoughts. She was disconnected, stunned, the rug pulled out from under her. Meredith wanted to help her by taking her career but—

Cassie hit Jasper's wheelchair with her left knee.

"Jasper. I didn't see you."

"What was the meeting about?"

With no words, Cassie just shook her head and began to walk off.

"Hey, Rhodes," she heard him call out. "I have the suicide video feed if you want to relive the experience. We all got a kick out of it. Including Meredith."

# INNER LIGHT

"Meredith. I didn't expect to see you."

"Do you have a few minutes for me, Nita?" the CEO said, two hours after drying her eyes from the meeting with Cassie.

Meredith showed just her head through the chief financial officer's open door. "I'll keep it brief." She paused then added, "I'm actually glad that you'll see me. I know you are disappointed about the letter."

She walked in to greet the CFO who had stood up from her half-eaten lunch to walk over. The jacket of Nita's jet-black pants suit was open.

"I am your employee. I am also your friend. I'm pleased we had the discussion."

"I'm disturbing you," Meredith said, smiling. "Your in-office lunches are legend here."

True to form, Nita gave nothing away, Meredith saw. But one thing she could not hide. The CEO broke out in a wide smile.

"Congratulations, Nita. When's the date?"

"January 23, 2017."

For the first time in five years, Meredith saw her CFO smile broadly.

"Boy or girl?" the CEO said, placing a hand on Nita's left shoulder.

"Girl."

"Well, let's not let business ruin this good day for you. I just stopped in for a refresher before our call in twenty. That is, if you have the time."

"Nope."

Meredith stopped midway down to the seat. "Oh. Well, maybe I can s—"

The CEO saw Nita throw her head back and laugh. "Just a tease, Meredith. Of course, I have time for you."

*Nita is really something today. Just as well,* Meredith thought, remembering the concerns for her CFO's multiple miscarriages and worsening depressions.

Smiling, Meredith walked to the chair on the passenger's side of Nita's desk, taking out her stylus and phone while looking around. The large windows, grey-beige walls, and white furniture gave the twenty-ninth-floor office an airy feeling.

"This backgrounder won't take too long," the CEO said.

Nita pushed her lunch aside. "Where do we start?"

The CEO turned to face Nita over the corner of the desk, turning on her iPad. "Remember we spoke about CiliCold and SSS last March? Cassie spoke to us about the—"

"Yes," Nita said, hands folded on the desk in front of her. "By the way, I heard Cassie was in this morning. How is she?"

Meredith put her stylus down. "I spoke to her for a while. It was great to see her, especially after this spring's terrible events. But," she continued in a softer voice, "I'm afraid she has a long way to go."

"Word has it she's going to resign. It's not my place, Ms. Doucette, but—"

Meredith covered Nita's left hand with her right.

"I am so happy for you today, Nita, and I know you and Cassie were close. Ask away."

"Will you accept her letter?" Nita asked.

"Confidence?"

"Confidence."

Meredith met the gaze of her CFO then nodded.

The CFO looked into the distance for a minute then back at the CEO.

"OK. CiliCold, right?"

"Yes. If I remember, we decided it was a good move for us not just because the product was good, but—"

"Could be good, right?"

"Right," the CEO agreed. "Could be good. But the real issue was to inaugurate the new direction. I think we called it 'molecule management.'"

"Yes." Meredith worked to get comfortable in the cheap inflexible chair. "That was Cassie's idea. We buy molecules then outsource their preliminary phase 1 and phase 2 studies. Much like we do phase 3 work. Jasper and Cassie fought over the idea."

*Careful here*, the CEO said to herself. It would be wrong to pull Nita into any coming fight with Jasper. The CFO had every right to pick her own side when the time came.

"Lots of debate over it, if my memory is correct."

Nita shook her head. "Cassie fought for it. I was pretty tough on her, but she had very good counterarguments. She'd really done her homework as always."

The CFO stopped for a moment, shaking her head. "I sometimes feel troubled about how I treated her then."

"What I learned from 911 was not to hold myself responsible for what I couldn't know."

Nita nodded.

Meredith stood. "Thanks, Nita. I remember now."

"Any time, Ms. Doucette."

"And when you have a name, I'd like to know."

"Ahana."

The CEO turned. "What does that mean?"

"Inner light."

"Well, may we will all have that one day."

Meredith watched with pleasure as another rare smile emerged from the taciturn CFO.

•

Meredith walked up the one floor to the conference room.

"Shareholder conference call in ten."

"Thanks, Jan."

*You'll need more than ten minutes to unravel this puzzle*, she thought as she sat in one of the luxurious chairs sitting around the long table. Meredith knew that Jasper didn't want the CiliCold product for molecular management. He didn't believe in it. So why was he so insistent on targeting CiliCold for destruction?

She tried to put herself in his head. With Giles, it was all about the dollars.

And revenge.

Some of it was personal. Jasper was an ugly man.

And he hated CiliCold.

Because he hated Cassie.

The CEO shivered.

The product wouldn't rake in much. It would be years before they even got to the FDA for review. Other companies would compete. Meanwhile, the cold and sinus division, C&S . . .

The CEO sat up straight. "My—"

"Time to dial in, Ms. Doucette."

# QUIVER

"Thank you for dialing into our interim shareholder's call," Meredith said, as Nita walked in, sitting by her next to the phone. "As this is an interim call, the discussions will be focused and relatively short. We wanted to let you know about the Tanner transition and also provide some preliminary information about other planned acquisitions.

"However, since we have you all on the phone and our CFO Nita Laghari is with us, I have asked her to provide an update on our financial position and projections."

"Thank you, Ms. Doucette," Nita said to the analysts and thousands of shareholders on the call. "If you will turn to page B1 in the packet before you, you will see—"

Meredith let herself mentally unplugged from the quantitative summary, following her own train of thought.

*Cold and sinus medications were a big winner for SSS. They brought in millions of dollars per year. Without them, SSS would be close to life support. New products were well down the bottom of the pipeline and—*

"Also, note that our debt load has—"

*Nothing was coming to their rescue anytime soon. A successful cold vaccine was years away even if the CiliCold idea worked. However, once word got out that we had it, shareholders and banks could read the same balance sheets and draw the same conclusions. A cold vaccine commits fratricide against over-the-counter cold remedies and treatments. They would face enormous public pressure to decrease the cost of the vaccine. Time would be running out for SSS.*

*On the other hand, if Jasper could deep six the partial antibody idea, C&S could continue to provide a solid revenue stream.*

*That's what he was doing.*

*He wanted to kill the goose before it laid the golden egg.*

She gasped.

31

"Can somebody talk a little more about the recent takeover of Tanner Pharmaceuticals?" a nasal voice asked.

Vee Novack.

Analyst.

*Always looking to show she knew more than anyone else.*

"Of course, Vee," the CEO responded.

"I heard that there were problems with the takeover. Gunfire at the facility, the police was called. It sounds to me like the transition was much rockier—"

"Let me stop you right there, Vee."

"I am just trying to figure out on behalf of the shareholders—"

"Then for the many shareholders on this call, allow me to answer you with facts, not speculation."

Meredith heard Nita inhale. "Yes, one afternoon in March, there was a serious event that led to the loss of life. A safety monitor for Tanner killed herself in a meeting with other Tanner and SSS representatives. It was a terrible day. Police and ambulance arrived on the scene. There was a full investigation.

"One of our principal attorneys, Cassie Rhodes, senior VP legal, sustained very bad scalp and face injuries during the suicide. She is still recovering for what I expect will be a substantial amount of time. Cassie was an important part of our team, my mentee, and we miss her terribly."

"I can see how this would impact your group's decision-making capability and maybe the June quarterlies," Vee said.

"I do not." Meredith drew closer to the phone. "This is May. Nita just effectively announced our June quarterlies. As you have heard, we are in a strong financial position."

The analyst persisted. "She wasn't shot, was she? I'm just wondering why three months later with only cuts and bruises she is not back—"

"Vee, when was the last time you had a mouth full of skull bits, brainstem, and blood?"

Silence.

"Let me know because I'm looking forward to reading your recovery manual. If you don't have one yet, then shut up. Please give our colleague some respect and some space."

The CEO, face now red, took a deep breath and sat back in her chair. "I have been very direct and honest on this call for the sake of our shareholders. We will answer your questions about our financials and acquisitions as long as you are willing to stay on the phone, but the personal lives and troubles of our people are their concerns. It is neither the interest of analysts, shareholders, or anyone else."

With no more questions, the call ended. Meredith looked up at the ceiling.

"Ms. Doucette. You just can't do what you d—"

"Nita," the CEO said, struggling to keep her voice under control. "If our shareholders are stupid enough to believe the injury of a single attorney will bring SSS down, then they should sell their damn stock."

"No, they shouldn't," Nita said, eyes closed, waving her left hand back and forth. "Sell-offs can lead to stampedes. By the way, its analysts who help to stop the panic selling and you just made an enemy of one of them."

Meredith pushed back from the smooth wood table, shaking her head.

"Plus, it's not stupidity," the CFO continued. "Shareholders look for stability. The more you talked, the more you signaled instability."

Meredith pushed her chair back and walked to the window. The sun was celebrating spring, filling her view with light.

A moment later, she said, "The thing is, Nita, I used to know that."

The CFO walked over, placing a hand on her boss's right shoulder. "I'm afraid, Meredith, that you have given your enemies another arrow for their quiver."

# TURNABOUT

**B**rake lights!

Breanna saw the blue Escort in front of her swerve hard to the left on Indiana SR 52. She jammed on her brakes, swiveling her head to the back to look at ten-month-old Jackie, strapped in her car seat.

*Breathe*, Breanna reminded herself. The CiliCold accountant closed her eyes, relishing the safety of her daught—

The screech of the white F-150 came from nowhere, bounding across lanes, now heading the wrong way.

Toward Breanna and Jackie.

The truck tipped over, slamming onto its side as it rammed into a red SUV, pushing it back into three other cars, the grotesque plastic, metal, and steel mass all headed in Breanna's direction. Breanna came off the brakes, hitting the accelerator for just an instant as she turned hard right then jammed on the brakes again and swinging left, bringing her Civic to a jarring stop against the right curb.

Her heart raced. When she saw no other flying cars or debris, Breanna, body drenched in sweat, jumped out of the car, raced around to the right passenger rear door. Opening it, she released Jackie from the seat. Then holding her close, she sat down on the curb, kissing and whispering her affection to the child.

Yet although overwhelmed with luck, Breanna couldn't stop her mind's eye from looking beyond to luck's end.

Cassie had paid Breanna's rent six months in advance as part of SSS's deal for the accountant to help betray CiliCold, handing the company over to SSS. That would take her to July. Utilities were paid through June as well, thanks to her Cassie guardian angel. Sweet life.

Then Cassie disappeared.

Nothing.

Like the earth had swallowed her whole.

So odd, Breanna thought, stroking Jackie's back. That this woman whom she had really only met once on a cold night at Perkins restaurant just four miles away on highway 26 had become so important to her. Economically and—

Her heart pounded at the rest of the thought.

She knew more about Cassie than Cassie had ever told anyone.

And that scared her.

●

An hour later, Breanna pulled into her apartment complex's parking lot.

A banged-up SUV sat in her assigned spot, motor still running.

No matter though. As long as she didn't have to clear snow to park, the accountant didn't much care where she parked in the clean lot on this warm, clear day.

"Hello," the woman said, getting out of the dirty SUV. "I am an attorney." Breanna watched the short woman, struggling with a bad limp, ache her way out of the car.

"How can I help you?"

"I was wondering if you needed assistance after the accident back there on 52."

Goodness. *A genuine ambulance chaser—kind of.*

Breanna smiled. "Thank you, ma'am, but we are fine."

"No need to check your baby for one of those neck injuries?"

"She was secure," Breanna said, still smiling, "and as I said, we are fine."

"OK, well, anyway, here's my card." The woman struggled back into the SUV, threw it into gear, and backed out of the parking space.

Cassie.

Standing there, on the other side of where the banged-up SUV had been, the West Lafayette wind whipped the short brown hair across her face.

# LIFE FOR A FRIEND

Breanna gasped, mouth open, her heart's hard cadence pounding through her.

Staring like her own life was at stake.

It was all Breanna could do to put Jackie's car seat down carefully in the sun on the warm pavement.

The accountant walked then ran to Cassie, stopping when the attorney tried to walk but stumbled. A moment later, Breanna caught the taller woman before she collapsed.

"I only remembered where you stayed," the attorney gasped. "Where we put you up. No idea if you were still here."

"We live here, Cassie." She was now down on her knees with the attorney on the asphalt. "We are home. And now, so are you," Breanna whispered into her ear

A moment later, Breanna picked up Jackie's carrier; and arms around each other, the women stumbled the short way to the apartment.

•

Cassie slept for over thirty hours.

Breanna closed the door to the attorney's bedroom, having made it a habit to pop her head in every few hours. She told herself she did it to make sure that Cassie was all right.

She knew that was a lie.

She looked in on her to convince herself that Cassie really had come back. That she was there.

With her.

And if Breanna had her way, to stay.

She was thrilled at the idea of a different future.

•

The next morning, Breanna was in the kitchen. Jackie sat at the large island, nodding her head and kicking her feet as the aroma of her favorite breakfast filled the room. Breanna couldn't blame her. The spices and popping bacon, the eggs, and brown toast had her own stomach growling.

"Well," she said to Jackie, "at least the morning sickness is over and I can look forward to these om—"

"What day is it?"

Breanna swiveled to face Cassie. There she stood in the doorway from the hallway to the large bright kitchen, wearing only black panties, the warm morning illumination falling over the olive-skinned woman, turning her breasts into mounds of lights and shadows.

Breanna swallowed hard.

"Thursday. May 27. Good to see you up." The accountant looked over at her daughter for a moment. Then turning back, she said, "You feel like break—"

The lawyer was gone.

Fifteen minutes later, Breanna took some orange juice and toast into the dark bedroom with its drawn curtains.

'You've been through a shock, Cassie," she said, holding out the plate with her right hand then sitting to the right of the quiet attorney. "What happened I don't know, but if someone is chasing you, you need to keep your strength up."

"Thanks." Cassie took the water, drinking it slowly. "I'm of no matter now. Inconsequential."

Breanna stroked her friend's dark hair. "Not here, you're not." She looked down at the pendulous breasts in the dark. "Let's first get you some clothes. There's no way mine will fit you. Let me get my phone."

Cassie gave her the size information.

"OK. You sleep, be back in ninety."

"Breanna, I have been in knots for weeks. What do I do." Cassie's voice was husky, her nose running.

"Take it a day at a time, and for today, that means staying here," Breanna said, sniffing the air. "Meantime, I bet a shower would feel good."

The attorney and accountant laughed together.

Breanna and Jackie dashed out to Target and, an hour and fifteen minutes later, had a cart full of underwear and bras, jeans and blouses, loafers and sneakers. She had little idea of makeup but did the best she could.

Breanna, singing to the phone track, Jackie nodding her head with her mom, entered the apartment.

"Cassie. We're back."

Silence.

"Bet she's asleep, Jackie," Breanna said, putting gentle pressure on the bedroom door to open it.

Bed was made and spotless.

"Cassie," Breanna called, now raising her voice. She went back to the living room then backtracked to the kitchen. The apartment door had been locked, she remembered, and Cassie had no key. She had to be here.

Somewhere.

A door thudded like it was being kicked.

Jackie started to cry.

Breanna took a moment to soothe her then went back to the guest bedroom.

Closet.

The accountant opened it, Jackie in her left arm.

Cassie.

On the floor in the corner.

Rocking back and forth, tears flowing.

*Like the thirteen-year-old back in Washington,* the accountant thought.

Breanna placed the baby on the floor in front of the open closet then crawled in, pushing the sliding closet door all the way back so she could sit with the attorney, cradling her head with the softest of touches as Cassie cried her life out.

Breanna didn't know the names or phrases the lawyer babbled but knew her friend was desperate. Perhaps sick. May be in trouble as she herself had been months before.

And just as Cassie, in that time, had given the accountant all that she needed, Breanna knew, whispering and placing soft kisses into the attorney's clean hair, that she would give her life to her friend.

# BURNING THE JUNK AWAY

He had hoped to get some thinking done before she arrived, but he was already late. He checked his watch: 6:05 PM.

*Maybe she won't even be able to meet me tonight*, he thought. *That would mean—*

He walked into the CiliCold office.

Rayiko, standing in the middle of the living room, turned to face him "What's up?" she said, hands by her sides.

He walked behind the brown sofa to pull back the curtains, letting the golden sunlight through, illuminating them both. He really didn't want to talk about this.

"Breanna called me last night." He cleared his voice then looked straight at Rayiko. "She talked to me about this Cassandra Rhodes, the attorney caught up in that bad suicide business at SSS."

"And the same one who co-opted our accountant," Rayiko added. She sat down on the sofa. Jon took the overstuffed red leather chair a few feet from her to his right.

"So I'm told." He could feel the anger swelling in him as he opened and closed his fists. "She actually wants me to consider hiring her."

"You look pretty pissed over there."

They sat in silence on the couch for a few moments.

"You know, the first nine of ten answers I got when I asked myself should I hire her were no."

"And the last one?"

"Hell no."

They laughed.

"I mean," Jon said, standing again. "What sense does it make?" He jammed his hands into his pockets. "She went out of her way to destroy us. I'd have to have a hundred pounds of brain damage to hire this woman." He snorted.

"She's untrustworthy. Plus, this is somebody I don't really know. I don't have any intuition about her. I have no experience with her. A traitorous stranger looking to get into our fold? The whole thing is laughable."

"You forgave Breanna," Rayiko said, crossing her legs.

"Yes, I did," Jon said, nodding. "I knew her, and I understood her situation before she let herself be used against us. I could bring that background to bear. This situation with Cassandra though—"

"I think she goes by 'Cassie.'"

His head pounded. "Maybe her friends call her 'Cassie,' but she's not a friend of mine."

"Sit," Rayiko said.

Jon stared at her. *What the—*

"Now, Jon," she said, smiling, gesturing to the leather chair across from her, now bathed in the sun's orange glow.

"You keep this up, then you're going to pass on the wrong person for SSS and the right person for us."

He hated these riddles. "What do you mean by that?" Jon said, struggling to control his voice.

"I mean that Cassie went through a hell that you don't know. Terrible emotional damage after the suicide. Plus, she has been cut loose from Triple S."

"Any idea why?" Jon said, feeling himself breathing easier.

"No, I don't. I just know that the tables have turned on her. I spoke to Breanna two nights ago, and she told me that Cassie just showed up at her door. Alone. Unkempt. A ruined person. You ever been down like that?"

Jon shook his head, and Rayiko leaned forward through the lengthening shadows toward him.

"How about during that bad business at the university?"

He exhaled. "Yep. Sure did." After a moment, he added, "And I didn't have one."

"And look at the pain you had to endure. No outlet. No venting. Nobody cared for you or about you. Keeping it all inside was eating you up. You know," she said, moving her hair off her shoulder, "some people have to go through horrid times just to have a chance to learn who they actually are. To burn all the junk away."

There was a truth in there that he knew he couldn't shake off. He sighed. "Even if I did reach out to her, what good would she be to us?"

"Well, having an in-house lawyer wouldn't be such a bad thing. "Look, I can't tell you what to do, but—"

"What?"

"If you hire her, then you must trust her. Openly. No reservations. No looks back, and no holding back. You have to let her know in everything you do that she is part of us now. If you don't, then she'll always be suspicious. Suspected. Isolated. She'll never be who she wants to be, who she is capable of becoming." She stopped then stood.

"There is no trial run. You do this, or you don't."

Jon stood. "I just . . . just don't know if I can do what you have asked."

"Then be the man who can."

He looked down at her for a few moments, anger gone, self-connected again. "Let me think about this some tonight."

They both turned to leave.

"Hey, how do you get into my head?"

"You know."

"No," he said to her back as she started walking to the door.

Rayiko turned around, taking a step toward him.

"I really don't," he said, shaking his head, walking up to her. "Never have."

She grabbed his collar, pulling his head closer.

"Because," she whispered, "that's where you want me."

# REBORN

"Stop it, Cassie."

"He's going to hate me."

"Calm down. You're on his side now. He's had a week to digest. He'll understand."

Breanna sat up at the head of the bed, legs spread, Cassie sitting between them in panties and a shirt. Breanna, stroked her friend's hair, face, and arms, settling Cassie down as she always did after a counseling session.

"What's this red rash on your arm?" Breanna asked.

"I keep it under my shirt."

"Hurt?"

"No."

"Itch?"

"Not really, Dr. Vaughn."

They both laughed.

After a moment, Breanna said, "Jon needs to know what happened at SSS. And about you."

"That's what you told me," the attorney said, head back on Breanna's chest.

Breanna, looking straight ahead, leaned forward so that her face was even with the attorney's. "Cassie, you make your own mind up, but when you talk to my boss, you tell him the truth. Be who you are now. Not the fake-out artist you used to be."

"When do we talk to hi—"

"Right now," Breanna said, play pushing Cassie off her.

Cassie twisted around off the bed, getting up to sit in a nearby chair while Breanna placed the old Galaxy S10 in front of them, putting it on speaker, dialing her boss's number.

"I should've had the company buy you a decent phone," Cassie said, laughing then ducking as Breanna threw a pillow at her.

"Breanna?" Memories flooded the accountant when she heard Jon's voice.

"Sure is. Cassie is with me." *This may not go so well*, she thought. By all rights, Jon should despise her and Cassie both for trying to immolate his company last March. She felt sweat's fine beads pop out on her forehead.

"Hello, Cassie," he said.

Breanna picked up no hostility in his voice. *I knew it.*

"Of course, you and I have not met. How are you?"

"Better," Cassie said. "Breanna is responsible for most of it."

"Breanna is special," he said, new softness in his voice. "Listen, it's after six, and I don't want to keep you long. Cassie, I have some decisions to make about CiliCold. It appears we have SSS enemies. From what Breanna says, you are not one of them anymore."

Pause. Then he said, "I'm going to choose to believe that."

Cassie exhaled. "Thank you, Jon. I am not your enemy now although I did target CiliCold on behalf of SSS a few months ago."

"Thank you for that. Can you tell me what your role was and why SSS is so interested in CiliCold?"

It took Cassie ten minutes to explain the entire ordeal.

"I am not part of SSS anymore. Your adversary there is—"

"Doucette? The CEO?"

"No. Absolutely not," Cassie said. "Jasper Giles. He's wanted to take the project from me. I'm not sure I know the reasons why."

"Breanna, anything to add?"

"I wanted to facilitate the sale of the company to SSS. We were floundering. But I was desperate. Despicable coked-up husband with one baby and another on the way. Cassie offered me a way out. I took it."

"I read the email traffic." He paused. "I was desperate as well."

"And brilliant, I hear," Cassie added.

"This is helpful to me," Jon said. "Breanna, of course, you are part of CiliCold shrinking's family as long as you want to be. Cassie, I . . . Let me just ask you . . . What would you like?"

"I don't know, Jon, but I like what I know of you and CiliCold."

"Then I look forward to seeing you both. Breanna, see you tomorrow. One question, Cassie. Why aren't you still with SSS? From what I have heard and read, the suicide wasn't your fault."

"The CEO doesn't believe in me anymore because she believes that I don't want to heal."

Breanna could barely hear her.

"Well," Jon said, "there's room for you to heal with us. I hope to see you soon."

*Click.*

Breanna looked at her friend, warm spring sun falling through the blinds onto the lawyer.

"That is how he is?" Cassie said, getting back on the bed. "And he's the owner?"

"Yes?" Breanna saw that Cassie's gaze was far away.

"How does he survive in the business world?"

"He doesn't. He's just . . ." The accountant shook her head. "Reborn. Over and over. And then some more."

The attorney shifted on the bed, resting in Breanna's warm embrace, stroking Breanna's arm.

"Bree, I think I'm ready."

Breanna nuzzled her friend's hair, stroking her right arm, watching Cassie's thighs move.

"Not yet, dear heart. But soon."

# RUNNING FOR LIFE

Jon rushed into CiliCold's downtown West Lafayette office, the sky full of deep blue and sun, certain he would be the first to arrive for the meeting.

He was wrong.

Rayiko, Breanna, Cassie, and Luiz were all in the company's living room that doubled as a meeting space for the company. Someone had opened the windows, and the clean spring air swept the curtains aside to get at them.

He looked around, smiling. "Doesn't anybody have any work to do today?" Jon asked, smiling.

"Not at this company," Rayiko said.

"I should have known. Did you all meet Cassie?" he said, gesturing to the attorney.

"We made the rounds," Breanna said.

"Tru dat, boss," Luiz said, the cell scientist taking off his leather jacket as he sat on the old wooden floor.

"Well, let's get to it."

Jon sat on an ottoman, the afternoon light from the window streaming in. *Love having my people back. I want so much to have it like it used to be,* he thought. "Let me tell—no. First, is everyone going to Wild Bill's wedding tomorrow?"

"Yeah. It's not far from here, right? Greenwich?"

"Greentown. Just east of Kokomo," Breanna said, extending her legs in front of her.

"How are you doing, Breanna?" Jon asked. "Pregnancy OK?"

"Five months left. I'm going to miss Wild Bill."

"I already do," Jon added. After a moment, he added, "And Robbie."

"And Dale. Sometimes," Luiz said, scratching his arm through his long-sleeved T-shirt.

45

"Dale's out of here too?" Breanna asked, turning to Jon.

"As of last week."

"So, Jon," the cell scientist said, scratching his head, "while we're glad to have Cassie, we still don't have much of a posse. What's the story."

Jon inhaled. "I spoke to Wild Bill, and he put me on to some people who got spun out of Tanner Pharmaceuticals when SSS acquired them." Jon turned his gaze from Luiz to the others. "But let's get to your question."

Jon began to walk the room. "Due to everybody's hard work, we now have a reproducible process that makes partial antibodies. These partial antibodies, once finally constructed in the extracellular fluid, defeat many of the viruses that cause the common cold."

"At least in monkeys," Luiz said, smiling.

"Right you are," Jon said, smiling at the younger scientist. "Wild Bill was starting to put together a regulatory pathway with the FDA that would permit us to begin human testing. Plus," the CiliCold CEO continued, "we are liquid. Breanna and Rayiko have seen to that. Problem is, Triple S is dogging our heels."

"What? Still?" Luiz said, head shaking. "They damn near ran us out of this place."

"What is it with those people?" Rayiko asked. "What are we to them?"

Jon turned to Breanna. "What can you tell us?"

"They want our product, don't they?" Rayiko said, staring at the floor.

"No," Breanna said. "They want us."

"Why?" Luiz asked, getting up from the floor and sitting on a couch. "Heaven knows that they've got far more resources than we do. They throw away glassware that we would fight over and probably have advanced equipment that we have never heard of. If they put their minds to it, they could make a product better than ours. No offense, Jon," Luiz said, shifting around to see his boss. "Just simply saying they have the firepower."

"But they don't have the ideas, Luiz," Cassie said, standing up. "They don't want you for your resources, but for your skills and ideas. Honestly, from what I heard, some scientists there couldn't pour piss from a boot with instructions written on its heel."

They all laughed.

Luiz, pointing to the attorney, said, "I like this girl."

46

"And you were part of this?" Rayiko asked.

"Yes, until a suicide turned me around."

"Well, I'm sorry that it took that, but we need all the friends we can get," Rayiko said.

Luiz nodded.

"I may not be the freshest butter," Cassie said looking at them all, "but I'm on your side of the bread."

"So, Jon," Rayiko asked. "We understand the problem. What's our next move?"

"I'm skedaddling," he said. "I hope you all come with me, but I can't make you."

"You're running?"

"Yeah. For freedom from these folks. For life."

"Where to?"

"Someplace nice and quiet."

"I thought West Lafayette was nice and quiet," Rayiko said.

Jon looked at her for a moment. Then drawing a deep breath, he said, "Not like pri—"

All jumped at Jon's loud ringtone.

"Well," Rayiko said, laughing. "At least now you have a phone that works, or at least rings."

Jon put it to his ear. "Hello?"

As Jon listened, he watched them sit on the edge of their seats like the call mattered to them.

*They were right*, he thought.

"One second please."

Jon put the phone down.

"Meeting adjourned. See you guys at the wedding tomorrow."

He waved the puzzled group goodbye then turned to walk quickly into the kitchen.

# MISBEHAVE

" Say that again please," Jon asked, sitting at the small kitchen table where he'd had so many arguments with his scientists before.

"Please hold for Meredith Doucette, CEO of SSS Pharmaceuticals."

"Very well."

Jon was amazed at himself. Calm. Even at peace. One of the most important people in the pharmaceutical industry was calling for him. Then he realized.

"Dr. DeLeon?" A gentle, smooth, even comforting voice. There was no threat here, Jon thought. Relaxing.

"Is it Dr. Doucette?" he asked. "I'm sorry that I don't know."

"'Mrs. Doucette.' We have not met, and it's late on a Friday, so I will not waste your time." Jon heard her inhale, as if examining some great concept in her mind one last time before sharing. "You and I may have the same problem."

"Well, OK then." After a moment, he added, "Mrs. Doucette, how may I help?"

She paused for a second. "I have a group here that wants your partial antibody project."

"Yes," Jon replied. "I have heard that from one of my own people. One of whom you know." He gripped the phone harder, struggling to keep the frustrations bred by the last six months of defeats and setbacks out of his voice. "I think you want it too."

"What I want, Jon, is for you to get on with your work. That will not happen here. At SSS, your project will die. My team will kill it." Jon rubbed his forehead. "I don't underst—"

"By bringing your project in-house and destroying it, my group will save a division that makes tens of millions of dollars a year treating colds that your advance would prevent."

Jon, putting the phone by his side, craned his neck up, looking at the peeling beige paint from the old ceiling. *What a madhouse. These people are antihealth.*

He brought the Android back up to his ear.

"Would you let that happen?"

"That's why we're talking."

"What can I do?"

"If you can go underground, go. And for heaven's sakes, get a patent for your work. You are ripe for los—"

"I have a better idea."

He laid out his plan.

The line was quiet for a few moments, and as the silence stretched out, he shook his head, fearing that she wouldn't buy it.

Then . . .

"Will your CiliCold team go along with that?"

"Yes. It buys us some time, and I think it would strengthen your position." He blinked twice. "Besides, we have some other scientific plans?"

"Beyond partial antibodies?"

"Way beyond."

They exchanged contact information.

"Jon, one more thing. I lost track of a colleague of mine. She was putting pressure on your company, was misguided, and has been damaged in the entire matter. She is no threat to you now. If you hear of or see Cas—"

"She is here and well cared for, Mrs. Doucette."

Jon heard Meredith's voice catch.

"Oh, thank you. Thank you."

"Mrs. Doucette?"

"I have to go."

"You know you're going to have to misbehave to get the folks coming after you, don't you?"

"I've seen their work."

# HEADED TO HELL WITH YOU

Jon arrived thirty minutes before the ceremony at First Presbyterian Church of Greentown and saw Wild Bill by a tree, well away from his bride, Emma, and her family. The CEO's old friend stood still, peering down into a tall glass.

Jon walked up. "You actually have to put your face into the glass to actually drink from it. You can't just will the liquid up into your mouth."

WB looked up, smiling. "If I'd known a wedding would finally get you out of the lab, I'd have married lots of times by now."

Jon shook his pal's hand. "You're dressed to the nines, Bill. Somebody would think you were the groom."

"Yep."

"I'm guessing nobody made it here from South Carolina?"

"Too long a trip." Bill shrugged.

"Of course. Plus, it's not free. Probably makes sense for them to have a party for you there. By the way, what are you going to do in Monetta besides being married?"

"Not to worry," Wild Bill said, smiling. "There are a few young biotech start-ups. You know the type. Aggressive. Full of ideas, but no idea how to get them off the ground and through regulatory approval."

Jon laughed. "Well, I'm glad that we could provide you the appropriate knowledge and training. Want a letter of recommendation?"

"Don't worry about me. Save your Dixie cups, my friend, 'cause the old South will rise again."     They laughed easily as they had always done.

•

"This relationship isn't going anywhere good."

Rayiko pulled off the side of the narrow asphalt road into a pasture. "What are you telling me?"

"Gary and I can't stay in Indiana."

*Gary and I?*

"He's my son," she retorted, eyes suddenly wet.

"Mine too, and no son of mine will languish here. We're going to need to make some changes. The question is, are you with us or not?"

She strained to pick up any thread of emotion in his voice. It wasn't there.

"We're not going to do this on the phone out of the blue, Richard."

"We just did."

He hung up.

•

"When are you leaving?"

"Tomorrow for Monetta, then heading to the Bahamas for a four-day honeymoon." Bill cleared his throat then took a drink. "You know, Jon, I'll be bringing Emma back here to see her family every now and again."

"Hopefully not in winter."

"Forget that, but"—the regulator took a drink—"whenever we come back, I'm not going to find CiliCold in West Lafayette, am I?"

"Nope."

"Smart play," WB said, nodding. "Somebody's got your scent. Don't know who, but they want to put CiliCold down. Any idea where you're headed?"

"Yep."

"Care to share?"

Jon whispered in WB's ear.

Bill snorted, pulling back so fast he spilled his drink. "That's impossible."

Jon shrugged. "Not impossible. Just unheard of."

"Damn, Jon," his friend said, nodding his head. "I'll give you this. Only you would think of it." Bill looked across the parking lot at the arriving cars. "The team headed to perdition with you?"

The CEO shrugged. "We'll see."

"Hey, Jon?" he said, seeing Emma wave him over. "Glad you could come. Tell them all that I said hey."

"Tell them yourself. I'm just the advanced guard. The rest of the CiliCold cavalry is on the way. We'll sit on your side of the church."

As he watched Wild Bill open, close, then open his mouth, Jon for the first time saw his regulator at a loss for words.

"We're with you today, Bill," Jon said, placing a hand on the thin man's left shoulder. "Will always be there." Jon pointed to the parking lot. "Here they come now."

They both watched Luiz—short, bald, competent, one of the best lab immunologists in the US—get out of his beat-up F-150.

Another car pulled up next to his, and two women got out.

"Who are they?"

Jon squinted, shielding his eyes with his left hand.

"Well," WB offered, "one is Breanna, the other . . . wow."

"Take it easy, bridegroom. That's Cassie Rhodes, our attorney." After a moment, he said. "I think."

"Well, you'll need one where you're going."

"I'll see to the attorney while you see to your bride."

Jon saw WB squint. "Is that Rayiko pulling in?"

Jon turned nodded, waved, then turned back.

The two friends studied each other.

"You're brilliant, Jon," WB observed. "But jumbled up inside. It's dangerous out there for your kind."

"Yeah," Jon said, shaking his hands. "I'll be careful."

WB, snorting as he always did, slapped Jon on the back and walked over to his new wife.

*I will miss him.* Jon walked out from the shade into the sun to greet his group as waves of grief, towering ever higher, waited to crash down on him. *God help me, I will miss them all.*

•

Rayiko pulled into the parking lot ten minutes before the ceremony. Stopping, she got out, waving to WB and Jon. Then she gasped and hurried back into her car, driving to a secluded part of the parking lot. There, stopped on new black asphalt surrounded by freshly cut Virginia rye grass, Rayiko rested her arms atop the hard and unforgiving steering wheel, put her head down, and cried for the second time during her Greentown drive.

•

Jon, seeing her hair falling over her right shoulder in shades of black, gray, and white, was in awe.

"Breanna, you actually stop time when you look this wonderful."

Turning, he now faced the tall woman. White dress cut below the knee, above white and tan sandals. No necklace or other distracting jewelry. *A smile that forces the sun to rise in adoration, yet eyes that opened into a world of sadness*, he thought.

She held his gaze.

Offering her hand, she took it with the slightest squeeze.

"Cassie? It is my pleasure."

"Thank you, Jon."

"Just where are you from, anyway?"

After a moment, she answered. "The Northwest."

"Well, nothing is better than an Indiana spring day. Almost makes winters worth it."

"And I have had enough of them," Breanna said, laughing.

"Got that right, Breanna. Well," Jon said, "we have a celebration to be part of. That," he said, pointing to WB, who was meandering toward the church entrance, "was our regulator. A great guy. We're here to enjoy the afternoon with him."

He moved closer to Cassie and Breanna. "You know," he whispered, "I spotted an ice cream parlor coming in on 35."

"Kelly's Ice Cream," Breanna said. "I scoped it. We were talking about going there when we're done."

"How about if we have a company meet there when the nuptials are done?"

"You better," his accountant said, pointing a tiny index finger in his direction. "You owe us a destination for CiliCold."

"Yes." Jon watched Cassie take a step back.

"Cassie," he said, smiling. "Where do you think you're going? I bought your ticket to this. You're welcome to ice cream and the meet if you want."

"I would like that."

He felt someone touch his arm.

"Rayiko," Jon said, making room for her. "I know you've met our attorney, but why don't you tell her what you do for us?"

"My full-time job is saving our CEO from himself," she said. "Nice to meet you, Cassie," Rayiko said, a glorious smile on her face.

"We were all talking about a postwedding meeting at Kelly's ice cream." He looked at Rayiko. "Interested?"

"That sounds like a plan. Count me in."

"Cassie and I are going in to sit down, Jon," Breanna said.

"Make sure Luiz doesn't roll his truck up inside the church."

Breanna laughed. "I don't know if he owns that old thing or it owns him."

"Rayiko and I will be in soon."

●

Rayiko watched the two women walk away, fighting her own emotions.

She felt Jon studying her.

"Bad day?" he asked.

"A bad start to it, anyway."

"A woman's beauty comes alive at a wedding," Jon whispered into her ear. "But you, sweetheart, are the star that outshines its galaxy."

Her heart leaped. She knew that he sensed her turmoil even though he couldn't have known the horrific fight with Richard. She had chosen to be open to only Richard in her life, only to have him bleed her heart dry with his criticisms and inattentiveness. On the drive to the wedding, she was nothing. Committed to a man committed to his work.

But her heart found new life with Jon.

"We had better walk over there too, don't you think?" she said.

Jon offered an arm. She took it before she could stop herself, heart pounding out its new hope.

# LAST PLACE TO LOOK

"**I** tell you that there are plain few problems that can't be solved with coffee ice cream," Jon said, tapping the table with a fist that held a wooden spoon protruding from the top.

"I just don't get how something that tastes so good, and makes your stomach feel great, can be so bad for you," Rayiko said, swallowing a spoon of vanilla pecan.

"In moderation, nothing is bad," the cell scientist said, sitting at the table.

"Philosopher Luiz is here. All hail."

Each of them bowed their head at Luiz, who just cracked up, almost spilling his dark chocolate.

*Who were these people?* Cassie thought, struggling to keep her mouth closed. Their company was being hunted by the most rapacious corporate interests. And what were they doing?

Horsing around at an ice cream store.

Outside, the tables were all full of Hoosier families enjoying the gorgeous spring Saturday.

Cassie watched Rayiko, who arrived at the wedding with recently dried eyes, spread an ice cream mustache across Luiz's mouth. All laughed.

*Incredible. Where are their troubles?*

"I call the meeting to order," Breanna said, raising both hands. "Jon, you have the floor."

"Can I taste your strawberry delight?"

"No, sire," Breanna said, laughing. "You can have your way with me, but do not touch my ice cream."

Everybody laughed.

"Gadzooks," Jon said, brandishing an invisible sword. "Well then, I hereby serve notice that I am moving CiliCold." He started to rise from the table. Cassie watched Rayiko place a gentle hand on his shoulder. Jon looked down at her then sat. "Who will come with me?"

"Where are we going, m'lord?" Luiz asked.

"The last place SSS or anyone will look."

"And that would be?" Cassie couldn't believe that she asked the question.

Jon, at once solemn, pushed his cup aside, and leaning forward over the old splintered table at his team, whispered, "Prison."

# HAY IN THE HAYSTACK

Three hours later, Breanna drove her Civic along SR 35 west back to Lafayette. The sun was just below the road to the south.

Cassie noted that Breanna kept the car's speed down.

*Just as well*, she thought. *So much to talk about.*

"I don't know what to say," Breanna said. "Jail?"

"Not jail, Bree. Prison."

"It's crazy."

"Not crazy." The attorney shook her head. "It's miraculous. The only question is whether he can pull it off." After a moment, she added, "And put together a team to go with him."

"I never thought about living in the desert."

Cassie almost said, "Neither have I," but choked it back. She could not believe how giddy she felt. Flushed from the inside out. Mouth full of sentences that were ready to stampede over each other. She struggled with the word to describe it.

"Think it through with me," Cassie said. "Florence is a small town in the middle of a nowhere desert and a Native American reservation. It's barely holding on to its existence. No self-respecting shoe repair shop, much less a biomed company would set up shop there. The high-speed internet challenges themselves will be considerable."

"They could be installed, though."

Cassie shook her head. "My guess is, he won't do that. Its effect on the energy grid would stand out to someone who is looking for one." Cassie laughed. "Bree, I have totally underestimated your boss. He doesn't want to be the needle in the haystack." The lawyer paused. "He wants to be the hay."

# FLYPAPER

"Let's just talk about what I do understand," the accountant said. "I'm going to need to slow down. This is one dark road."

After a minute, she continued. "I get the city, all right," Breanna said. "Small, forgotten. Ignorable. But a prison?"

"Think of it this way," Cassie said, hands moving in the darkness. "It's already abandoned. Lots of space that can be reconfigured. Plus, the electricity and water supply are already part of the infrastructure. That means little utility work. Sure, it would need to be cleaned, but given he would be paying the city for what would otherwise be dead space, they would likely support any small infrastructure changes that he would want to make. We need to turn here, right?"

"No, not 19. We'll go on to 31 then south at the light to 26."

"OK."

"You know," Breanna said, looking over at the attorney. "I never asked you, Cassie. Do you drive?"

"Well, before SSS yes, but not for years. I've been limo'ed around too much. But I would like to try again if you'll let me."

"OK, here's 31."

Breanna turned south in the twilight.

"And why's he leaving the partial antibody project behind? The breakthrough is invaluable."

"You're right, Bree, but my sense is that Jon is becoming quite a chess master."

"Maybe he's leaving the project behind as a decoy."

It hit her. "No, Bree. Not a decoy." Cassie squeezed Breanna's leg in excitement. "A deflection."

Cassie watched Breanna squint, as she thought it through. *She's always so—*

The accountant saw it. "Flypaper." Her mouth dropped.

"Agreed," Cassie said. "SSS will find it, declare their fight with CiliCold over, and march triumphantly back to Maryland with the prize and make it work. Meanwhile, CiliCold escapes scot-free to Florence undetected to ensconce in a prison and get back to work."

"The question is though, what does he need the space for?"

"You got me. I'm not a scientist," Cassie said. "Any guess I make will be a bad one?"

Breanna shook her head. "He's got something in mind. He wouldn't leave partial antibodies behind unless there—whoa."

The low tree branch reached out for them from the side of the twisting road.

"That was close."

"You're sweating," Cassie said. "You OK?"

"Just startled. Anyway, now you know why I love working with these people."

Cassie stirred, a new hunger back. "How good is the babysitter?"

"The best." Breanna looked over. "You should know. You got her."

"Well, she'll be asleep when we get back."

They rolled to a stop at a red light.

Breanna turned to look at Cassie. "She will keep her all night."

Cassie unbuttoned her seat belt and leaned over. Breanna's lips were waiting for her. Full, warm, open. She rubbed her own over Bree's, memorizing their textures and contours.

She felt Breanna's hand rub over then inside her blouse. Urgent small movements. Cassie's heart pounded as she stretched her chest up to help, nipples swelling to—

Green.

She moved back to her seat, leaving the seat belt off. Both opened their window.

Breanna looked over at her. "Yes?"

"Already started."

# WELCOMING

Cassie walked into the apartment in front of Breanna, heading to her own bedroom. Breanna stopped in the kitchen and called the babysitter. Then heart pounding, she locked up the apartment and followed the lawyer, putting on "Holding Back the Years."

There Cassie lay, shifting to the right a little, the dim light revealing only blue lace underwear.

Breanna removed her own blouse and pants, then with an index finger traced her finger over and around Cassie's panties.

"Did I buy you these?" she said, looking up at Cassie, laughing.

"No, silly. This is not my first seduction, you know."

Breanna looked up at her and, with soft hands, pulled the panties down and off. She almost passed out from the smell of Cassie, her heart trip-hammering. Sweet moments she yearned for.

She looked at her. Bare. Needing. Yearning.

*I will please this woman for the rest of her life.*

Breanna moved up Cassie's body. She stopped at her left breast where she kissed and nuzzled the soft flesh, teasing her left nipple with her right hand. Then she moved up Cassie's neck, passing the scar on her chin to her mouth where she kissed then sucked her lower lip, playing with her tongue while still caressing Cassie's nipple.

"You believe life is all pain. I know why," Breanna whispered into the right ear, sucking on the sweet lobe. "Tonight, dear heart, welcome to tender love." Breanna came back to her mouth, kissing it tenderly, then moving to her left ear. "And the only thing for you to do is to enjoy it."

Breanna roamed over each of Cassie's cheeks, laying kisses like wreaths. Gently. Perfectly placed. Then Breanna entered her mouth.

Breanna stayed a step ahead of Cassie's need for the feel of their tongues together. Then she stopped and surrendered to her lover, sharing her long tongue. Let it chase her, catch it, press it, squeeze it, then escape again.

"Your tits are so soft, your nipples so hard," Breanna said, running her left hand between the breast flesh and then below, then back up to a nipple to squeeze and play with. "I want them now, Cassie. I have always wanted them. Since we met in the restaurant for the first time, I have wanted them. To lick. To please. And I am going to suck them as they were meant to be sucked. Love them like they were meant to be loved."

"But I need you to—"

Breanna moved her right hand down to and below Cassie's belly to her lips.

Wet. Swollen. Ready.

"I am going live in your lips."

Breanna had her face in Cassie for ten minutes before Cassie was racked by a contraction that lifted her body off the bed. This was at once followed by another. A minute later, she had a final huge explosion, pushing Breanna's face into her, wetting her with herself.

As Cassie relaxed, Breanna moved up to Cassie and held her tight in the soft light, kissing her tenderly. "When I say I love you, Cassie, that is one of the things that I mean."

The two lovers lost themselves in each other until the sun rose, finding the exhausted women wrapped in each other.

# SPINNING THE BALL

"Kevin," the female ex-reg exec called out from the sidewalk, backing away from the car, one hand across her full chest. "You should be ashamed of yourself. Thinking such nasty thoughts about me."

Kevin, ex–senior VP marketing for Tanner Pharmaceuticals, sat up straight in the white Infiniti, watching in horror at the two women to her right, who first stared at Olivia, his ex-colleague and new girlfriend, then glared at him in the driver's seat.

The sixty-one-year-old opened and closed his mouth twice, then once more, watching Olivia in her sneakers, jean skirt, and black vest over white blouse bounce her carry-on onto the car's backseat, then climb into the passenger seat.

Earlier, he had been at absolute peace with himself when he arrived at IND airport in the heart of Indiana. Thoughtless, experiencing a post-RIF freedom high.

Now his heart was in his throat, watching this delicate woman, hair in lush gray waves, lean over to him, saying, "You really should be more careful. Such strong, wicked impulses." Her luscious Georgia accent lifted each syllable heavenward. She kissed him on the cheek, then sitting back in the seat, declared, "And the adventure begins."

He felt like he had a sixteen-year-old heart in a sixty-one-year-old chest.

And loved it.

"Olivia, I swear the earth stops spinning when you dress like this."

"Well, aren't you sweet today." She closed the car door and threw her purse in the backseat. "Take us somewhere."

"I've never followed the Ohio River before."

"Sail on, sail on, oh ship of state."

Kevin guided the Infiniti out of the airport to 465 towards 65 S.

"You know," he said, glancing at her, "we've been unemployed now for three mon—"

She put her fingers across his lips.

Cinnamon. He almost licked them.

"You and I have been full up these days with the past. Not this trip."

She faced straight ahead. "We have paid our prices, Kevin. Your sweet Dana's death. Our company's destruction. What we have to show for it is—"

"Intact hearts."

She looked over to him with a smile. "I was going to say 'time and money,' but hey, that works."

He reached over to hold her hand, and she took his in her two.

His heart raced. He was full of the day, full of the sunlight, full of her spontaneity.

They turned onto 65 south, headed to Louisville, silent for a time.

"I used to talk up starting my own business, but—"

He heard Olivia start to giggle.

"What's so . . . She told you?" Kevin shook his head.

"Dana really thought that was funny," he finished.

"Dana admired you for trying, Kevin, and I thought it was sweet, but—"

"I had the books and tried to follow the rules," he said, looking over to her.

"Lots of pitchers spin the ball, but very few actually curve it." Olivia shifted in her seat. "So, Kev, what's your intuition tell you? What do you want to do?"

The speed of his answer astonished him. "To enable the intuition of others."

"There you go," the ex-reg expert said, rubbing her thigh. "I think mine is to hang on to being a regulatory expert."

He glanced her way. "You've been on that for twenty-five years."

"I love the work. I just can't abide the corporate side anymore."

"God knows you were good, Olivia. If they had a *Regulatory Monthly* magazine, you'd be the centerfold."

She looked at him.

"Just speaking metaphorically."

"Uh-huh." She brushed his thigh. "Wicked man."

Sitting back, the ex-reg said, "Anyway, I'm hearing some rumblings. You know William Cantrell?"

"Reg guy?"

She nodded. "Not noticed by the reg giants in the industry, but known for honesty. Anyway, he called me about something happening in immunology."

"In Indianapolis?"

"Not anymore. Someplace in the southwest."

"Desert stuff? Really?"

"Smart people." She stared at the green fields hurtling by. "I love this land in early summer. Anyway, this new group is not so savvy business-wise though."

She shifted her legs.

He had to notice. Delicious calves. And the promise of soft thighs.

*Back on point, Kev,* he thought.

"Lots of groups are like that," he said, refocusing on the road. "Great ideas. Wandering the land, eating locusts and honey. Very few ever get to put it together."

"Like you?"

He looked at her. "Yeah. Maybe."

"Well, would you like to spend some of your freedom helping others, or do you want to use it all staring at the clouds?"

He was quiet.

"We've got time, Kev. No worries."

"Just show me the way home, Olivia."

She pointed to Storming Crab's Seafood. "Let's get a bite."

"Fine with me."

She stroked her hair. "I need to stop at a Target. Not tonight. Maybe tomorrow."

"OK, I forgot a couple of things too."

"I didn't forget anything,"

"So what don't you have?"

She leaned over and whispered, "Panties."

# HEADLOCK

"Listen, Giles, I can't get th—"

Jasper tapped the iPhone off. If he weren't in the tiny elevator hurtling him up to the thirtieth floor where the board meeting was scheduled to start in three minutes, he'd hurl the phone to the tile floor.

Stennis had promised him details on the partial antibody project.

It was to be Jasper's demonstration to the board. His great triumph. He would show them that wheelchair or not, Jasper Giles was the man of action at SSS.

Now, without the CiliCold project details, he'd have to rope a do—

The door swooshed open, directly into the boardroom.

Richly finished maple tabletop with metal name holders in front of each of the chairs.

No space for him and his wheelchair.

He almost spat on the thick carpet that bedeviled his wheelchair's movement. His right thigh howled in pain.

He pushed forward, ignoring the several members who smiled and nodded at him as he jibbed and jabbed the chair forward. Everyone else was already seated, taking out their packets.

Meredith walked in and sat at the table. At once, Jasper felt the stress level in the room increase, the tension between the CEO and senior VP legal known to everyone. Like a painful abscess, no one wanted to touch it.

All greeted her. Giles snorted.

She had more equity than most of the board, and she had the power, he knew. However, everyone had heard of her recent behavior on the interim shareholders' call. He was looking forward to using that knife to cut her heart out.

Usually, that was enough to give him a chromium steel boner. But for today of all days, his right leg pain was driving him out of his mind.

Starting years ago as just a flea flicker of a nothing in his right toes, it had swelled, marching up his leg unabated. Now it was just below his knee. Nobody could diagnose it or stop it. Some said it was "granulomatosis." What did he care? It was General Sherman's march to the sea, tearing up his l—

"Hey, Jasper. Let me help you with this."

"Uh, thanks, I—"

He looked up.

Meredith.

Looking down on him.

In a moment, she took hold of the chair's handles and smoothly pulled the chair out from its crooked position under the table then wheeled him forward.

"If you would prefer, Jasper, we can have someone here to help you."

Silence.

He watched her turn to the board. Sweat poured off him.

"I would like you all to know how honored I am to have Jasper here," she said. "Despite how he feels physically, he never fails to attend a board meeting. The least we can do is graciously offer him a warm, encouraging environment, respecting his effort to attend."

He saw her look down at him. "Please feel free to ask for whatever you need, Jasper."

"Sounds like an obituary, Meredith," Phillips said.

Jasper turned to Stella Phillips, head of advertising and a member of the executive committee. Sharp-tongued as always.

Everyone held their breath as Meredith stood then closed the distance between herself and the dyspeptic board member. "Stella, I prefer to show my affection for people when they are alive, not when they're dead."

Jasper wiped his wet brow with a wrinkled dirty Kleenex. *What universe was this?*

●

The meeting convened and worked though the details of the financials. This proceeded smoothly as always, Giles noted, squirming around to find a comfortable position for his right leg. SSS board members were selected both for their equity stake in the company and their financial acumen. There were the usual sharp exchanges. Income statements. Profit margins. Just push and pull, he observed, twisting his right leg one way then the other.

Three hours later, after lots of punches were thrown, he observed that none had landed. Everyone was pleased with the dividend payout ratio.

Next.

His name on the agenda.

And he had nothing.

No printed plans. No "zone five" escape. His pulse rate jacked up. *What—*

"Let's take a break, shall we?" Meredith offered.

"Agreed."

"Amen."

"Jasper," she asked. "Can I walk out with you?"

Jasper nodded. She wheeled his chair out of the meeting room to her office around the corner. When they were there, she leaned back against the desk, looking down at him. "I want to know how to support your presentation on the partial antibody project, Jasper."

He stared at her. *What the devil is she up to?* "First, thank you for your help with the wheelchair. Most days I can manage, but obviously, not today."

He watched her close her eyes and nod.

"Anything I can do?"

At once, Jasper was enraged. What did she think he was, some pitiful crip? He would do fine without her.

"Hey, Meredith, I have it under control. Really."

She sighed. "OK then, let's head back."

•

Meredith called the board back to order. "Jasper?"

"Yes. Thank you. This is an opportunity to discuss—"

"One second."

Donald Trapes.

He had a sizable share in the company in addition to being a CEO of his own.

"Can we discuss what happened on the interim shareholder's call last month, Meredith?"

"Of course. What would you like to—"

"From what I heard, you disgraced yourself, insulting an analyst, an analyst that we rely on to inform our shareholders. She's typically plea—"

"She wasn't pleasant then—"

"And she damn sure is no friend to SSS now, thanks to you."

Meredith leaned over the table. "I accept your point for the time being, Don. After answering all of her questions, the analyst began a deep dive into the impact of the suicide on one of our senior attorneys. She resisted my entreaties to stop, so I overcame her resistance."

"By insulting her."

The CEO raised her head. "Were you not there? You're a shareholder and have every right to be on the call."

"I wasn't, but I know what I was told."

"Well, let's put that to the test, shall we?"

Jasper watched her stand and walk around the table.

To him.

*What the hell?*

"Please gather around so that you all hear," the CEO called out, taking out her phone.

All crowded around Jasper, listening to the faint audio on the recorder of the interim board meeting exchange.

"Well," Scott Sare said, moving his right hand through his dark hair when it was over. "I may not have used the same words you used, Meredith, but her questions went beyond the pale."

"I disagree," Stella said. "Meredith, you represent a corporation. It's the corporation that has to be protected. Not individuals."

"Straight from the twentieth century, Stella," Judith Cosure interjected. "Individuals have a right to privacy too."

"Not when they put the company at risk, they don't."

"And how exactly did this lawyer put the company at risk, Stella?" Scott asked. "Our attorney did no wrong. She didn't pull the trigger, for Christ's sake. If I remember what I read, the assailant first pulled the gun on her, then killed herself."

Stella leaned past Scott to stare at SSS's CEO. "You were wrong, Meredith and you know it."

The ornate room was quiet.

"She was already emotionally damaged," Jasper interjected, relishing the moment. "You released Cassie from SSS yourself. What harm could have been done by a more genteel, revealing response to the analyst?"

"Little from the company's perspective," Meredith replied. "But a lot from Cassie's."

Meredith walked back to her seat. "It's bad enough that Cassie's been emotionally damaged by this. I was not going to allow what was left of her to be dragged through the street."

"Would you do that for anyone else here?"

"No." The CEO looked up. "I would do it for everyone else."

"Her questions were good—"

"They were a salacious inquisition. OK," she said, sitting and folding her hands on the table. "Anything else about this? No? Let's return to our seats." She turned with a smile. "Jasper?"

"Thank you." Jasper was stunned at Meredith's tough demeanor.

He began, sweat pouring off his forehead. "I'm going to take the unusual tack of describing a project that we don't have—"

"I didn't see it in my packet," Scott said.

"Neither did I," Donald added. "What's it called?"

"We call it the partial antibody project."

"OK, what does it do?"

Jasper took ten minutes to work through an explanation. He noticed that the sweat was pouring from his brow when he was done.

"Jasper," Scott said, scratching the skin above his eye. "I don't understand. The human body makes complete antibodies. It does this essentially for free. Why are we purchasing a system that only makes partial antibodies?"

"Because these will cure the common cold, so I'm told," he said, reaching for his right leg.

"How can partial antibodies kill anything?"

"Guns kill," Stella said, raising both hands. "Partial guns are harmless."

Somebody laughed.

"Well, where is it now?" Donald asked. "Who owns it?"

"A company called CiliCold. We are pursuing them."

"Never heard of 'em."

"I have," Stella said. "They've been trying to raise money up and down Indiana for over a year. So far, nothing to show for it."

"Is that right, Jasper?"

"I'm not really sure," the VP legal answered, licking his lips. He noticed the door open and Meredith's assistant walk into the room.

"Well, does the stuff work or not?" Stella asked.

"We would have to obtain it, then test it."

"Why should we buy a product that has not been shown to work, just to see if it does work?"

"Are our competitors interested in it?" Scott asked.

"No."

"That's not a surprise. We shouldn't be either."

"How much will it cost.?"

"About a mil."

"Hmmm," Scott said, shrugging. "Not much."

"It's too much if it doesn't work," Donald said, standing up. "Look, folks, we have a fiduciary responsibility to our shareholders. Which one of us could look those folks in the eye and explain the advantages of this deal?" He turned to VP legal. "Jesus, Jasper, the least you could do is give us a complete br—"

"I have all the details of the project right here," Meredith said. Her assistant distributed the 125-page document to each board member.

"Jasper and I have been working together to get our hands on this. We finally did today."

Jasper looked at her. Shocked, he nodded.

"Well, Meredith," Donald asked, "can you explain this?"

"First, let me say we are obviously going to have to make any decision about this now," the CEO began. "None of you have had the opportunity to read, understand, and raise informed questions about the document containing the details that you need.

"You are right, Scott," she said, nodding to him. "Full antibodies are made by the body. But if the body hasn't seen the virus before, it can take weeks to make them. During that time, the virus can do great damage to us. The idea of the partial antibody product is to give the body a head start."

She leaned forward. "The concept here is that you have two factories making the antibodies in sequence. First, the cell undertakes partial construction based on the instructions that we provide to it, releasing these partial antibodies. The extracellular fluid modifies this partial antibody, allowing it to change the virus into a noninfectious, harmless particle that is cleared by the body."

She turned to Jasper. "Is that about right?"

He nodded, speechless.

"Does it work?"

Meredith turned to Stella.

"In rhesus, yes. Resoundingly."

"FDA?"

"Not even close. Frankly, I'm not sure this project is even on their radarscope."

"How will this affect CS&A?"

Stella again.

"Jasper?"

"Well, I'm glad Meredith has given me a chance to speak about my own project here. My sense is that it will kill our Cold, Sinus, and Allergy Division."

"They make millions."

"But this could make billions," Scott offered. "If approved."

"But once the analysts get hold of it, we will be in their headlock," the CEO said. "They will discount our CS&A department at the start because they assume it's dead in the water. And every little FDA glitch, every little regulatory hiccup, they will downgrade our shares."

"So," Donald asked, turning to Jasper, "you are suggesting that we buy this partial antibody motivated only by a fantastic piece of speculation and hopefully kill it?"

Jasper, spent, shrugged his shoulders.

"Well, it's an interesting time," Meredith interjected. "I know Jasper and the infectious disease team headed by Dr. Stennis will get to work on this right away."

"There are lots of exciting, even dangerous questions to ask. You all are the best to get the answers. Remember, this is all confidential."

"Any other new board business? Then we are adjourned. Safe travels home, everyone."

# FOR OLD TIMES' SAKE

Emelio Cultour, chair of biology, couldn't believe his shirt had soaked through so quickly. It was just a simple posttenure meeting review with the candidate.

Unfortunately, a candidate that didn't make the tenure cut.

Desperate to buy time, he examined the faculty member's folder again.

Emily Nuson, associate professor of computational biology, sat before him quietly. Tall, just a little on the thin side, dressed professionally in a red blouse and slacks.

Yet her clear eyes and articulate voice unnerved him.

They were solid.

Purposeful.

"Can you explain to me about yesterday's negative vote?" she asked again. He saw her eyes wander over the cabinets full of books, the walls crowded with degrees and awards.

"Sure, Emily." He sat up in his chair, adjusting his tie. "Remember that nobody doubts your abilities. In fact, your colleagues rave about you."

"Well, sir, something went wrong, didn't it?"

"Yes," the chair said. He took a deep breath. "With the three foreign students."

"The cheating scandal is what it was."

He noticed the change in her voice. Before, it was light, enjoyable. Now it was peppered with anger. He swallowed. "I remember," he said, leaning forward over the desk. "You identified three students talking during an exam in your class. You interrupted them, took their papers, and asked them to leave."

"That was in accordance with the policy, right, Professor?"

"Yes."

"Right out of the rule book, in fact."

He nodded, pulse ratcheting up.

"Where I am confused," she said, putting her small black purse on the desk, "is how these miscreant students affected my tenure vote. It's policy that students caught violating university ethics rules are expelled, correct?"

"Not in this case."

"I know." He saw her eyes fix on him. "Can you tell me why?"

"The associate dean of students thought they had not been treated fairly by you."

"And how was I unfair? I warned my students at the beginning of the semester about the hazards of cheating on exams."

"Well," the chair said, wiping his palms with a handkerchief that he pulled from his pants pocket. "I wasn't there so I don't kno—"

"Of course, you know," she said. Her voice was now raised. "Have you forgotten that other students in my class were interviewed after the cheating scandal and avowed that I gave fair warning to them all about cheating? In fact, those were their words, right?"

"Yes, of course."

"And the website that I created for the course explained what behavior was permitted during exams and what was not, right?

"And isn't it true that before the exam in question, I warned students about the hazards of cheating, correct?"

He drew back from the desk as he watched her snap open her purse.

"Emily, the feeling was that the students didn't speak well enough English to understand your warnings."

"Well, sir, they certainly asked coherent questions during the lectures. No problem with comprehension there, right?"

He shook his head. "Uh, I'm not so s—"

She placed the revolver on the desk.

"Go on, Professor."

His mind raced, sweat pouring off his brow. Heroic moves would lead to violence. He inhaled, deciding that gun or not, Emily was rational. Angry, but rational.

"These same three students were allowed to petition the tenure committee, were they not? Explaining what they believed happened. And without giving me the opportunity to defend my actions, which were entirely within the scope of the university rules, these students swayed enough votes to deny me tenure."

He saw that her eyes were fixed on his. "Is there anything more to it than that, Professor?"

"No. Emily, I am so sor—"

She picked up the gun and pointed it at his head. He could see the points of the bullets in the side cylinders.

His eyes shot open. "My God, Emi—"

She jumped up and was around the desk in a flash, pushing his wooden chair back on its rocker, the chair and professor crashing to the floor. Then sitting on his lap, she yanked his head sideways, putting the gun to his left temple.

"How dare you, Professor. You ended my career."

He lost his bowels, the thick, filthy liquid soiling his pants, filling the room with the smell of the desperate.

"Reap the whirlwind."

She pulled the trigger.

He screamed.

Nothing.

He fell back on the floor, and the associate professor in the red blouse and smooth slacks walked out of the deanery and off the university campus for the last time.

But not before she took the chair's picture.

For old times' sake.

•

Three hours later, at Terum's just off of 82, Emily received a mess of text messages that she ignored. She was calm, enjoying the end of her meal on the western balcony, watching the red sun disappear behind thin gray clouds.

She knew the university would be too embarrassed to press charges against her, to bring the entire disgusting spectacle to an—

"Hey, sweet cakes, how come you—"

She turned. "Get lost, shit for brains."

The drunkard turned and hustled back to the safety of the diner.

She hated administration. She had tried to tell people who advised her on taking the academic career route that she hated it. But they were persuasive, so she tried.

And this was the result. She was a big-brained comp biologist but not a good citizen.=

Text message.

*Heard about it,* it read. *Wanna stop horsing around and work for a living?*

Emily called.

"Been a while, Rayiko."

"When I was your student, I liked you. I follow where my mentors wind up."

"Where am I now?"

"Easy. At a bar watching the sunset."

"Just taking it easy for a stretch."

"Well," she heard Rayiko say. "Do you want to barhop the rest of your life, or do something up your alley?"

"Both."

"Then I'm hanging up."

Emma's heart jumped. "Hold on. Wait. Work?"

"We need what you do."

"Tools?"

"Got 'em. Plus, what you need that we don't have, we'll get."

"Rayiko, is this legit?"

"Both legal and under the radar."

Emma relaxed. "Ha. Where is it?"

"Hole in the wall. C'mon, Em, stop playing around and ask the one question you need answered."

Emily smiled at the use of her nickname. "Has anybody ever done—"

"No. And most people think that you can't either."

"Well, hell then, Count me in."

"Be in touch. Have one on me."

"Already there."

# PRISON GARB I

June 16, 2016
Luiz, Rayiko, Breanna, Cassie

I am leaving for the Arizona State Florence Prison Complex on Monday, July 11. Should get there by the 16th.

I have no authority to ask you to follow.

You each have your own lives, your own ways. Many of you like Indiana. Actually, I did too until I was introduced to Mother Winter.

But it's time for a change for me, so let's first talk about the easy things.

I felt compelled to send this note snail mail. An email, once sent, is out of my hands, and it can wind up anywhere. That wouldn't be a good idea given that I want CiliCold to live on the down low for a while.

The need to leave Indiana is urgent. SSS has a bead on me, and the more I have to fight them, the less I can develop new ideas into preventive products.

So staying shreds my spirit, but leaving you all breaks my heart.

People tell me this issue of moving is something I should be able to manage. After all, folks leave companies all the time, commonly for good reasons, right? Robbie left us, and we moved on without her. That was more painful for me than I think I let on, but I lived with her being gone.

Now I see that the next hurdle will be working without some of you. I can take a sip of this bitter liquid every now and again, but cannot down all of it.

So let me change topics for a moment.

I know that you trust my decision about giving up the partial antibody approach. I also know that it came as quite a shock for you, especially since we worked impossible hours to have it come alive.

76

Remember the sweet days in frigid February and early March? We were so ecstatic at its success.

In Luiz's hands, the concept works. Viruses that attack us, once inside our body, can now be rendered inert.

But while theoretically elegant, it has flaws. I believe only Luiz can make the B cells do their magic at this point. To the rest of the world, that means the work is not reproducible.

So given the uphill fight for reproducibility, and in order to get SSS off our backs, I worked with an insider there to give them our work product. We are done with it, so I am OK using it as a distraction to them as I slip away. While they are chewing on what we have done, they will leave us alone.

But really, the main reason I was willing to throw the SSS dog a bone was because I know that I can make a better product. My ideas on this are forming up now. Why trust the body to design the antibody that can take weeks? Let's design it ourselves from scratch. Externally. And rapidly.

Anyway, I will be thinking hard about that as I drive to prison.

Why Florence? Because it's an agricultural spec on the Gila Bend River Reservation, draws no attention to itself, and can provide a secure, affordable home for our business.

It will be exciting. Way different. Challenging.

Rayiko, I know that you have not decided on whether you are coming, but you all should know that Rayiko has contacted on our behalf a computational expert who calculates three-dimensional chemical relationships. Also, thanks to WB's help, there is a regulator and a facilitator who will be heading our way as well.

These are three new people, and they bring new skills that we will need for the next project.

I'm saying all this because this is your company too. We are part of each other.

For some of you, the move will be impossible. For others, it will be easy and welcome. If this is one of the times to be uprooted in your life, then I encourage you to seize it.

Arizona is waiting for you. It's a buyers' market with many nice surrounding communities. It's taken Arizona a long time to recover from the housing crisis of 2007-2008, so homes are still priced to move.

Plus, all the sun you could want. And unless you really crave higher elevation, mountain living, winter, as you have known it, these past frigid years are over.

There are many communities to choose from. San Tan Valley and Queen Creek are relatively closer to jail. Great prices, lots of land, but far from Phoenix and Sky Harbor airport (not that we fly all that much). Gilbert and Chandler are farther north. A longer drive, but better developed. Mesa and Tempe are farther still and kind of on the expensive side.

As far as commuting goes, for the most part, you will drive many miles exceedingly fast in very little traffic. Police south of Phoenix are solid professionals. Same with the reservation police, but you do *not* want to mess with them.

And it is hot. Daily temps this time of the year are over 100. By August, about 110, threatening 115–120. It is dry to be sure (temps drop to the upper 70s at night and humidity can be as low as 5–15 percent), but make no mistake. Hot is hot.

I have Zelled each of you $15,000 to help with moving expenses. This is from my own kick, not the company's. If you move, it will be difficult logistically and financially. I can't help with your personal logistics, but the $$$ may make them easier.

If you move, it'd be good to do it quick. Why don't we meet at 9 AM local time on Monday, Aug 1st, at the main gate of the prison complex? That's in six weeks. We can begin to set up then, and I can share our next project with you.

But really, if this is a move that you can't make, then for those who can't, let's meet at the old Perkins on SR 26 in West Lafayette on Saturday, June 25, say, 7 PM. We can say our goodbyes then.

If you stay, I doubt that I will see you again. If that is the case, I will devote myself to my recovery from our separation. And in a new locale, maybe it will be easier than I think. But I will never be the same without all of you.

I don't know how to end this. It's too late, and too sad.

Jon

P.S. If I can find some prison garb, will send you all a prison selfie. Should be a hoot.

# ESSENCE

"What is with this man and money?" Breanna, three days later, asked. "He's always giving it away."

Cassie, Jon's letter in hand, looked up from their kitchen table. "Always?"

"He pulled this when we were going to lose our administrative assistant early this year and then again when we had an HVAC issue." Breanna jumped up from the kitchen table in jeans and a bra, brown skin gleaming as she walked around the table. "Money's valuable, Cassie. He owns a company for heaven's sake, and he acts like money is nothing."

Cassie thought for a moment. "Bree, money is not valuable. Not to everybody." She sucked her tongue. "My guess is that Jon just places more value in other things."

After a moment, she added, "Like you first told me."

Breanna whirled. "He's a businessman, and he should know better. Whether he's going to Arizona, to Arkansas, or to Alaska, he's going to need this money."

"And you are an accountant, Bree. You understand the thrust of money, the power it wields. Jon just feels the power of his thoughts." Cassie thought for a second then said, "And of the meaning of his own team."

She reached up to touch Breanna's bare arm.

"He sees the money stacked up in his savings account. Doing nothing. Helping nobody." Cassie uncrossed her legs under the table. "Then he sees his team suffering through the idea of a move with little money, so he gives it to us. It is just an"—she paused, gesturing for Breanna to sit at the table—"an elemental . . . no, a reflexive reaction. He can meet the need of his team, and so he does."

Cassie picked up the letter again as Breanna plopped down at the table. The lawyer scanned the correspondence again. *Have you ever known anyone so different as Jon?* she asked herself, shaking her head.

"What do you suggest that we do, Cassie?"

"Well, we don't need the money, but he won't take it back." The lawyer dropped the letter on the table, reaching for a half-full pitcher of lemonade.

"Who else do you think will go? What about Rayiko?"

"Rayiko?" Cassie poured a fresh glass.

"Yes. Thanks." Breanna took a swallow from the glass, rubbing her brow. "I don't know if she'll move or not." Breanna shook her head. "She's frugal, and this would be a game changer for them. Plus, I don't know it all, but her home situation is complicated."

The accountant paused for a moment. "The money would help them, of course. This is really nice lemonade."

"Learned to make it years ago. You want Rayiko to go, Bree?"

"I hadn't thought about it that way." Breanna gave the glass back, thinking for a minute. "Yes."

"Why?"

"I guess because while we would be lost without Rayiko, I think she would be lost without us. There's a part of her that we fill. Maybe she didn't know it was empty, but we're in there now."

"And you, Bree?"

"You first, dear heart."

"Absolutely," the attorney said. "I'll go. What I have known with this group is"—she shifted on the chair—"connection."

"But weren't you connected to SSS?"

"Sure," Cassie said, sitting back in the chair. "To money, to business masochism, to character destruction.

"But the relationships in CiliCold I have never really been part of before. They have such . . . such power. You all take my breath away."

Breanna felt her gaze and looked up. She saw Cassie exhale then say, "I'll go to hell before I give that up."

Breanna sighed. "Well, guess I'm coming along for the ride."

"You bet you will," Cassie said, holding Breanna's right hand in hers. "But I should not be on the payroll out there. You should get paid for what you do. Not me."

"Not you?" Breanna tilted her head. "We'll probably need an attorney out there."

"I'm fine."

Breanna leaned forward, smiling. "How fine?"

"Five-point-two-mil-in-the-bank fine."

"Liquid?"

"Just sloshing around. Another five mil in investments."

"Wall Street?"

"For the greedy and the suckers. Too crazy."

Breanna stroked her own hair. "So we're in on this?" She shook her head then smiled. "I think my babies can stand Arizona."

"Great because I bought some new things."

"Cassie. Desert things? Already?"

Cassie stood and touched Breanna's arm. "Come, check 'em out, girl."

●

Luiz read the letter alone in the small converted office in his two-bedroom apartment. The window was open, the light streaming in from the north turning the room light pink and orange.

His wife used to call it "love light."

The truck accident seven years before took that light from her.

And from him.

Standing in the light, he shook his head. He and Dale worked hard on the partial antibody project. Luiz remembered the failures, the arguments, the threats to leave, and above all, the mind-killing fatigue.

To turn that work over to SSS lock, stock, and barrel was just so, so odd. Dale would have had a seizure over it.

Luiz stood up from the desk. He was not far from Dale on this. How could Jon just . . . just give his work away for nothing? No acknowledgment of a major breakthrough. No paper with his name on it. No presenta—

*Leave something behind for somebody.*

"Thanks," he said to no one. To the universe.

Jon would only give up one idea if he had a better one. And who was this new scientist coming in? A computational biologist, he said.

They were going to calculate antibodies?

Incredible.

But one thing was sure. Somebody would actually need to test them in mammals.

That's where he came in.

He had a badge.

"Soy viejo," Luiz said, laughing, remembering the old *Dragnet* TV show line.

He put the letter back in his pocket and headed out to get a salad before the chill of the June night took over.

•

As Rayiko put Gary to bed, Richard sat in the apartment living room, letting his right hand holding Jon's letter fall by his side.

*I hate this place.*

The small apartment, so ideal for a young childless couple four years ago, was now bursting at the seams. Gary's things, Richard's computers, Rayiko's workspace. He'd been arguing with her for months to find a bigger place, but Rayiko the Frugal wouldn't budge on the moving issue.

Now this.

Gary was quiet now, and Richard read the letter once, then twice. His heart was pounding.

*This is perfect*, he thought.

But he didn't want Rayiko to know how excited he was. With her, it was either manipulate or be manipulated.

He could manage. He'd heard that there were some database ups. gr—

"So, Richard. What are you thinking," Rayiko said, walking past him to sit on the small brown couch opposite him. Already in black pajamas, she had a sheaf of papers in her right hand. "What is this, Rayiko?" he said, waving the letter. "Are you all married to each other at that company?"

He watched her exhale. "No, but we are all closely involved in the work."

"Well," he said, letting the letter fall to the floor. "Sounds like a Manson thing."

He watched Rayiko for a sign and caught only a cold, studied neutrality hurled back at him.

"Your strength is different than his," she finally said, as she began to flip papers in her lap.

"Damn right it is," he snorted. He took some breaths and then walked over to sit on the worn sofa with her.

"Well, wife of mine?" he said, index finger pointed to her. "What next."

He watched her keep her teeth together. *Wants me to make the next move. OK then.*

"I did some checking while you were with Gary a few minutes ago," he started. "We can get out of our lease, and you and I have already been talking about getting a house, maybe down in Noblesville. But really . . . Arizona?"

"That was my first reaction too," she finally said. "Sounded kind of . . . desperate."

"Well, I have two acquaintances from the Grand Canyon state. One from a town named Superior, which is north of Florence, but the other from Casa Grande, which is just west of the prison town."

He turned right to face her. "It's dry gulch country. Deserts are dangerous. Do you know that a scorpion sting is worse than that of a wasp? And in the spring and summer, they can get anywhere in your house. They crawl on kitchen floors. Up onto bath towels. Into beds.

"People use black lights to hunt them down in their home at night. 'Search and destroy' for Christ's sake."

He leaned over toward her. "Beds, Rayiko? You want to check your bed every night for scorpions? And how about Gary. He'll be four years old. One day, you'll find him on the floor trying to play with two scorpions on his thigh. Do you want to deal with that?"

"And let's not talk about coyotes, what they do to pets . . ." He shook his head, giving his best performance.

Rayiko looked at him. "Phoenix is the fifth-largest city in the nation. I'm sure there are tips for dealing with scorpions, just as we follow advice for dealing with roaches, Richard."

"I'm sure that they do control it. But this letter," he said, waving it back and forth in the air, "doesn't say 'Phoenix.' It says 'Florence.' Sixty miles south of Phoenix in the desert. On an Indian reservation for heaven's sakes."

"We don't have to live in Florence."

"Fine. Queen Creek, Apache Junction. Whatever. All the surrounding communities have the same issues."

"I—"

"Look, I'm not saying it's a bad idea," he said, leaning toward his wife a little. He hated touching her. "It's just going down the rabbit hole. And if it doesn't work, we'll probably be able to sell our property. Housing prices are barely back from the 2008 catastrophe. Anyway, it's always boom or bust out there." He shrugged.

"Where do you think you would work?"

*Clever girl*, he thought, changing the topic.

He had already checked. There were three groups in the LA area that were already sucking his kneecaps for the position. But he didn't want to be too eager.

"I don't know." He rubbed his forehead. "Well, nothing south of Phoenix for me. Just cows and cotton there. There may be some action in LA. It's not so far, actually. Just a commuter flight from Sky Harbor to the West Coast. I could fly out in the morning and be back just after evening rush hour."

They sat quietly for a few minutes.

"Did you ever stop to think," he said, watching her carefully, "that if he liked you and your 'team' so much"—he air quoted "team"—"that he wouldn't leave you high and dry?"

She looked up at him. "If Jon didn't leave, he would be destroyed."

Richard guffawed. "Please. Such freaking melodrama with you folks. I just don't get that."

"No, Richard, of course you don't, and you never will. I love you, but I also recognize that you are made up of a different essence than him."

Richard straightened up on the couch, letting the letter drop to the floor. "What exactly does that mean?"

"To you, focusing on money is everything. We need it, I know. But the result of your dollar concentration is that something with no financial value is dead to you. An idea or concept with no financial value to you is dead. Companies and people you can't do business with—dead. Stone, dirt, flowers, birds, animals, sky—it's all dead to you. The only thing alive is money.

"To Jon, everything is alive. That approach has its problems to be sure, and there have been times when he really flails, but his approach to life itself fills him like money fills you. Those that work with him believe that in the end there is an order to what he does. And strength behind it. It is why we work so hard with him. And it is why scorpions, snakes, coyotes, hot sun, and every other little obstacle that you bring up simply doesn't matter."

"Gary matters to me," he said with a smile.

"For which I am thankful," she said. "And thanks for bringing him home."

"So are you going?" he asked, lifeless eyes conveying little.

"You mean are we going, right?"

Richard studied her studying him, saying nothing.

# NOBODY

Friday night.

Jon was spinning in two directions at once. Dread and exhilaration. *This is life*, he thought.

Unpredictable and frightening.

Since his letter, he'd heard nothing from his team.

In fact, Jon wondered whether they had even received the letters. He'd checked the addresses over and over.

Yep, they were right.

And here was Perkins.

He pulled the Cherokee in to a spot by the side of the restaurant and walked in.

But like so many times with his team, he was in the dark. He knew he would learn nothing until he went inside.

Where he would learn it all.

He did receive a call from a Ms. Olivia Steadman. She wanted to know his itinerary.

Sounded strong. Assured. He checked her out. Solid reg background. WB treated reg like a hobby, he thought, walking into the restaurant. But he got the job done. If he appr—

Luiz.

"Hey, Jon, just heading back to my seat from the head. Come on," he said, moving ahead, motioning Jon to follow down the dark aisle.

*Luiz.*

*He wasn't going?*

He understood the complications for the others, but Luiz? Like Jon, he was footloose and fan—

Jon stopped.
Rayiko, Breanna, Cassie.
All there.
Nobody was going.

# PRISON GARB II

Jon's eyes fluttered for a minute, his back slick with sweat. Nothing was on automatic. He had to make himself breathe wondering if his heart would continue to beat on its own. He sat down at their table.

*No one was coming.*

*It changed nothing. It changed everything. If total rejection was right, nothing is—*

"Jon," Rayiko said, tapping him on the shoulder. "Your idea was stupid."

"What? I—"

"Really? Coming out here to say goodbye for only those who are staying behind? What sense does that make? Maybe the rest of us wanted in on the action. Check out your text messages."

Jon dropped his Android then fumbled to pick it up, completely at his team's mercy.

Not a message.

A picture.

Luiz, Rayiko, Breanna, and Cassie.

Loose-fitting white-and-black-striped shirts.

Numbers across all chests.

Prison garb.

Jon leaned his head back, closing his eyes. "All of you? Seriously? We are all going to Arizona?"

"Not if you tell the world," Rayiko said. "I thought this wagon train was supposed to be deep and dark."

Jon was breathing deep, trying to catch up to his runaway breath. "There. It's settled," he said, looking around. "Arizona."

"Can we get some menus please?" Cassie said to the waitress passing by.

"Good. Dinner," Jon said, famished all at once. "I'm buying."

"You bet you're buying," Breanna said. "Somebody snatch a pitcher of margaritas."

"Cassie," he said, a moment later, looking at the picture again. "Of all people. You're an attorney."

"Just wondered how the other half dressed," she said, smiling.

Everybody fell out.

•

Two hours later, Rayiko looked across the booth at Breanna who was fast asleep against Cassie who was dozing against the sleeping Luiz.

"They're hammered," she heard Jon say.

"I'm the designated driver, so they're good."

She followed Jon's eyes as they moved toward her. He took a sip of tea then said, "Are you really OK, Rayiko? I imagined that your decision would be the toughest."

She felt his arm around her and let it stay.

"Yeah." She was quiet for a second. "It started out that way, but Richard found a new job in Los Angeles and—"

"LA?"

"Yeah. He will work there Tuesday through Thursday, work from home Monday and Friday, and be home during the weekends. Seemed like a good deal."

She knew, hurting some with the thought, that she was less sure then she sounded. The discussions at home were a little too smooth for a Richard talk. He was trying to play her. Not that she couldn't read him anymore.

More like she didn't like what she read.

A small headache appeared.

"Anyway, he's not so sure about life in Arizona."

"Which is why most people leave Arizona alone with its heat and droughts and, of course, why it's ideal for us now. Who looks to the desert for computational scientists."

"Guys who like to drop the big bombs?"

"That's New Mexico. In Arizona, the desert has a peace that you don't find anywhere else."

The desert was the least of her problems, or at least she hoped so. Night lights for scorpion search-and-destroy missions? Ugh.

"Well," Jon said, "thanks to you, we are getting a three-dimensional computational chemist."

She looked up. "Is that what Em calls herself?"

"Got it from her online CV."

"I told her that you will have the computing power she needs. Is that possible?"

"Sure is. By a brother named Kevin. He's coming in with Olivia who's the reg person Wild Bill talked us up to. I'll get Kevin the specs before we get on the road."

"But look at what's on you, Jon," she said, resting on his chest. "Building a team again, this time half of them not knowing of the existence of the other half. Converging on a deserted prison. And to do what? Work on a project that you haven't even articulated yet."

"Yeah, I know. Somehow, it doesn't seem quite big enough, does it?"

She smiled, feeling him nuzzle her hair.

"It was good that you pushed your departure date by two weeks."

"Seemed like everybody needed more time."

"How about SSS?" she asked.

"Thrown off the scent," Jon said. He took a deep breath. "That won't last forever, but it will buy us the time that we need."

"To do what? What's the project?"

He leaned down, whispering in her ear.

The tiniest flush spread across her face, and her heart jumped.

"No, we are not. Be serious."

He whispered again.

Rayiko straightened up. "Jon, that's crazy. Nobody's ever done that."

"We can, with the right team."

"And if we don't, we're stuck out on a limb in the heart of Gila River Indian Reservation?"

"Well, if the team falls apart, I figure we can have some lively shoot-outs in the prison."

"You play too much." He lifted his left arm, and she sneaked under it, resting against him.

He kissed her hair. "This is a day for play."

# GLOVE ON THE HAND

Luiz heard Jon bounce up off the torn black passenger seat after a nasty jolt.

"Time for me to drive, Luiz?"

"You're just saying that because the driver's seat is more comfortable."

"Tru dat. This seat is terrible. I thought Hertz had good trucks."

"They do. Just bad seats." Luiz pulled the small truck off the road, turned off the engine, jammed on the parking brake, and threw the hazard light switch.

It was Tuesday, July 15, 7:16 PM, day two of a five-day drive from Indy to Florence that by Luiz's map should have taken twenty-five hours. They had already spent one hotel night in Rolla, about ninety miles southwest of St. Louis. Now they were in Cherokee country, eastern Oklahoma.

Although there was still plenty of light in the sky, Luiz knew that Jon would want to stop soon.

"Tell me again why we are taking the leisurely route at a leisurely pace."

"Well, it's not for the good cuisine," Jon said, laughing. "That seafood back in Joplin liked to slay me." He got out and walked around the front of the truck, stopping for a languorous stretch.

"To remind you," he called out to the cell scientist, "we're hauling the equipment that we can't afford to replace. Plus, we can't go fast because I already lost one crown and two fillings to this truck's bouncing all over the road. And we are hauling my beloved Cherokee. Anyway"—Jon checked his phone map then got behind the driver's seat—"we're not far from Tulsa. Thirty-five miles."

"Great, I could eat again."

"You would be," Jon said, belching. "You had the burgers in Joplin. Good choice. I may never be hungry again."

"Don't blame Desenex. Tried to warn you, amigo." Luiz got in, then reaching over, put his hand on Jon's arm. "I know that you'll fill me in soon on what's really going on here."

Luiz saw the intensity in Jon's eyes. "Now's a good time, my friend. Thanks for your patience."

Jon started up the fifteen-foot truck, flicked off the hazards, released the brakes, and eased out onto 44 west.

"I needed time to think, Luiz. That little maneuver we pulled with SSS will buy us time, but not all that we need. When they wake up, they'll come at us hard."

"Why?"

Jon paused then replied, "Because they kill that which resists them."

"Sounds like a *Star Wars* thing."

They both laughed.

"When we get to Arizona, we'll have to settle in fast and plunge right in."

"Plunge into what? Better put your lights on."

"Thanks. I forget that they're not automatic."

"Like they were in your Cherokee?"

Jon smiled. "We're jumping into synthetic antibody generation."

Luiz shook his head. "We already have that, Jon. They're called B cells. I've been studying them for years. They make antibodies automatically. Been doing it for over a billion years in mammals. We don't make them do it. They don't go on strike, don't need smoking breaks, and don't need money."

"No," Jon said, turning his head to the immunologist for a second. "I mean in vitro production. Mass quantities rapidly."

Luiz was quiet. Jon horsed around some, but never about his ideas and especially when he was in the process of building them up. Luiz remembered that the worst fight Jon and Dale ever had was when Jon began to describe a concept that Dale tried to dismember during the birthing process.

He had seen Jon angry before but never fury like that. So he borrowed a tactic he'd seen once.

"Mass quantities rapidly?" Luiz said, repeating Jon's last comment.

"Yeah. Maybe later we can give the B cells the tools to build them on their own, but first the antibodies are built outside the body then injected into the host."

*Dios mio*, the cell scientist thought. *We've been doing this for years.* He took a moment then sat back in the seat.

"I think you made this seat worse. I just cracked two vertebrae," Luiz said. "How is this different from tetanus antitoxin?"

"Antitetanus antibodies are made from horse serum. So the horse has to be infected, generate the immunity, and then we siphon it off and give it to humans. There, the horse is the production engine."

"Here, we'll have a two-part issue. Design and production," Jon continued.

"Oh, Wilbur," Luiz said.

"You and Mr. Ed."

"Watch the road."

The CEO squinted. "Yeah, we need to stop soon. Anyway, the antibody is really a short but complicated chain of amino acids. Once we have designed the right sequence of them, we can mass-produce 'em. Taking that end of the bridge is easy."

Luiz grimaced. "So the question becomes 'How do you find the right sequence?'"

"Random searches take far too long," Luiz said, nodding his head.

"Right. By the time the right sequence is found, the patient would have been dead for a hundred years."

They both laughed at the exaggeration.

Luiz put his head back on the seat. "So we find it intelligently, eh?"

"Which means?"

"AI," they said at once. Luiz smiled.

"There are two parts to this operation," Jon said shifting in the seat. "You know, this seat is really rough too."

The immunologist closed his eyes. "Keep talking."

"The first is mapping the viral surface. But that to me seems kind of straightforward."

Luiz nodded. "Agreed."

"Yes. That's—" Jon paused for a moment. "What's that smell?"

"Dust, dirt, and cow manure." Luiz closed his window.

"The second is taking that map and building an antibody on it."

Luiz pursed his lips. "That means reverse engineering the antibody from the surface of the virus? From the antigen?"

"Yep."

"Well, how would we do that?" Luiz was really perplexed here, anxiety sliding into his voice. "You're taking a three-dimensional surface of a collection of proteins on the viral surface then trying to engineer a combination of amino acids that fits that combination of proteins in a three-dimensional configuration so that it can fit all over the virus, denaturing it. Am I right?"

Jon smiled. "Trying to build the glove onto the hand."

Luiz made himself take a deep breath. "Very tough."

Jon nodded. "I know. That's what the body does, and without our help. The first time the body is exposed to a virus, the immune system has a devil of a time building the first antibody that successfully attaches to the virus. It's got no history to guide it. Definitely not an AI approach." Jon exited the highway.

"Where're we staying?"

"Navigating to South Bolder Avenue and Seventh. Holiday Express there."

"Anywhere that the bed is softer than these seats."

"Anyway," Jon continued, "it takes from days to weeks for the body to first develop an antibody. And in the meantime, the virus has its way with the body.

"Ask yourself what will happen when the Big One finally comes, the killers that are on the way like tomorrow's sunrise. Sephus Keller III retrovirus. Celphoid-zeta."

"I've never heard of those names."

Jon looked over at him. "Just made them up."

"Like Captain Trips?"

"You watch too much Stephen King. But whatever it's named, it would have not just high infectivity, but high mortality as well. People will die by the hundreds of millions while the body hunts and pecks for the right amino acid combination to defeat them."

"The virus doesn't respect our body's timelines any more than it respects our woes and sufferings. They just . . . slam home." Jon shook his head, dropping the visor to shield his eyes from the setting sun in the red sky.

Luiz scratched his neck. "How long will it take to produce the antibodies once it's operational?"

"After we get the viral protein map, a day for the first retro map."

"A day?"

Jon stopped at a light. "Two to three to start mass production."

Luiz dropped his head then looked over at his boss. "You're dreaming, Jon. I don't mean that as an insult."

The light changed.

"Not dreams, Luiz. Mathematics and computing."

Luiz had felt anxiety swelling in him for several minutes. He licked his lips. "Listen, I appreciate your faith in me, but I do the biology. I manipulate B cells, not beta coefficients in some link function."

"And we'll still need you to do the B cell thing. Once artificially produced, some undifferentiated B cells will have to be convinced to accept the sequence as their own so they can produce them when the body needs."

Luiz smiled. "I can pull that off. But not the first part."

Jon pulled into the Holiday Express. "That's why we need help."

"And when will we be getting it?"

"Tomorrow 7:00 AM at breakfast."

# KEKULÉ

Luiz never liked taking a problem with him to bed. So tonight, he sat in the small chair by the small desk next to the small window in the small hotel room.

And just thought.

"How would they be able to pull this off?" he asked out loud. His mind whirled through his mastery of molecular biology and, ultimately, chemistry and physics. Jon and whoever they would meet tomorrow were trying to tightly combine small amino acid chains together within a chaotic environment.

But there's so much movement at the molecular level. Like trying to find a shoe that fits a foot that jerks around hundreds of times a minute, you never get to see if it fits because it won't keep still.

Here, the molecules oscillate billions of times a second, bombarded by trillions of atoms from every different direction. Even if you kill all the jigs, then you'll find "a fit" that might not even fit in the real world. Too much movement.

How can you produce something stable in this whirlwind?

Of course, he remembered that the body does it all the time. It has huge molecules that combine with smaller molecules changing them, sometimes adding energy, sometimes releasing energy.

But these enzymes were billions of years in the making, and we don't have that kind of time.

Kekulé.

Luiz jerked at the memory, remembering that the German scientist had to figure out how carbon atoms stayed tightly bound without enough electrons. One night after another failed effort, he left his office, climbed onto a bus, and exhausted, went to sleep.

And dreamed of monkeys.

Six of them in a ring, representing a carbon atom apiece. But they kept the carbon atoms from flying apart with their tails.

Overlapping each other.

What kept the molecule from tearing itself to pieces was that the tails were shared.

Gripping each other for strength and support.

Luiz's head snapped out of his doze. He didn't need to match a molecule to a molecule; he simply needed to match a collection of constructed molecules to the viral surface. Even if the fit to the virus wasn't strong, it didn't need to be. The strength of the larger molecule attached to it would be sufficient to hold.

*Tal vez*, he thought. Perhaps, but he was tired now. Rolling into bed, Luiz thanked God that he was here and part of this mess.

# KNOCKOUT BLOW

CR30-R. 11:00 AM.

That's all the text message said. But it was enough.

Jasper wiped his brow. CR30-R was the main thirtieth-floor conference room.

SSS research and development territory.

Something was up.

Jasper put his iPhone back, as he turned to face Stennis in the scientist's office. It was an exaggerated motion these days, leaning all the way to his left in the wheelchair to expose his left shirt pocket under his jacket, then reaching with his left hand to sweep the jacket aside and drop the phone in its pocket with his right.

Giles sniffed but didn't have to wonder at the odor. It was the smell of defeat.

"Stennis," Jasper said, as he rubbed his right thigh in vain. "I need to know where we are with the partial antibody construction."

"We're going to start our tenth monkey tomorrow," the tall scientist said, thinning brown hair lying across his forehead.

"Tenth?" Jasper shook his head. "No production yet?" VP legal began moving air through his mouth in big gulps, spittle accompanying each exhale. "We've had the project in our hands an entire month now. This is the best we can do?"

"Jasper, this is a project designed to be executed by CiliCold scientists. The concept is easy. Just make the $F_c$ part of the antibody and release it into the extracellular fluid. In fact"—Stennis shook his head—"it's miraculous. The trick is getting the B cells to make partial antibodies. That we can't do yet."

"Well, you have all the materials they had. What do they have to do, hold your damn hand?" Giles hated the defeatism seeping from this man.

"Look, it's a com—"

"Don't give me PC bullshit to cover your group's incompetence. We must move forward with this project so it's the Doucette knockout blow when her incompetence becomes clear. What's the holdup?" Giles waved his hand at the swath of white coats moving through the lab doing . . . lab things.

Stennis shook his head. "Not having the right people who can program the B cell. In fact, it may take us months to get those cells to do our bidding, if at all."

Giles whirled his wheelchair around. "Are you telling me that SSS can't finish it off?"

"I'm telling you that we will do what we can, but it may be all for nothing. And don't forget," he said, Giles seeing the wrinkled index finger pointed his way, "we won't even be able to tell if the process transforms viruses until we can get the body to make the $F_c$ fragment."

Giles swallowed hard. "They'd better damn well do something. Triple S' financials need new drugs flowing through the line, and this is one of them. Lots of people right up to the board level are expecting good results. If it's good, then we have a blockbuster that we hold on to for a few years, bilking the system first for millions from our Cold and Science Division. If not, well, we kill it before it damages C&S."

"You threatening me?"

"Threatening you?" Giles rose as far out of the chair as he dared. "Threatening you? I'm promising you. You didn't even have to come up with the idea. You only have to execute it. Count on this—you don't make the partial antibody productive, and I'll make an argument that your research team be cut by 60 percent within the year."

"You can't make up immunology as you g—"

"CiliCold seems to."

"Maybe I should work for them."

"They don't exist anymore," Giles called behind him as he wheeled his chair out for the nearest elevator. "Scattered like ants after we got the product. You work for me. Get it done. Or find them and get them to do it."

# HANGED

Meredith walked about the corner and right into her VP regulatory, Monica Stephens. "Monica, I am really so sorry," the CEO said, apologizing for the stumble. "I think that you and I are headed to the same place."

"I don't know, Ms. Doucette. I am heading to an urgent 'dovetail' meeting with reg in CR30-C."

"Dovetailing marketing and regulatory? Well, I'm going to the sister room, CR30-R," Meredith offered. "I must tell you that I don't know what it's about, but . . ." The CEO paused for a second, wondering if she should continue her thought train out loud. *If I can't trust my VP reg, then I'm really screwed.* "I've no ideas about the audience or the agenda. I'd guess it's a research development issue."

"Neither do I. I didn't even know that there was a CR-30R meet."

Meredith studied her reg chief, knowing that they were thinking the same thing.

"How can we not know about both?" Meredith knew that she and Monica were cut from a different cloth. Meredith shared her own thoughts. Monica was taciturn, always keeping her thoughts to herself. Even when she spoke, she used words with painful efficiency, as though she was paying a price to utter each one. Her behind-the-back nickname was "Dr. Dour."

Yet here, walking into the elevator, Monica, trim as always in a beige pants suit and white blouse, drew the same conclusion.

"We'd been cut out," Meredith said.

"I agree. The why or how of it I don't know, but the fact is undeniable."

Meredith decided.

"Monica. Please do me a favor and come to my meeting with me. Things appear urgent, and neither you nor I know what is happening.

If we are being pushed to some kind of hasty decision, I will need your counsel."

Monica looked down. *Odd*, Meredith thought.

"I will attend with you, Ms. Doucette." Monica pulled her Android out and called her assistant, asking him to attend the other meet.

"One moment." The CEO called her admin assistant.

"Jan, please cancel the CR30-C meeting and reschedule for a time that I can attend."

The VP reg focused on the elevator floor, saying nothing.

*Odd*, Meredith thought.

•

Conference room CR30-R was one of the most electronically sophisticated conference rooms in the SSS building. Far too complicated for most of the attendees, a technician's presence wasn't just recommended, but required at all meetings.

Meredith walked through the auto doors that swished open, noticing that Monica was close behind.

Each of the thirty chairs was already taken. Meredith took a quick census.

Peterson, Casper, and two others from research and development. Jacks and his team from clinical research. Two from project management. Two from IT. Plus Jasper. And another six from marketing including executive VP marketing, senior VP marketing as well as VP marketing executives for Asia, Latin American, Europe, and North America.

Nobody from regulatory or quality control, she noted. Yet not an empty seat.

*The deck is stacked*, the CEO thought.

*Time to kick it over.*

Meredith walked over to the two seated IT department members. "We require these seats. I'm very sorry."

The short bespectacled man and taller woman got up and walked away in a crouch. The CEO and VP reg took them, as she saw Robert Peterson, VP research, smile at her before he began his presentation.

"Good morning, everyone. We have some exciting news from one of our early phase 1 clinical trials that we wanted to share with you because of the implications." Then he stopped, and Meredith watched him turn to her.

"Glad you could make it. This may be a bumpy ride toward approval."

*He tipped my office off about this meet*, she thought.

He had concerns about this program.

The CEO was stunned. Judging by the heavy marketing presence, they must have wanted to push this project along. She took a breath and interjected.

"Which is why you in research and we in senior management and regulatory must retain control," she said, looking directly at the large marketing contingent in attendance.

"Meredith, we thought it was premature to bring senior management in at this time," Denise Cowars, VP marketing North America, deadpanned.

"Senior management will decide what and when senior manager will get involved," she said. "Is there a problem?"

Cowars said nothing. The room, tight with emotion, was silent.

"Rob, I think that we are all ready," Meredith said, looking around the room, her voice betraying nothing. "Please share what you have with us."

"You all probably don't know the identities of the compounds on which we are working," Dr. Peterson began, turning his head so that all could hear. "One of them is SNW17012. It's a compound that we acquired as part of our new molecular management initiative." He nodded to Jasper.

"What does this compound do?" Barry Jacks, a physician, asked.

*A clinician. Always to the point*, Meredith thought.

"We initially believed that it would be a useful adjunct seizure therapy, but the initial biochemical studies suggested that its activity on the white matter of the brain might prove useful in degenerative neurodisease of adults."

"You mean Lewy body stuff? Huntington's chorea? Those diseases?" Jacks said, leaning forward.

"Yes, but we were wrong. So we turned our attention to children."

"Can you please speak louder?" the VP marketing Asia called out.

"Of course. We turned our attention to the treatment of ASD."

"Autism? Was it effective?" Jacks again.

"In treating it? No."

"Well, what are we doing—"

"It was effective in preventing it," Ron said.

Meredith didn't breathe. Neither did anyone else.

•

Rob began to go through the numbers. "This was a phase 1 study in two- to three-year-old children who were believed to be at risk of autism spectral disorder."

"I know this study," Monica said, "Essentially, it used this new compound with an unknown side effect profile in children to treat a disease that they may not even get. It took over a year for the FDA to sign off on the protocol."

"And what are you here to tell us, Rob?" the CEO asked, leaning back in her chair.

"We studied thirty of these young children who were at high risk of ASD based on behavioral measures," Ron continued, lasering a line on a PowerPoint slide. "In the placebo group, you can see that of the fifteen high-risk children who did not receive the compound, eleven were exhibiting clear signs of ASD a year later."

"My God," Jasper said, pointing to the screen. "Are those the active group numbers right next to them?"

"Yes, in the active group, only three moved forward to ASD."

"You are telling us that eleven of fifteen untreated children were autistic in a year, yet only three of fifteen treated children progressed to autism at the same time?" Cowars asked.

"That rate is too good to be true," someone called out.

"Or maybe treatment doesn't prevent autism but merely postpones it. How long did you follow these children?"

"Two years."

"Pretty long for children this age."

The room was dead still.

"Phase 1 studies must be interpreted carefully," VP research said. "But there is something else." He turned to an assistant. "Cindy, can you start the video please?"

The lights came down, but even in low light, it took a few moments to make out what was on the screen. Not just because of the light, Meredith realized, but because the image was impossible for the brain to accept.

It was a child who had melted into itself.

Not really melted, but completely collapsed on its own body. One could only guess at the age. The child's head was tilted back at an impossible angle, unsupported by a neck that was unsupported by spine or thoracic musculature. The legs were at about 140 degrees apart, impossibly bent at the knees, and the arms were bent back behind the entire body.

The child was motionless.

Dead.

Again, the room was quiet.

"This is a child that was administered the compound two days ago," Ron explained. "We are lucky to have this video. A nurse had the presence of mind to shoot it when she discovered the child this way. What that same nurse tells us is that this flaccid paralysis was preceded by opisthotonus for thirty seconds."

"What is that?" VP marketing Latin America asked in a hushed voice.

"It's when every single muscle of the body suddenly contracts," Jacks said. "Neck, arms, back, legs, everything. The person looks like they are trying to stretch out as far as they can. If they were on their back, then the only parts of the body that are on the bed are the back of the head and the heels."

Meredith turned to Rob, knowing that everyone in the room was struggling with the image. "So you are telling us that normal health in at least one child, after ingestion—"

"IV injection is the rout—"

"Was followed by total opisthotonus, then total flaccid paralysis, then death within twenty-four hours of therapy?"

"Yes, twenty-four to forty-eight hours."

Jacks shook his head. "Therapeutic triumph and catastrophe from the same medication."

The room erupted, many arguing for the intense fast-track approval with certain provisions and cautions, others arguing that the drug was dangerous and testing must end at once. The conversations grew loud and heated.

"Knock it off!" Meredith shouted, suddenly on her feet. "This is not some damn debating society. Everyone sit down and be quiet now."

Stunned at the CEO's outburst, all returned to their seats. "Have the parents been notified?" the CEO asked.

"Uh, yes, they have. Last night."

"What about our safety department and the FDA?"

"We thought talking to this group here would be notification of our safety team and ultimately of the FDA," Diane said.

"The agency should have been notified at once," Monica said, jumping up. "Check your protocol. There are some instances when a death is required to be reported immediately. We may already be out of compliance with the FDA."

"Calm down, Monica," VP marketing Asia said. "It's only been a da—"

"Who the hell are you to tell her to calm down? You don't know the obligations and responsibilities of safety and regulatory," said the CEO, "and do not presume that you do. In fact, the agency should be contacted electronically at once. In fact, someone should phone them today."

Meredith saw that Rob looked to be at a loss.

"Rob, I want you to see that Monica, in the next thirty minutes, has all the information about this death that you have."

"You mean both deaths, right?"

The room was dead still.

Meredith felt her heart beating hot and angry, the gray hair on her neck standing straight. "Do you mean to tell me there have been two such deaths and the FDA has not been informed about either?"

"Meredith," Cowars said, "we wanted to be sure what we were dealing with in this circumstance."

"Ms. Cowars, I am less and less interested in what you and your team think of this situation." She turned to Rob.

"When did the first child die?"

"A week ago."

"And this second child, whose image we see here, was injected after we knew of the first death?"

"Meredith," VP marketing North America said. "How could—"

"Please stay out of the way of my question," Meredith said. She turned to the presenter. "Is that right, Rob?"

He nodded.

"So we, after knowing that an injection caused the death of one child, knowingly gave a similar injection to a second child who is now dead, right?"

He said nothing.

She turned to Monica. "I want you to personally step in and take charge of this debacle. I am stunned that our protocols have not been followed. The FDA is to be notified at once. Call the FDA officer in charge of our IND and speak in person with him today."

"Of course, Ms. Doucette."

"I want a meeting between safety, reg, and me at 3:00 PM today with an update on our progress."

Monica turned to Rob. "Has the study been stopped?"

"The investigators are consid—"

"The study is to be placed on clinical hold at once," Meredith said.

Somebody gasped.

"Meredith, don't you think that we sho—"

"Every moment that you delay in taking decisive action in the face of a clinical debacle," Meredith said, standing, "adds to the sense that SSS is not taking every conceivable measure to ensure that this tragedy does not happen again."

"Ms. Doucette," Cowars said. "Really? We don't want to kill the goose while it's laying the golden egg, do we?"

"Ms. Cowars, your neolithic incompetence may have already done that," the CEO said, locking eyes with the executive VP marketing. "What do you think the media will say about this? We will and should be crucified for this travesty. That means you as well, Cowars. I am now going to ask you and your marketing teams to leave this meeting at once." She turned to VP reg. "Monica, please call our lead safety people and tell them that they are required here in five minutes for an initial update."

Cowars sat, stunned. "You have never ejected me—"

Meredith, eyes blazing, walked over to her, leaned into her face, and shouted, "Eject you? I should hang you!"

She sat down in the shocked room. Meredith, her head pounding, walked back to her seat, sitting still for a moment in the stunned room. Then she declared, "The people responsible for this tragedy will not work for me anymore."

As the meeting broke up, people talked in hushed whispers.

Meredith was confused. Grabbing the VP reg's arm on the way back to their offices, she asked, "Monica, how could you not know about this?"

Monica looked up at the CEO.

"Because you didn't want me to."

# OUTLAWS

Not quite on the run from but not heading back to Stanford, Emma followed Rayiko's instructions.

*And here I am*, she thought as she walked into the Holiday Inn breakfast buffet. *Tulsa*.

"Rayiko tells me that you're an outlaw."

"Only to the boring," she responded, heart jumping but voice steel smooth. She turned.

The tall, thin man laughed. "God help me if I ever become boring. Right now, I am only Jon. Jon DeLeon."

"I'm Emily Nuson."

He smiled like it came naturally. Actually, like he couldn't help it. She smiled back.

"I won't beat around the bush nor talk to you about 'opportunities' and 'challenges.' Let's leave that talk for the academics in our past."

Emily nodded. "Tore off my rearview mirror a long time ago." *This will be fun.*

"We simply have a problem that you can help us with," Jon continued, grabbing a flimsy white plate after her. "I can promise you serious computing boxes, a paltry salary, and no administrative overhead. You report only to me, and the only thing I want to hear from you is how I can help you. Oh yeah, this all takes place in prison."

*Prison.* She smiled. "Well, like you said, I'm an outlaw."

"Let's walk over and get some breakfast." He walked with Emily through the buffet room. "The eggs are a little runny, but—"

"It's OK. I don't complain about food I don't pay for."

"I am starting to enjoy you, Emily."

"Because Rayiko told you, or in spite of it?"

"Both. And you're buying."

They laughed and he walked her over to the table where Luiz was seated.

She saw Luiz stand. "Emily Nuson? I am Luiz Calderone."

*Luiz Calderone?* She had heard of him at Stanford. He looks so young for all he has done in immunology, she thought.

"No, the honor is mine," she said, reaching for and shaking his hand. "I have done my best to follow your work. In fact, I have tried to mimic your work with my software. Badly, I think."

"It's my hope that we can work together now."

Jon motioned for her to sit next to Luiz as he sat across from them. "I don't know how much time you have, and I don't want to waste it."

*Time?* She'd spent her time in one budget hotel after another, looking to lose the defeat demons who dropped her off at night and were there, waiting bright and early in the morning for her.

This new human company she could use.

"Well, let's get started then."

"First," Jon said, leaning forward over the table, "I confess I do not know you. I only know about you. What I think I've learned is that you are a computational biologist who does not do well in academia. Your work record is exemplary. As a faculty member, well"—he shrugged—"you don't play by the rules."

"So far so good."

"I, on the other hand, am a renegade scientist. I was accused of intellectual dishonesty, exonerated, but still wear the scarlet letter on my shirt. I have only a small but exceptional team and some interesting ideas."

Emily studied him carefully. There was not a dishonest nuance on his face. He'd been hurt in academia and it showed. The openness and sincerity, like a ray of sunshine, was getting through to her icy heart.

"How did leaving feel?" she asked.

She saw him study her carefully. Saw his eyes water. "I felt like a part of me that I liked so much had been slashed away. They cleared me of wrongdoing, but it didn't matter. The accusation was the crime. The confiscation of my computers, the depositions of my research team and of me. Altogether, it tore the academic heart out of me."

"I may know what you mean."

He leaned forward. "I know but also know, Emily, that you will recover. You can't ignore the pain. That is true. But there comes a time when it . . . it doesn't find you so easily. The trick is to not be so fond of it that you pull it back in."

Emily, suddenly close to tears, shook her head. "Not there yet, Jon."

He nodded. "Let me know when and I'll help."

He cleared his throat. "Look at me, boring Luiz who has already been away from his work far too long. You two eat your breakfast and I'll talk."

•

By Emily's count, Jon spent the next thirty minutes laying out what he had in mind. He answered Emily's questions carefully, saying both what he knew and also laying out what he did not.

"So," she started when he had finished, "you are asking that I be part of a project that will be confronted with a virus. Our job is to map the viral surface molecularly, identifying all the chemical moieties, then translate that structure into mathematics. This mathematics will then be used to identify a string of amino acids, the beginning of an antibody that will fit the moieties in three dimensions. The entire process, once working, is to be completed in one day. Once finished, we will produce the antibodies in tremendous quantities to be used as a passive vaccine." She tilted her head at Jon. "That it?"

"Not quite," Jon said, putting down a glass of what to Emily looked like grapefruit juice. "Actually, we will not be in the antibody production business. That's for Big Pharma to do. We will give them the final structure, and they will reproduce and distribute."

"So we will be, what, vigilant for new viruses? And when one is identified by who, the CDC, we will obtain it, beat it to death mathematically, and distribute the working antibody to somebody who will get it to Big Pharma? Why aren't the companies doing this all on their own?"

"Two reasons," Luiz said. "First, they have no confidence in the process, and second, they don't have you."

She scratched her head. "Actually, I don't know if I have the confidence. So many moving pieces."

"Such as?"

"One is the chemical environment. Antibodies only work if the neighborhood is right. Right pH. Right buffers in the right concentration. If I'm off by seven hydronium ions around the virus, then anything I make won't fit in the real world."

Luiz nodded.

She shook her head. "There are millions of interactions between the electrons of the amino acid, sialic acid, and carbohydrate molecules on the surface of the virus. All those electrons jiggling around between atoms within a molecule and between different molecules only billionths and trillionths of a meter away. Seems overwhelming."

"I'm no mathematician," Luiz said, "but what you describe are electrostatic and covalent attractions. It may take some time, but the ones we are not interested in we could describe as a constrained Brownian motion and move them out of the most intent part of the model. We only have to model the amino acids on the virus that pass an initial test for our chemical affinity. Then use a tight organic sheath that can bond to enough of these on the other side to stabilize."

They both looked at him.

"Or something like that," he said, shrugging. "Anyway, these are physical forces whose strengths are known. They can be mathematically described and reproduced, right?"

"That's what the math is for." She pursed her lips. "You know, I don't know if I can do it, but I can see how it would be done." She slumped back in her chair. "Luiz, it would have taken me six months to say what you just did in six seconds. Anyway, Jon, I'd like to try if you'll take me."

"No worries. I hired you at the buffet bar."

They all laughed.

"Listen, Emily—"

"Em. My friends call me Em."

He smiled. "Well, Em, if you want to hitch with us, we are on the way to our prison lab, eight hundred miles away."

"Sure," she said, picking up her bag. "Let's go."

"What about your other things. Lug—"

"You really don't want to know."

They looked at each other.

"Outlaws," he said, smiling.

Smiling back, she grabbed his arm.

# COMING DAYS

Meredith was dizzy. "What do you mean? How could I not want my regulatory chief to know about this SSS research calamity?"

"Not just me, Ms. Doucette. The safety team as well. Here."

Meredith all but snatched the paper from her compliant VP reg.

> June 4, 2016
> To: VP Reg Monica Stevens
>     Safety Chief
>     All Marketing VPs
>     Research Director: Robert Peterson
>
> From: Jasper Giles
>
> All decisions concerning our SNW17012 molecule will go through research, legal, and marketing departments from this day forward. Final determinations will be shared with senior management, regulatory, and safety when I am satisfied that all of our performance criteria have been met and we can go forward with agency application for approval. All senior management communication will be through me. This is by order of Ms. Doucette.
>
>                     Jasper Giles
>                     VP Legal

The CEO studied the memo. This was not a work-around. It was a coup.

# GNU

"Kevin, where are your hands?"

Olivia twisted around from lying on her left flank, her high heels, shapely legs, and makeup promising access to delicious mysteries.

"These hands are for you, Olivia," Kevin said, lying her on her back.

"Show me."

•

An hour later, they lounged in the sitting area of the luxurious hotel suite.

"These Ritz-Carltons just kill me with kindness," Kevin said, putting the room service menu and phone down.

"I'm going to get fat."

He sat up and shrugged his shoulders. "So?"

In a flash, the pillow was flying through the air. His left hand snagged it.

"Where are we with the wagon train timing?" he asked. This was such a wild thing they were getting into, traipsing out to Arizona. Like tumbleweed.

"What?"

"You know, everybody head west. All points converge on Flossie, Arizona."

"Florence," she corrected, sitting up on the sofa. "And it will be a while." She paused. "I can't say that I understand it all, actually. Nobody has the entire picture."

"'You come see me now,'" he imitated in his best Mother Abigail voice. "'You and all your friends.'"

"Hey, watch it. I liked *The Stand*."

"Sorry. Me too."

"I think it's best that we get there early," she said, lying back on the sofa.

"You're right. Jon gave me an extensive list. Apparently, he's not really crazy about security. Just speed. He needs three high-speed servers, each with two Intel Core 8 Xeon 2.1 processors."

"With a one-and-a-half twist off the ten-meter board," Olivia said, sitting up, brushing gray strands from her face.

"He's going to need a fire hose to keep the temps down on those babies. Do you happen to know what she's programming in?"

"I couldn't understand what he said, Kev, so I wrote it down. Here." She pushed a small paper over to him.

He looked. One word.

GNU.

He sat up. "Sweetheart, this can't be right."

"What does it mean?"

He shook his head then shook it again.

"GNU stands for 'GNU not Unix.' It's basic-level coding that does not involve UNIX level . . ." He stopped. "Olivia was many delightful things, but she was no programmer. How in the world will the programmer do this in GNU/Unix level code?" he wondered. "She's got to be thinking of millions of lines of code. And when it expands, it will be hundreds of millions of machine language lines.

"What's wrong with that?" Olivia asked. "Sorry, I can barely manage my iPhone."

"It's used to assemble the backbone of Linux, the operating system of, well, many commercial and scientific projects. Advanced languages are built on top of it. Nobody programs in it anymore. It's way too tough and takes way too much time to code. Plus, debugging can be a nightmare."

"Jon said three years ago that some company built a special platform for her to use. They had to burn the midnight oil to find the teams." Kevin sat on the edge of the bed. "That's some serious pull. I wonder how she convinced them to support a GSU project. I'm not sure that I—"

*Knock.*

"Room service."

"Hush, Kevin," she said in her lovely Southern lilt. "Get the food. Conserve your strength."

*GNU?* he thought, bringing the steaming pasta plates back to the sitting room. *Just what kind of team was this?*

# UP TO US

$5$:00 PM.

For a change of place, Meredith and Monica met in the VP regulatory's office.

"I took the liberty of informing Nita," Meredith said, walking in. "She will join us momentarily. She has one of the best minds in the company."

"I agree," Monica said. "And here she is."

"Hello, everyone," Nita said.

They greeted each other as Monica waved them both to chairs.

"Maybe you can update her on the 3:00 PM meeting we had today," Meredith asked.

"Happy to," Monica said.

She laid out the previous meeting that allowed the safety group and regulatory to coordinate their information and to be clear on the chain of communication. All information about this event that went to the FDA would come through regulatory and from regulatory to the three of them.

"Are you comfortable with our current regulatory situation vis-à-vis this event?" Nita asked.

VP regulatory shook her head. "I am not. While we have met our notification requirement to the FDA, that was only preliminary. We must still send them all the information that we have about the two children. The entire medical histories—illnesses, vaccinations, prior medications, hospitalizations. Everything."

As Meredith watched Monica, it became clear to her why Nita wasn't included on Jasper's memo.

She wouldn't have stood for it.

Nita would have come to her, and the plan would be blown.

And Jasper knew that.

"What did the child die of?" Meredith heard Nita ask.

"Nobody knows."

"How could that be?"

"Because," Meredith began, "no—"

The phone rang. Monica picked up, listened, then muted.

"Ms. Doucette," she began. "Mr. Giles would like to know if he can stop by."

The CEO shook her head. "Like him or not, the man does have a sixth sense when something is going on that he doesn't know about."

"Maybe I need to develop that," Monica said.

"You and me both."

"Please tell him I would like to meet with him tomorrow morning."

VP regulatory repeated the message into the phone and hung up.

"The reason nobody knows why the child died, Nita," the CEO continued, "is because it's only been seen in a small number of cases, separated by decades of time."

Meredith sighed, stretching her legs out. "It's been a long day, and I don't want to keep us too late." She turned to Monica. "This coup almost worked."

"What do you mean?"

Meredith closed her eyes. "If they could go forward with a drug that ultimately became a blockbuster and show that I knew little about, it would have been much easier to sack me. Unfortunately, it blew up in their face because this drug has terrible side effects, and it turns out that nobody in the coup knew how to handle that." She shook her head.

"How about sending to the agency a family video of what the child was able to do before he died?" Nita asked.

They both looked at Nita.

"It would be a good baseline, reflecting his prior motor abilities," the CFO offered.

"Great thinking," Monica said. "I'll do that."

"Everything we know, I want the FDA to know," Meredith said, sitting up. "We are going to need their help to move forward. Anything else, Monica?"

"We haven't notified the IRBs yet."

"Quite right," the CEO responded. The Institutional Review Boards were groups of scientists and ethicists who review the scientific progress at the local level. Each clinical center has to report regularly to its own IRB, and that IRB has authorization over whether that center can continue in the study or not.

"IRBs have their own rules about when events should be reported to them," Monica added.

"I think in this circumstance, they should all be notified at once." The CEO turned in her chair. "Monica, what do you think of sending the same report that went to the FDA to all the IRBs tomorrow? We can tell them we will share all future FDA correspondence with them on a timely basis."

"Not good enough," Monica said, shaking her head. "We should be specific. Let's say that we will send to them all agency correspondence on this issue within forty-eight hours of our sending it to the FDA or within forty-eight hours of receipt from the FDA. I will task two people in my group to manage this."

"Agreed," said the CEO. "This event is so tragic it is impossible to think of a scenario where an oversight board would not want to know about this as soon as possible."

"Some of the investigators will be called before their own IRB to give a report on these cases," Monica said, leaning forward, rubbing her forehead.

"The advantage is that all the investigators will have to know exactly and in detail what happens at any of the other clinical study sites," Nita added.

"The steering committee will need to communicate with its members regularly so that all principal investigators understand the issues being raised at another PI's IRB."

"We can't bring the two children back, but at least we can show that we are acting responsibly in the face of a terrible tragedy," Meredith said. "Anything else, Monica?"

VP regulatory shook her head. "This event will be on our radarscopes for weeks, but for right now, given our plan for tomorrow, we are good."

"One other thing," Nita said. "Investigators, IRBs, FDA. That's a lot of people. I think we must assume that at some point along the line, the media is going to be notified of this catastrophe."

"Maybe we should loop public affairs in?"

"No," the CEO said. "I have to question just who I can trust in this company right now. So any public statements come from my desk."

"I don't think that's a good idea."

"You can't do that."

"I don't have any problems sharing it with both of you before I say it. But what the public hears will come from me officially. Not public affairs, and God knows not legal. Legal is the enemy now."

"OK," Meredith said, standing. "We have some difficult decisions about this drug going forward. The promise of an amazing benefit, but a hideous and deadly side effect must both be carefully considered."

Nita asked, "Can the FDA take the bat out of our hands and demand that we must stop developing the compound?" She looked at Monica.

"Yes, but I don't think that they will, Nita," Monica said in a quiet voice. "The FDA is not just a regulatory overseer. It sees itself as a partner with the drug industry. That means they like to see major blockbusting drugs be approved and are eager to expedite winners. More than that, they like to be associated with a winning drug. To be seen moving forward arm in arm with SSS when this compound is approved—"

"If approvable—"

"Yes. Another reason they won't stop," Monica added, "is public pressure. ASD is a problem that affects almost one in eight families. That translates to tens of millions of children and adults. Parents are desperate for new therapy. You only need spend fifteen minutes on social media to assess their anxiety over the absence of an effective treatment."

"So," Meredith added, "when they learn that a promising drug whose preliminary data suggested that ASD could be prevented was killed because of an initial 'mistake' or 'unfortunate outcome'—"

"The FDA will have the devil to pay. They will be hauled before Congress, and that will not be pretty."

"There are members of the House and Senate whose children, nieces, nephews, grandchildren have ASD in one of its forms," Nita said, rubbing her temples.

"So," Meredith said, "it will be up to us."

"Ms. Doucette," Nita said, looking up. "I think it comes down to the data. If the phenomenal success in preventing autism is sustained along with no further occurrences of what we just saw, then approval would be justified. However, if the rate of this flaccid paralysis stays as high as one in thirty, then, well, that suggests another answer."

"So waiting for more data would be optimal," the CEO said. "But more data means more treatment. And more treatment runs the risk of another treatment death."

They all nodded.

Meredith stood. "You have no idea how much I rely on you both. Thanks for helping me to get through this and for protecting me from my own thoughts."

"Good night, ma'am."

"Good night, Ms. Doucette."

"Oh," Meredith said to Monica, touching her sleeve. "May I use your office for a moment? I'd like to take one or two notes."

"Of course."

After they left, Meredith wrote out two options, then after a moment, a third.

Anxiety consuming her, she tore the third option up.

Then she wrote it out again.

# SINGING SONGS

Olivia sat up in her seat at once, as the rain pounded the car's roof.
"Desert squall," Kevin said, patting her thigh.

"Squall?" She shook her head. "Look at that rain. Seems like the end of days."

Kevin couldn't blame her. It had taken all of three minutes for the still-blue New Mexico sky to go gray then black. The rain didn't just fall; it blew across the car from south to north. He was never so thankful for empty roads as he steered along the highway barely visible in the headlights.

Four minutes later, the tempest ended. He looked north as the tail end of the storm moved over the hot sand, claiming its short-lived title over the hot sun's reign.

Two hours later, they crossed from New Mexico into Arizona. He knew he was crazy, but he just wanted to put the top down to let the dry heat enter him, become part of—

"Kevin."

He turned, surprised at her tone, and saw a face he hadn't seen since they'd been at Tanner together.

All business.

The look on her had been that she had no room for nonsense when regulatory issues got thick. That was the face he saw confronting him now.

He glanced at the rearview that revealed nothing but asphalt as he slowed the car down. "What's on your mind—" he added. "Dr. Steadman?"

"What am I doing out here?"

He'd sensed something had been rumbling under the surface of their lives for a few days. Never fully present, but not fully absent. Leaving signs of itself in incomplete conversations.

"That's a hard question." He looked at her. "I don't like hard questions. I like easy ones. Let's take an easy one first. Kind of a warm-up."

"Let's have one, then." Clipped. Ready for a fight.

"OK, what is my role?" he said.

She sat up straight for a moment. "Kevin, you may have been marketing VP, but everyone knows you as a 'can-do' guy. You have a contact list that extends from Canada to the Caucasus. You get things done, not because you know how to do them, but because you know how to find the right people who can."

He smiled. "Let me accept your flamboyant characterization as correct for just a moment. That doesn't answer my question."

She rubbed her hands in exasperation. "You will do what these people need to have done before they know they need it. You size up problems and solve them. That's what I see that you offer them. What is that?" she said, squinting.

Kevin peered to the right where she was gazing, hand over her eyes. "Buzzard, I think."

She rolled down the window. "Sorry," she shouted out the window. "We're not dead yet."

"Maybe, it's a hawk," he said, as he touched the control, watching the window roll up. "And maybe it's after you because you think you're dead."

"What?"

"You think that you're useless now."

She pursed her lips for a moment. "I'm an OK regulator."

"If self-condemnation is what this is about, then don't throw in the towel by selling yourself short. You were a AAA regulator. National, repeat, national reputation. They were singing songs about you."

"Name one."

He started, but the car filled with a new rising song.

A siren.

# REDLINE

"Well, what we got here? Little salt and pepper, huh? What you doing over there with this mug, pork chops?"

The leering police officer, face dripping with hot perspiration, pushed his face into the car. Kevin remained still, looking straight ahead. Anger pulsed through him, and he closed his eyes. *Not now.*

Finally, he turned to the big face of the policeman, dropping his hands, and asked, "How can I help you, Officer?"

"First, you can put your damn hands back on the steering wheel there, buck. Then you can tell me how fast you were traveling."

"Sixty-five," Kevin answered, sweat popping up on his brow.

"Good for you. I clocked you at sixty-five in a sixty zone. Know where you are?"

"On Arizona SR 70 now, heading northeast to Globe." Kevin paused, slowing down his delivery. Then he said, "Halfway between Fort Thomas and a town called Bylas."

"Nice job. Guess I should call you 'Professor Buck.'" The cop laughed, showing a patchwork of gnarled yellow-and-white teeth.

Kevin watched him look over at Olivia. She seemed perfectly calm, sunglasses off, looking straight back at the police officer. "It's not so bad to be just a little over the speed limit, Officer," she said, meeting his stare. "We haven't seen another car for about fifty miles. And the ones we do see are going much faster than we were."

Kevin watched the cop lick his lips. "You saying you weren't speeding, ma'am?"

"No. I'm saying it wasn't speeding that you'd ever notice out here."

Kevin saw the police officer's face stiffen. "License and registration please. And I need some ID from you too, ma'am."

"No insurance?" Kevin asked, leaning over to get the registration from the glove compartment.

"Did I ask for it?"

"No."

The constable pulled back for a second, giving Kevin some space. "Biggest problem we have out here is not the speeding. It's kids and spics running guns and drugs."

Kevin took Olivia's ID, placed his driver's license and the registration over it, then handed them over. *Maybe there was a chance here.* "I understand I-10 between Tucson and Phoenix is the most highly patrolled section highway in Arizona because of the guns, drugs, and money."

"I didn't say anything about money, sambo."

Kevin kept his teeth together. This was going to end badly. The question was only who would get hurt the worst. His heart started pounding.

"Hmm, both from Illinois. Kind of the wrong time for a vacation drive out here, isn't it?" The policeman put the ID in his upper left pocket.

"What's your name, Officer?" Kevin asked. "I can't see a nameplate." *He's going to keep our licenses?* Heart pounded harder.

"Siphod." Face back in the car, right arm leaning on the windowsill.

Kevin laughed. "Well, we are not vacationing, Officer Siphod. We're moving."

"Where to?"

"Looking for a house in Queen Creek."

The cop snorted, snot flying out and onto Kevin's left shirt sleeve. "That's south and west. Why you headed north on 70?"

"Well, believe it or not, we heard it would be a cooler drive."

"That's a fair statement. But fact is, I don't know what you two are doing out here. Why don't you both get out of the car."

Kevin opened his mouth to complain but felt Olivia squeeze his hand. "This officer's being kind, Kevin. Let's just do as he asks, OK?"

Kevin got out slowly. He wasn't looking for a fight. But doing nothing enabled idiots like this.

*Figure out your redline,* he thought. He got out and stood in front of the officer.

*Know what you'll do before you do it.*

"Let's all go back to your trunk now, buck. Won't take too long."

*If it means jail, then jail it is.*

"You're videoing this on your dashcam, right?"

*Olivia would not be touched. If he had to grind this idiot to powder, Siphod would not put a hand on her.*

"No, we have no need for that up here. Hey, just open your trunk, will ya."

*And if you die, then he's unlikely to go through with a rape on the open highway.*

"No problem."

*Plus, at the gunshot, Olivia would run, if she couldn't outright steal the cop's car.*

*Plubunk* went the hatch, the familiar noise seeming louder than usual to Kevin.

Siphod reached for his flashlight, the late day draining the sunlight. Beam moved left and right all over the trunk.

Then he stood up and ran it up and down Olivia once.

Then again.

"What's your name again, sugar britches?"

"Olivia."

"Why don't you go to my car? I'm going to leave sambo here in his ride with the clean trunk, then you and I will have our own talk."

•

Olivia walked over the dusty road to the passenger side of the police car and went to open the door.

Locked.

She saw Siphod's shadow behind her and jumped.

"No worries, sweetheart," he said. "You just get in the backseat. I'll be back directly after I deal with Buckwheat here." Leaning over her, he craned his neck around to look at Kevin. "I know he's forcing himself on you. Doing it for days, I bet. Seen it before. Don't worry. I'll pluck his wings. Then I'll be back here with you, OK?"

"No, it's not—"

He shoved her in the backseat. "Before long, you and I'll be good friends." He dribbled spit on the top of her blouse. "I guarantee it."

•

Olivia's heart raced as she watched Siphod through the dirty windshield slowly walk up toward Kevin.

Like he was stalking him.

"An animal," she said to herself.

*And animals need to be put down.*

The thought took her breath, but just for a second because it was right.

And up to her.

She loved Kevin, but he carried no gun and was no fighter. His full sweet life might end in a few moments, and then her fate was in her own hands.

She faced an enemy that would brook no compromise. No negotiation, no "understanding the other side."

Kill or be killed.

And all of a sudden, she was furious.

Angry at a universe that put her in this position.

Sick of it and its randomness.

*Yes, someone would die today, but it will not be me.*

Siphod will fall. She'd be doing the world a favor.

Her heart pounded, as she reached into her purse and found a pen.

Kevin gave it to her. Inscribed was "my favorite reg girl" on the barrel.

*No time for that.* When Siphod came back, she'd stab him in the throat. Maybe the eye. If he took her pen, she'd bite his cheek so hard she'd rip it off.

Then with his gun, she'd kill the animal and watch the motherfucker bleed out on the dirty road.

"If it's either fuck me or fuck you," she hissed, "I say fuck you."

•

"Turn back around there, buck,"

Kevin began to walk toward the driver's side door of his own car when he felt two hard fingers jab the middle of his back. "Move on, boy."

*Redline.*

Kevin turned at once to the left, letting his left hand swing out, catching the officer's jaw with the back of its closed fist. When the turn was complete, Kevin unleashed a hard right roundhouse, catching Siphod on the bone just below the left eye. Kevin heard the bone crunch as the cop staggered to the left, but stayed on his feet.

Kevin got to Siphod's holster the same time he did.

*Got to . . . get the gun . . . first.*

Kevin picked his head up and butted Siphod, thick blood flying from the cop's broken nose.

Kevin saw the elbow coming.

*Move, man.*

Too late. He sprawled backward.

Sitting up, he saw Siphod.

Gun in hand.

"I get to kill me a nigga today, then enjoy his tasty dish." Kevin leaned forward, but out of position, fell to the side.

He heard the gun cock.

*Jesus.* He exhaled, looking around desperately.

Weird noise, like the air was full of metal Slinkys.

Singing wire, Kevin thought.

Siphod fell to the ground and seized, his feet scraping up and down the hard gravel, chest bucking, eyes alive with fright and pain.

Kevin scrambled up, fists still clenched. *What just happ—*

Suddenly, Olivia was beside him; and as he put his right arm around her, he saw a second police car behind Siphod's with an open door. Kevin squinted in the diminishing light to read what was painted on it.

San Carlos Reservation PD.

Kevin turned back.

There was a man behind Siphod. Massive. Had to be six foot five, three hundred pounds, stretching the uniform to bursting. Shoulders may be three and a half feet across.

This guy was somebody who'd get what he wanted.

And he wanted Siphod.

Tased him.

Kevin began breathing again.

"Thank you," Kevin said. "We wanted no trouble with this officer, but he was threatening my partner so—"

"What he was doing to you, he's done to other people," the tall man said, voice even. Solid. No emotion, and unhurried. "Most are our people. Some are yours. Tonight, he gets what he deserves."

"I . . . I don't understand," Olivia said. Kevin felt her quaking under his arm.

"You folks crossed over onto San Carlos Reservation land a few miles back. Here, we take things into our own hands."

Kevin, heart finally slowing, didn't want to ask too much of these strangers, but he had to know. "How did you find out about tonight?"

"Heard he was coming our way, tailing a car with a couple inside." The tall officer shrugged. "Obvious Siphod MO."

Kevin straightened up. "What can we do?"

"Get going," the massive man said. "You'll be on reservation land right on into Globe. It's getting dark, but the elevation is good and the moon's bright tonight." He looked up at the deep velvet sky. "Good light."

Kevin reached over and shook the huge man's hand. "We are so very grateful."

Out of the corner of his eye, he saw two other police cars with the same reservation title pull up, quietly parking across the road. One of the emerging men walked over then started and drove Siphod's car off the road. Other officers had long, flat blades in full display as they walked over to the cop on the ground.

The officer looked down at Kevin, handing them back their IDs. "We have some work to do here. You folks get going. Welcome to Arizona."

# DIE TO LIVE

" How are you?"
"Fine, Kevin. I am fine." She wiped her wet brow with a Kleenex. "I know what you did back there. For me. You almost died."

"I—"

She patted his hand. "Later, OK?"

She returned to her own thoughts on a road illuminated by the brightest moon she'd ever seen, reviewing what happened just ten minutes before.

The cretin Siphod had done her a favor.

Ever since she'd left Tanner, she'd been footloose and fancy-free. No responsibility for anything.

And it was glorious.

At Tanner, she'd been responsible for new drug applications. With page numbers running into the tens of thousands, these documents were required by the FDA to approve Tanner's new compounds.

They all went in over her signature.

Her signature had gone on each of these NDAs.

Then the SNDAs were submitted, she recalled. Her signature.

Major safety reviews. Her signature.

Responses to FDA queries. Her signature.

She was the grease that oiled the Tanner regulatory wheel.

She was good at it, and she'd been sick of it.

She'd never told Kevin that if it weren't for his wife's illness, she'd have left Tanner months ago. She didn't need a damn SSS takeover to drive her out. She loved the people, her team, her "troop."

Stedman's soldiers.

But at 66, she couldn't bear the crushing boredom anymore, each hungry day after five thousand other ones chomping away at her stomach lining.

Now with all of Kevin and no responsibility, life was open and free. And rootless.

Feckless.

And boring again.

Besides Kevin, she meant nothing to everybody.

Life had become a video of her own funeral. This new coffin she lived in, closing down a little every day, was tangible. Looming. The nauseating smell of the flowers, knowing that someone outside was giving a fake eulogy in the cloying Savannah air that no one heard.

But tonight, it was shattered.

During the beginning of the constable's assault, she did not know what Kevin would do.

But she knew what was coming.

It would be death or life. No middle ground. No bullshit.

And the new blinding insight showed that she was alive. Ready to commit.

She would not go down like some cute and docile sixty-six-year-old fighting for her vanity, giving in at the first punch.

For the first time ever in her life, she had been ready, even eager to get hurt in order to hurt back.

Ready to feel pain. To lose teeth or have an eye gouged or a finger jammed up in her. She would die in order to kill.

Every cell was alive. On notice. Devoted to die in order to live.

It was new life coursing through her.

And as Kevin began a slow curve to the south, the moon now fully upon her, she saw her mission—her last one. And for now, it was for her to be ready.

Vigilant.

To engage.

"Olivia."

She snapped around.

"My left eye can't see."

•

"Pull over."

Kevin pulled to the right erratically, half the car on the shoulder, the other in rocks.

He struggled to find then turned on the interior lights.

She maneuvered until she was sitting on his lap facing him. For the first time ever, he didn't squeeze her, and she rubbed against no erection as she carefully looked above his left eye.

"You're bleeding over your eye, with blood draining down into it." She fought back the urge to vomit, instead asking, "How much farther?"

"Eighty miles down the Superstition Mountains."

"In the dark? Not doing that now."

She acted, getting off him, then tearing the bottom of her dress into two long strips. After a moment, one more.

"Get into the backseat, Kevin."

He got out and managed to get in the backseat. She followed.

"Now, head in my lap."

He did as she said.

"We don't have any bandages," he said, coughing.

"We do now."

She balled up one of the strips and placed it over the cut above his left eye, creating some pressure.

"How long you going to do that?"

"Long as it takes."

Neither sensed the two cars, headlights off, slowly approaching from the rear.

# DEATH HOUSE

"You have got to be kidding," Cassie said, shielding her eyes from the blinding Florence sun. The entire town was a furnace. It was like an air fire, where the air was so hot she thought her lungs would catch fire.

And here she was, broiling, standing in front of a huge slab of a facility that would now be her workplace.

"No wonder this is 'Butt Street,'" Breanna said, in shorts, flip-flops, and a blouse. "And how many suns are up there in that sky anyway? My goodness, it's got to be 110 degrees out here."

"It's 'Butte Street,' and no," Cassie said, "more like 115 degrees. And the forecast points to three more weeks of this."

"Well," Breanna said. "Jon was right about one thing. No one will find us here."

*Hope that's right*, Cassie thought, but she didn't believe it.

•

Cassie took short careful steps through the double doors, emerging into what she saw was a huge darker room. *At least it's cooler*, she thought, putting a hand on Breanna's shoulder as she squinted to see.

They walked through a huge open area. Up ahead, some people were huddled together. *With some walls, this could pass as a—*

"Well," Breanna said, looking up. "I guess we'll be working on the first floor."

Cassie followed her gaze. Huge spotlights first brightened the large gray ceiling then moved down past the upper two floors filled with dark bars.

"Unless," Cassie said, "we do something wrong and we end up behind bars there." She shivered as the old recurrent nightmare raced through her.

They both walked to the center of a U-shaped area surrounded by temporary rugged walls. Cassie guessed they were about eight feet high. There were several desks, two of them supporting computer workstations. In the midst of it all were some people milling around.

"I don't know everybody here," Breanna said.

"Well, we'd better introduce ourselves." Cassie walked ahead. "Hello, Jon."

Jon stood up and smiled. "Hello, devil. Welcome to hell."

Cassie laughed along with Jon and Breanna.

"I don't know what you have in mind, Jon, but this is going to be one heck of a place to work," Breanna said. "What's it like eating here?"

"In jail?"

"Heavens no. In Florence."

"Well," Jon said, scratching the back of his head. "Luiz has tried both the River Bottom Grill and the LB Cantina. Really authentic food. But that's Luiz talking."

"Authentic what?"

"Dunno." He shrugged. "But he says it eats good. People in town seem to be pleasant enough. What do you think?"

"Well, we found one couple who was willing to look after my baby just north of here, and that was a godsend," Breanna said.

"Ah, look who else is here," Jon said, pointing to the double doors. "Hey, Rayiko. Good to see you."

"I wish I could tell you it was good to be here," she said, pointing a finger behind her. "But damn, it's really hot outside."

"Fortunately, we're working inside," Cassie said, spreading both arms out as far as she could then lifting them up.

Rayiko looked around. "Do you think that's fortunate? This is a jail."

"State prison. Even worse," Luiz said, scrambling out from under a tipped-over workstation. He looked up, wiping his brow. "Can you imagine what it was like being incarcerated here with only fans? No AC?"

"Hey, Luiz," Rayiko said. "I'll skip the grand tour. By the way, where's your striped suit?"

"I've been pardoned. The Florence authorities asked me to stay on to keep a watch over you guys," he said, pointing to them.

"Oh shit. We're in trouble now."

"Well, I hate to ask where my office is. Just keep it off of the second and third floor. Hi, Emma," Rayiko said.

"This is Emma, everyone," Jon said, smiling. "I guess you would call her our chemical modeler. Seriously, we are lucky to have her. She'll be a big help on our next project."

Cassie walked over to the tall thin woman with short blond hair. "As the attorney of record here, I'm formally welcoming you to prison."

"Shoot," Em said, shaking Cassie's hand. "I just got to Arizona."

"That's all you need to do to go to jail in this outfit."

"And," Breanna asked, "just what is our next project?"

"Don't know, but if you fail, you don't just go to the pokey," Jon said, glancing at the upper floors. "Oh no. It's execution for you," he finished, pointing a finger Emma's way.

"You mean—" Rayiko said, walking toward the tall modeler and looking up.

"Yep," Luiz said. "Gas chamber and electrocution. Take your pick."

"Jesus, Jon, you brought us to the death house?" Cassie asked.

"Which is where you belong, bitch."

They all turn at the new raised voice from the entryway.

# WOLF IN THE FOLD

Olivia, flushed and eyes wide, pointing at Cassie, said, "What the hell are you doing here?"

•

Fifteen minutes later, Kevin caught up to Jon as he arranged four chairs around a large desk holding a single Dell workstation.

"Been meaning to ask about that eye patch," Jon said, bringing the final chair over.

"Been meaning to tell you," Kevin replied with a smile. "Let's just say Arizona can still be a pretty tough place. We're only here because new Native American friends shepherded us through their reservation."

"Temporary or permanent?"

"Eye patch?" Kevin shrugged. "Just another week."

They all sat down. Olivia and Cassie sat across from each other, all others having been excused for the day.

"How long have you been here, Cassie?"

"I think maybe three weeks, but—"

"Jesus, I'm just saying," Olivia said, waving her left arm in the air as she took her seat. "Why is Cassie here at all, Jon? You don't know her like I do. Like Kevin does." She pointed to Kevin.

Kevin stared at Olivia, mouth open. Confused by this attack on Cassie, his heart raced. He closed his eyes, looking for some equanimity. Then a moment later, he watched as Jon shook his head, waving his arm in the attorney's direction, and said, "Olivia, I have spoken with Cassie and know something about what you—"

"Jon, you know nothing." Olivia banged the table with her fist.

The room fell silent at Olivia's retort. Kevin started to nudge his girlfriend then stopped.

"She's an accomplished corporate lawyer, true enough," Olivia said, leaning forward on the thin folding chair. "But truth has very little to do with what she represents, and nothing to do with what comes out of her mouth."

Kevin felt his brow break out in a sweat as he turned to face the regulator. "Olivia, you and I are new to this organization. They don't know who we are either."

Olivia whirled around to face Kevin. "They know that we are not liars, Kevin. We have superb backgrounds, but more important than that, we have good principles. We are honest. Sometimes right, sometimes wrong, but we stood for moral conduct. We were productive at Tanner. Yet we were thrown out of our jobs by Team SSS and Missy Rhodes here."

Kevin watched Olivia turn to face Cassie across the table, her arm outstretched, shaking with rage. "Who do you think you are? You orchestrated the destruction of our company, Tanner Pharmaceuticals, throwing away good people who would have been able to adapt to a new home at Triple S. You didn't even consider keeping them."

Kevin looked at Cassie who sat staring straight ahead, saying nothing. *Not this lawyer's reputation at all*, he thought.

"—decapitated Tanner Pharmaceuticals," Olivia continued. "And after that, Jon, she then went to our safety department and drove one of our best safety officers to suicide."

Kevin heard Jon in hushed tones say, "I understand, about the su—"

"No, you don't," Olivia said. "SSS is a reckless drug company with an abysmal safety record. And if that wasn't bad enough, Ms. Rhodes went to Tanner Safety and downsized it with . . . with prejudice."

Jon said, "Well, the suicide aside, Tanner was their organization, right? They purchased it, and they had the right to—"

"I don't care if it was legal or not," Olivia said through clenched teeth. "They had no moral right to take steps that led to the death of a safety officer. And we," Olivia continued, "have no business bringing Ms. Rhodes, the instrument of that policy, in here with us.

"And if that's not enough, remember," she added, now looking straight at Jon, "that it was Ms. Rhodes here along with Triple S that tried to dismantle CiliCold last March. That is one hell of a cosmic coincidence. My God," she cried out, "how much evidence do you need that the wolf's in the fold?"

Jon nodded his head. "Yes, I do know that Cassie played a ro—"

"I led that assault on your company Jon, as we discussed," Cassie said quietly, looking down at her folded hands. "SSS was trying to take your best idea by any means necessary, and I was their agent."

Kevin stared at Olivia who with opened mouth, pushed back from the table then leaned, hands on hips, forward into the attorney.

"Well," Olivia said, pointing a finger at the attorney. "The miscreant speaks. So what are you going to do, Cassie, 'lawyer us up' with smiles and soft phrases?"

"Olivia," they heard Cassie say. "I'm here to tell you that all you say is true."

# ABSORPTION

So," Olivia said, wearing a smile that Kevin could only call a sneering mask of victory, "you admit that you took apart Tanner."

"Yes."

"That you fired good people."

"Yes."

"That you were all for reducing Tanner's safety department, a move in contravention to helping SSS's sagging reputation?"

"Yes."

"And that you were complicit in the suicide of a safety monitor."

"That is true as well," Cassie said. Kevin watched her remove a handkerchief from her pocket and dry her eyes.

She turned to Olivia. "Yes, I was there for the Tanner firings. You know I was there, Olivia, because I remember seeing you. Kevin too. I did all that you say. And," she said, tears flowing again down her face. "I'm not going to say that I was just following orders or that it was the right thing to do.

"I had a job to do at Triple S, and I executed it to the nth degree. I was ruthless. In fact, I was trained to be ruthless, and I loved it. I've done things that are unmentionable. Things that you can't possibly know. And I did them all for Triple S and my own career. And in the end," she continued, weeping now, "I murdered my own heart."

"Then," Olivia said, jumping up, the chair falling over behind her, "where do you get the temerity, the gall to show up here like you are a trustworthy colleague, ready to work on a project that you don't understand and would demolish at the drop of a hat if you still worked for SSS?"

"Olivia," Kevin said, reaching out to touch his girlfriend, "That's en—"

"The part of my life that you describe that was so despicable is like Cristen's blood on the floor." She paused for a moment. "Or on me. I wipe, but it's never gone."

"I'm lost," Cassie cried out, crying openly. "My life is an ash heap. I have no value."

The room was still, and Olivia, sitting back in her chair, uncrossed her arms, letting them fall by the side.

"Olivia," Kevin said, reaching out to touch his girlfriend. "Don't you thin—"

"Well," Olivia said, brushing away Kevin's hand, but speaking in a softer voice. "What makes you think that being here is the right thing to do? And how can we trust you now if you couldn't be trusted before?"

Kevin watched Cassie drop her head into her arms that were resting on the cold table.

"I am groping my way out of this mess as best as I can." She looked up now. "And you are right, Olivia. I'm not even sure I understand what this group's new project is. But I do know that this organization is interested in bringing forward the best science it can. Here," she paused, "it's about people and not about the money."

She looked up at Jon. "Not about the dollars, right?"

Jon nodded. "I don't worry about duckets here."

"I would like to be part of this group. Being about and for people—for friends is the clearest track that I can follow to fix, to heal myself. I have never tried this before. Frankly, I don't know if it's going to work."

"But you are my role models." She smiled. "Like it or not."

All four smiled.

"Anyway, I am here. Open for you all to see and ready to help you in any way that I can. Maybe, Olivia, you and I can ultimately become friends, maybe not. But I will always be open to your criticism, and I commit that I will do my best."

The room was still. Kevin looked down, overcome by sympathy. He watched Olivia first glance away then back at the attorney.

Kevin looked at Cassie. Licking his lips, he said, "Cassie, what do you think you will be able to do for us here?"

"Well," Cassie said. "For example, if you're interested in getting a patent for this work project"—she looked over at Olivia—"whatever it is, I can help with that. In addition, I fully expect that Triple S ultimately is going to find where we are."

"Not here they won't," Jon said. "A least not for a while."

"Sooner than you think," Cassie said. "You don't know them, and I've seen their teeth. Plus, their attorneys are going to use any legal means necessary to disrupt us and take your work."

Kevin watched her lean forward, dry-eyed. "We also have to keep in mind that while finances may seem tolerable now, they become very critical very fast. We have to begin to plan for that. And," she said pushing back from the table, "decide how we are going to respond to any queries for absorption by Triple S."

"Absorption?" Olivia and Kevin said at once.

"Yes. They're not going to be able to take your ideas without absorbing you. That war's not over yet."

All were quiet.

"Don't lose heart," Cassie said, leaning forward to cover Jon's hand with her own.

"Success is only transient, and failure is not fatal," Cassie said. "The only thing that counts is the courage to try. And if you are prepared to keep me and fight for this company, then so am I."

# SMALL RATES, BIG SAMPLES

" Meredith, they'll make you feel like Herod's beheading of John the Baptist was a mercy killing."

Meredith sat quietly in Nita's office, putting her iPhone with its three hundred new unread messages down on Nita's clean desk. Her VP reg had placed Meredith's draft FDA response on the new autism drug down. To the CEO, Nita's eyes filled with sadness. She almost looked like she would cry.

"Meredith," the CFO, head covered in a tan hijab, said. "Your feelings about SNW-17012 run deep, b—"

"And I want to resurrect our safety program here."

"But you do understand that many people on ECOM will resent this. And you also know that Jasper has friends on the board. He will see to it that the board reacts negatively to your stand on this drug."

"We pay a price to rise out of mediocrity," the CEO said, shaking her head. "Many will object to the maneuvers I suggest."

"Meredith, the board will throw you into the Delaware River over this. Well." The CFO sighed. "Give me a few minutes to look this over again to be sure that I can present it clearly at the executive meeting."

Meredith shook her head. "No, I will present it. I need for you to understand it. And to be able to support it."

"I don't really know if you intend to kill this drug with this plan. But I do know that you will kill yourself in this field," Nita said in soft tones.

"Well," Meredith said, checking her watch as she stood up. "I did not ask for this fight, but the fight is here."

Meredith watched Nita study her carefully.

"Yes, I will support you all the way," the CFO said.

•

139

Nita entered the thirtieth-floor conference room first, followed by Meredith.

The room was packed. Meredith noted that the heads of the research and marketing divisions were there with their aides, in addition to the executive and senior vice presidents. Of course, Jasper was there, his wheelchair already scooched in under the wooden table.

*So much the better*, Meredith thought. *Everybody needs to understand my thinking on this.*

"I appreciate your attendance today," she began, heart pounding. "I am also thankful for your patience, allowing me to take the time to consider carefully the implications of our new ASD compound and its consequences for the treatment of autism spectrum disorder. This drug holds great promise, but also holds great peril—"

"Well, are you going to move this drug forward for expedited FDA approval or not," Vanessa Seymour, executive vice president, said.

Meredith used her right hand to gently stroke the skin under her right eye. "Vanessa, you have been patient for several weeks. Please honor us all by holding on for just a few minutes more."

The CEO then looked around the crowded room, taking her time. "There is tremendous excitement about our new compound. Even the FDA regulators that Nita and I spoke with would like to be part of the approval process for this drug."

"You bet they would," Jasper said, smirking. "They—"

*The class clown*, Meredith thought. *And I'm giving him a hand grenade with my name on it.*

She had dressed him down like a schoolboy after she found the email cutting her out of ASD drug development meeting.

Didn't faze him.

For a moment, the implications of what she was going to suggest ripped through her, and her stomach flipped, throwing bile up into her throat.

"—know a winner when they see one."

She watched him smile at the nodding heads around him.

"Most of our clinical investigators want to move forward with the approval of this drug that looks like it's a preventive therapy for autism."

*Time to cross the Rubicon*, she thought. She took a deep breath. "However, the catastrophic findings in two children must give us all pause."

"You know," Kauer said, "we have been pausing for a month now."

Meredith stared at the senior VP. "You will be pausing for a little longer."

Nobody spoke. Even Jasper was silent. Then Meredith saw Jasper write down a note and show it to Seymour who read it, shaking her head.

Meredith continued. "We must be absolutely convinced that we understand the frequency of occurrence of this adverse effect—"

"NCD for neurologic collapse disorder," someone from research added. The CEO couldn't tell who.

"Thank you," Meredith said, "and that means that we need more data. Without it, neither regulators, nor physicians, nor parents can make any determination about the benefit risk of this drug."

"But we do know something about the rate, right?" Jensen asked.

Meredith smiled at VP marketing Japan. "Actually, we know very little about the rate because we have a small number of patients we've studied. And that's the great dilemma." She turned her attention to the full room again. "Making a data-based determination on a sliver of data is an oxymoron."

Cowars, VP marketing North America, said, "Not to me. I think you're making too big a deal out of this, Meredith. We can certainly put on the label that 16 percent or 1.6 percent or 0.16 percent or whatever percent of patients had this neuro-finding thing. That's fair warning to the regulators and also to patients. Let parents make their own minds up."

"I agree," someone else added. "Why not just move forward with approval for this on an emergency basis status." Meredith watched as he stretched his hands out to her. "After all, autism is at near-epidemic proportions in this country. Parents are frightened out of their minds. Are we really going to deny this benefit to children who would otherwise get autism simply because we're not sure of the rate of what looks like a rare disease? Most people won't get this neurodisease anyway."

Meredith heard others murmur in agreement.

"So," Meredith said, rolling the thumb and index finger of her right hand together as she first looked at Cowars, "you think we should go forward with the drug, representing the small data sample as the truth?"

"I never understood this small sample fear anyway," Cowars said, laughing and looking at others around the room who Meredith noted smiled back.

"Well, these families can't afford the luxury of your ignorance."

The room fell quiet.

"Small rates in small studies can easily turn into larger rates in larger studies and then into tremendous numbers of affected patients in huge populations. I am sorry that you both were so loosely trained in this matter, but weak training or not, that's the fact."

"Meredith," Jasper said, "I think all they meant was—"

"Thank you, Jasper," the CEO cut in. "Nobody here needs a translator."

Meredith looked at Cowars. "Suppose we treat fifteen million children in this country, and three million of them get NCD. Our drug will not be seen as a therapeutic triumph but as a debacle because most children treated would not have gotten autism anyway. Plus," she continued, staring at Jasper and his legal team, "we'll need buckets to catch the lawsuits."

"We can build the cost of lawsuit payouts into the cost of the drug," Pinson, one of Jasper's assistants offered, Jasper nodding.

Meredith stared hard at Jasper. "Not on my watch, you won't."

"OK, OK," senior VP research said, holding both hands up. "We know what you won't accept, Meredith. Why don't you tell us what you have in mind?"

# THIS IS WHAT THAT LOOKS LIKE

"First," the CEO began, "we are going to modify our informed consent. From now on, every patient family that signs up for our SNW-17012 studies must understand that there is a risk of a new disease, NCD. The language will be specific and detailed."

She watched as Cowars, shrugging, looked at Jasper. "That won't help recruitment."

"But it will ensure that each family has a chance to understand the risk their child is going to assume," Meredith said. "As we sit here today, they do not.

"In addition," the CEO continued, "we are only going to recruit additional patients in very small groups. I am suggesting that that group be no more than five. I am open to other ideas about the cohort size. However, the cohort size must be small."

"Jesus, Meredith," somebody said.

"Don't invoke the Almighty yet," the CEO replied, smiling. "It gets better. Each patient recruited in these small cohorts will be followed for six months. Then the study will be placed on clinical hold again."

"You mean, we will place our own study on clinical hold? Again? Not wait for the FDA?"

"Yes, that is exactly what we are going to do, Jim," she said to James Duny in R&D. "It's our drug that caused this problem, and it is up to us to move cautiously."

She turned to face the room again. "The data will be sent to the FDA for their review. We will then work with the agency to review our experience with SNW-1701I. If we both agree that the drug appears safe, we will then lift the clinical hold and recruit another five patients, follow them for six months, go on clinical hold again, and review the drug with the FDA. And we repeat the cyclic process until the study is complete."

"So," VP marketing SA said, "it will take six months to recruit five patients—"

"Maybe longer with the new informed consent," someone added.

"And another six months to follow them so it will take a year to recruit and follow five patients. Then we're going to be placed on clinical hold while we tabulate the data and review with the FDA. And if they approve, we'll do the same thing the next year. Is that what you're suggesting?"

Meredith looked him in the eye and said, "That is exactly what I'm asserting."

"That will take forever," Cowars said. Meredith watched Jasper shake his head.

"Then let it take forever," Meredith said, letting her voice rise. "This is not a game of financial optimization that we're playing here. We—"

"Yes, it is," Cowars said.

"—are on the cusp of a major discovery, and we want to make sure that it's not going to be the source of a nationwide or a worldwide debacle as hundreds of thousands, if not millions, of patients are subjected to this drug."

"Well, Meredith, the parents of the children who were born with autism during this entire 'cycle' process will not forgive you. They're going to suggest that we are a company that is withholding a new critical therapy from children who are going to be very sick."

"Really? And what would those parents say," Meredith asked, "if in fact one of their children had NCD. Whose fault will that be? Will it be their fault?"

The CEO looked around the room. "No, they will say that they were just being responsible parents, taking advantage of a drug that was approved by the FDA as safe and effective.

"This drug right now may or may not be effective, but it certainly is not safe. We need to know for sure what the NCD attack rate is as soon as safely possible."

"So this is what you are asking us to do?"

"I'm not asking you to do anything," the CEO stated, enunciating each syllable carefully. "I'm telling you what this company is going to do. It's important that you line up behind it. If you can't, then I need to see your resignations."

"Has this gone into the FDA yet?"

"It has not," Nita answered.

"Do they expect to hear from us about this?"

"No. The FDA will usually make its own mind up—"

"Well then, why not just let them come to their own conclusion about this."

"No."

"And why not? That's what we always do."

"Because I'm not sure that their standards are going to be high enough. Look, folks, this is our damn molecule, our damn problem, and our damn responsibility." She turned to walk out then came back.

"Oh," she said, "I want each of you to take the Drug Safety courses. Finish modules one and two, and send me your results."

"Not doing that," Townser, VP marketing Europe, said.

"One second." Meredith pulled her phone out. "Jan, can you come in here please?"

The admin assistant came in, breathless. Looking at Townser, Meredith said, "Jan, I want you to call security to escort Mr. Townser out of the building. We will send him his personal effects. Also, inform IT that he is off the net as of"—she checked her watch—"3:50 PM today. Have HR collect his laptops, tablet, and his car immediately."

"You can't do that, Meredith," Cowars called out.

"Check your own contracts. You can be discharged at once due to gross malfeasance. This is what that looks like in my book. Please complete the course as discussed."

The CEO pivoted and left, leaving the room in shock.

•

"So, Nita, how did that go?"

"I tell you in all honesty, Meredith, that this is a disaster for you. Although it may help to resurrect the company's reputation."

"I couldn't live with myself if I did otherwise."

"Was that whole Townser episode necessary?"

They turned a corner, almost to their offices. "The only way to get compliance here is to demonstrate the consequences of no compliance."

"OK," Nita said, shaking her head. "But shareholders aren't patients' shareholders. They have only a passing interest in autism, and most couldn't put two sentences together about it. Shareholders want to make money, and you've just taken money out of their pocket."

Nita paused then gently touched the CEO's arm.

"If you can't live with the company as it's been and as it is, then seriously, maybe you shouldn't be CEO anymore."

●

Jasper, whispering into his phone, said, "I think we have enough to go to the board now."

"From what I've been hearing from people and based on their text messages, I think you're right. In fact, I think you have an obligation to go to the board. Isn't that a hoot?" Stennis cackled.

"Well, hoot or not, I'm going to the board, and she's going to be out of here."

"Are you going to call an emergency meeting?"

"No," the attorney said. "I'll wait till one more clear screwup. And then take it to the next scheduled board meeting."

"Why delay?"

Jasper shook his head. "Because, Nimrod, I want to be sure that we have an undeniable collection of evidence." Also, Jasper knew that because the evidence would speak for itself, he wouldn't have to come on so strong verbally.

"How do you know they'll choose you?"

"When you find CiliCold, I'll let you know."

# HEART TASTING

On the drive home, flying past the rugged terrain laced with beige rocks and dry scrub grass, Cassie worked and failed to control her own breathing.

She knew that Breanna was angry.

In fact, watching Breanna grip the wheel with both hands, she knew her lover was furious.

Cassie knew that word had gotten around about the tough conversation the principals had with Cassie's CiliCold involvement.

And Breanna probably had heard a lot about it.

She sighed as they pulled up to their three-bedroom house just west of S. Ellswood Road. Breanna protected her, defended her, watched over her, and hurt for her. Cassie's stomach clenched.

"Let's go right through to the backyard," Cassie suggested.

"Fine by me," the accountant said, shrugging.

They got to the backyard that Cassie, after a month there, still couldn't get used to. The yard was huge by her standards, a half an acre, with two large ironwood trees that stood their own against the end-of-summer scorching temps.

They sat close to the house under its overhanging adobe roof, the north wind lifting Breanna's salt-and-pepper hair.

*I hate to argue with her*, Cassie thought, sitting on the sofa, the gray-and-black patio between them.

"It's mid-September, and I can't believe it act—"

"What do you think you were doing?" Breanna asked, staring at her.

Cassie leaned forward, resting her elbows on her own knees. "Breanna, please sit down so that I can explain this. Please?"

Cassie watched as Breanna turned her back on her then sat in the lawn chair next to the black lounge sofa.

147

"I was telling people . . . your friends . . . the truth that they needed to hear about me."

The attorney watched Breanna's head shaking. "Opening up is one thing. Evisceration is another. Olivia gave you a horrible time, and all that you really accomplished was . . . what?" Breanna raised her arms in the air. "Describe what a horrible person you were, then ask for a kumbaya moment."

"I wanted them to t—"

"And the thing is," Breanna said, twisting her left knee over her right, "I get where Olivia was coming from."

"So did I," Cassie said, head down, rubbing her stomach.

Breanna sat back in the chair. "Then honestly, Cassie, why couldn't you just keep quiet about it, or at least talk to Olivia in private?"

Cassie lifted her head up. "Because as soon as she saw me, she reacted. As well as Kevin. There was no time for privacy."

Breanna rubbed her left eye. "So what's next?"

"Let them accept me," Cassie said.

"What?" Breanna snorted.

"Breanna, when your Triple S work was revealed, why didn't Jon and the others react with scathing indignation?"

Breanna said nothing.

Cassie leaned forward. "Because they knew you. Had known you for months. And your terrible situation with that tramp of a husband. They had a context in which to judge what you did."

"For me, they had no context. No one knew my background." She paused for a moment. "Except Olivia and Kevin, who had seen my perfidy up close with the Tanner dismemberment."

"So," Breanna said, "you let them taste your heart."

"Do what?"

"You bared your soul to them."

"Yes," Cassie said. "I guess so."

"Maybe you can use that phrase in court one day."

They both laughed.

"That's all I knew to do. They embrace me for who I am or not."

"And if Olivia feels better tearing into you?"

"Then I live with it," Cassie said, sitting back on the sofa. "But she had a reputation for being both straight and fair. Plus, she knows more of who I am now. The worst and best of me." Cassie leaned down to scratch her leg.

"Others will have questions."

"I've had lots of questions to answer for a while now. It's about time I got to the job of dealing with them." She rubbed Breanna's right arm with soft back-and-forth strokes.

"Cassie, I just don't feel for you. I hurt for you." The accountant raised her head as tears flowed freely. "I don't like to see you bring such pain down on yourself."

"And I'm tired of hurting, Bree," Cassie said, crying as well. "I must get right with people." She stood. "I believe that being honest will f—oh."

She coughed and vomited onto the Bermuda grass. *What is . . . this?* Passed out.

# TRAIN SONG

"How do you feel?"

Cassie gathered her thoughts. Awake now, she sat up in the passenger seat as Bree drove them home. After a trip to the local urgent care center, an hour of fluids, and a battery of tests, she felt better.

"Doing OK. In fact, I could eat something. Maybe the doctor was right, and I was just dehydrated."

"No doubt with all the blood that they took."

"And all of it normal too."

"I'll just drop you off at home then get Jackie."

"No, you won't," Cassie said, patting Breanna's knee. "I'll go with you and we can all eat."

Breanna smiled. "Red Robin, here we come."

They smiled at each other as Breanna turned left, heading to the sitter.

"What was that song you were humming?"

The attorney turned to face her. "What do you mean?"

"On the gurney at the doctor's, you were humming."

Cassie smiled. "My favorite."

"And it is?"

"Just know a little of the tune, not the title. Strange," she said, looking out of the window. "I heard it once and it never let go of me. I call it 'The Train Song.'"

Breanna laughed, turning her head to look at her. "A top-dollar attorney who amasses voluminous data in complex cases, devastating opposing witnesses on the stand in court, and you can't remember the title of your favorite song?"

"Lover, there's much I don't remember."

Breanna looked back at the road. "Going to rain."

They drove in silence for a while. When the rain started, it quickly pelted the car with huge drops.

"Well, hum it for me," Breanna said, slowing down and hitting the lights.

Cassie started.

"I know that song," the accountant said, squinting. "Just give me some time."

# EXTRACTION

"You were pretty worked up about Cassie."

Kevin flattened up against the apartment door, letting Olivia walk by.

She threw her purse on the gray couch.

"Well, weren't you?" Olivia knew this was coming. Kev was too civilized to let her outburst on the floor just go by without a reaction. As always, he gave it a day or so to settle, but—

"The difference is that I was willing to give her a chance. You jumped down her throat at first glance. Didn't even give her a chance to speak. That's not like you, Oliv—"

"I get it, Kev. Really, I do," she said, sitting on the couch in their San Tan Valley apartment, head down, putting her hand out, palm facing him. "I know better than to put on that display." She pounded the couch three times. "I am full of anger and full of vengeance." She plopped on the couch.

Kevin sat next to her.

She turned to face him. "Thing is, that ordeal with the sheriff broke something loose in me, and I've been trying to figure out what it means. What I sometimes wonder is—"

Her phone rang.

Rolling her eyes at the interruption, she looked to see who was calling then collapsed back on the sofa.

"I was afraid it would be Jon. It's an old girlfriend. Do you mind?"

"No problem," Kev said, standing. "I was going to head to jail anyway."

She smiled, kissed him, and he walked out.

"Heather?"

"The one and only. How are you at . . . well, wherever the hell you are."

Olivia opened her mouth but stopped.

"Here and there," she decided on. "With Kevin."

Heather laughed. "Ah. I knew there was something about you two. He's a catch."

She closed her eyes. "You have no idea. How are you? You're at SSS now, right?"

Heather smiled. "Triple S is a hornets' nest. Nuthin' but the dollars count, but I'm managing."

She paused.

"I think we could use your advice. Actually, I mean, management could. I heard today that there was a fight over a new drug here. Prevents autism."

Olivia leaned forward. "Sounds like quite a find."

"Safety is in some hot water though,"

"Aren't they always at Tripl—"

"Not this time. Now, from what I hear, they've found some gumption and are trying to hold the line against moving ahead too aggressively."

Olivia pursed her lips. "What's management's take?"

"Doucette is with safety on this one, but the wolves be circling."

Olivia felt more than heard her friend's voice drop.

"I know you're not in the industry, but maybe you could help her out."

*What's the harm in that?*

"Give me the VP reg's number."

●

Two hours later, the Triple S CEO and Nita, hung up from the three-way call.

"Do you know her?"

"I know of her," Meredith said. "What do you think of her idea?"

Nita shook her head slowly. "Isn't your finger deep enough through the meat grinder, Meredith?"

"I'm not looking for extraction. I'm all in." She paused for a minute then looked back at Nita. "Why don't you write it up for the exec meeting."

"As you say, Meredith."

# FLY HEAD

"What I don't get," Jon said, turning all the way around, taking in the changes to the first-floor prison, "is how you actually got them to remove some of the cells?"

It was November 1, and Jon and Kevin were in what Jon would call his office. *In fact, nobody really had offices here*, Jon thought to himself. Everything was open, everybody had space, and everybody was everywhere.

People didn't make phone calls to each other; they just called out to each other.

*If somebody wants personal space, then they can just go to a cell on the second floor*, Jon smiled.

"It's Saturday," Kevin said, "and it's gorgeous outside. Why don't we join it." Kevin used his hand to usher Jon out first.

"Just answer my question on the way out," Jon said.

"I just convinced the powers that be that it was in their own best interest to help us."

"And how, pray tell, did you do that?"

Kev turned around, now facing his friend. "I told them we were going to make them famous."

Jon laughed. "Or infamous. But I guess the state prison already has done that for them. There's nowhere to go but up."

"That's what I thought."

Jon was just amazed at what Kevin had done for the group, as they walked to the prison exit. In the space of two months, Kevin had turned the disheveled group into a smooth operation.

The entire work of CiliCold now revolved around Luiz and Emma, Jon reminded himself. They needed Emma's know-how, software, and insight to plumb the depths of the antibody.

But Kev was the mortar between the bricks. People needed desks. He got them. Computers. Go to Kev. New cellphone. He was the communications guy from purchase to setup. The computers worked seamlessly on a small network, separate from the internet. No ins and no outs for the sake of secrecy and security. They had one and only one computer with an outside line to the web that Breanna managed.

"Even Cassie and Olivia are slowly and steadily working together." Jon shook his head.

"That's not me, Jon," Kevin said, turning around. "That little miracle's on you."

Jon stopped in his tracks. "I thought you and Oli—"

"That kind of communication only goes so far. You, on the other hand." Kev shook his head. "The effortless sacrifice of your own time for them engenders in them a kindred spirit."

Jon laughed. "OK, sounds like something from Proverbs. But let's talk about the tender subject."

"Emma."

Jon nodded, his stomach starting its anxiety roll.

Emma's work had not gone as smoothly as they had all hoped. Sure, her immense GSM programs and subroutines were smooth operators, running flawlessly on the sleek servers that Kevin had bought for her, but the solution she was getting for the antibodies remained elusive.

"It's not for lack of trying." Jon scratched his full head of hair.

Kevin nodded, opening the door to the bright Arizona light. "She's making antibodies, all right. $F_c$ and $F_{ab}$ chains are as she designed and hold their integrity in the extracellular fluid. But Luiz's work shows that they just don't have the killing power we need—"

"Look who's here."

Luiz ambled over. "Coming outside to warm up?"

"Hardly," Jon offered. "Just talking some about Emma." After a moment, he added, "And her difficulties."

Luiz nodded. "Em works hard, and I love her devotion. But no kill shot yet. Her antibodies don't have the viral affinity that we had hoped for."

"How long does it take to make them?" Kevin asked. "We were hoping for forty-eight hours."

"Four days." Luiz shrugged. "And they barely denature the virus."

"Does she have any new ideas about how to work herself out of this corner that she's painted herself into?"

"Know what?' Luiz said, leaning back against the warm red wall. "I guess my job is just to make sure that what she comes up with works, but"—he paused—"I've been wondering if Emma is overcommitted."

"What do you mean?" Kevin and Jon said simultaneously.

"Guys, you ever see a fly in a car? Fly comes in and goes to the windshield that it now climbs, trying to get out. But it can't, so it flies itself into it. Just banging that ole fly head against the windshield again and again until it exhausts itself. Even though a back window can be wide open.

"So," Jon said, his head nodding slowly, "it keeps trying the same approach bec—"

"Because it can't figure out why that approach is failing," Kevin finished.

Jon's heart leaped. "I can give her a new idea that I've been playing w—"

"Hold up, Jon," Luiz said. "If Emma has locked herself into a place that's making it difficult for her to function, then somebody should reach her first on an emotional level."

"Well, do you th—"

Luiz shook his head. "She's friendly, and like I said, I admire her. But she reveals little of herself. The emotional talk had best be good. Who can do that?"

Jon looked at Kevin. "I know a guy."

Kevin shrugged. "Do my best."

# SPARKY

"No time."

Emma and Kevin were in her workspace the next day. *She's going to explode*, he thought, noting her clenched fist, rapid eye movement, and clipped talk.

"I know," Kevin said in a low voice. "Let's take the nickel tour."

Kevin watched her eyes narrow.

"Am I going to be fired?" she asked.

Voice now tough.

Defiant.

He smiled.

"Absolutely not, Em. Let's you and I go to the real prison."

She scratched her scalp through her short blond hair. "I thought we were already in jail."

"I mean, the interesting part. Old Sparky."

"Who?"

He leaned in and whispered.

Watching the smile spread across her face was like witnessing a glorious sunrise.

"Now you're talking."

•

They walked out the back then into another building, Kevin leading the way.

"How long have you and Olivia been a thing?"

"Well, there's a question," he said, without turning.

"Come on. How long?"

Kevin slowed his climb up the dusty steps. "Not long, really. Four, five months."

"Really?" She rushed to catch up to him. "That's it? A hundred twenty days?" she said as they climbed the steps, passing the third floor.

"We spent a lot of time together after my first wife's death last year."

"Didn't know." She exhaled.

"She's in a better place now."

"When was the last execution?"

They turned a corner.

"Two years ago. Ah, here we are."

They came to a long row of cells.

"This is where the condemned inmates stayed."

Kevin opened one of them.

She entered and sat on the bed, lifting her feet in front of her onto the bed, resting her chin on her knees. "Kind of small. How long were the inmates here?"

"Seventeen years on average. Just waiting for their execution. Or reprieve."

"Creepy."

"Guess there's no electric chair," he said, looking down the long corridor. "Just a lethal injection room and gas chamber."

"No Sparky?"

He shrugged. "They must have taken it out. Probably sitting in some old dude's den.

"So how are you, Em.?" He turned to face her. "The real story."

"Well . . ." He watched her move her head, giving it a slow twist, left, then right, then back again, then stop. Over and over. Then she said, "Nothing's really up. That's the problem. The math's not working. So my programs are really hoofin' it, but chasing the wrong solution."

She put her legs down and leaned back against the brick wall. "And I'm not clicking like I should be. This is a much tougher problem than I expected."

"That's why nobody has ever attempted it, much less cracked it."

"Well, I thought I could, but maybe my name has to be added to the failure list."

*Not a chance*, he thought.

"Well, I don't know what else to do," she said, jumping to her feet, right hand rubbing the skin of her brow.

"Everything I know about ionic and covalent bonds I built into my models. And in fact, they are leading to fascinating new antibody structures. The hydroxyl groups and disulfide bond structures are incredibly intricate, but sadly, they don't really hone in on the virus or anything else for that matter. Their affinity is not a killing one."

"So your new antibodies don't really denature the virus? They, like, make friends with it?"

The computationalist laughed. "Right. But we need to murder it. That's the goal. Not play footsie with it."

"How old are you?"

"Twenty-nine."

"You've got a lot of energy and a ton of insight into this problem. I don't believe there's anybody as capable of solving it as you."

"You lie," she said, smiling. "You don't know everybody in the field."

"Well," he said, holding his hands palms up as he leaned back against the dirty bars. "I know enough about science to know that some of the best ideas come from the field's youngest." He smiled. "You youngsters develop in days what old-timers take months or years to work out."

"Are you saying that I'm out of insight now?"

"No. Just stepping on it."

She cocked her head. "What d—"

"You haven't put any energy into failure."

She cocked her head. "Who wants to fail, Kevin?"

He came off the bars. "It's not 'who wants to fail.' Everybody fails, like everybody breathes."

Her head shook like the death wobble of a spinning top. "I'm not into failure."

Kevin walked over to her. "Oh yes, you are. And you'd better get used to it if you want to find the solution you seek."

He sat next to her, stretching his long legs out, leaning his head back against the wall. "Em, there's no book written for what you're trying to do. You're creating a new path. How can you not fail as you go about finding it? You're a trailblazer. What, you think pioneers had maps? They don't read them, Em. Th—"

"They drew them."

"Precisely. Your quest must be full of failure."

"I hate failure."

"But have you ever really known it?" He leaned forward. "Look at you. You've been working hard and successfully since you were a kid. If it weren't for that student-cheating issue, you'd have gotten tenure at one of the youngest ages for your department."

He watched her squint. "How do you know that?"

"I have a good source."

"Rayiko." Em nodded.

"She's the best."

"Well, what do I do?"

"Start by getting out of your own way. Don't fear failure. Anticipate it. I'm not saying you have to be proud of it. Just stop being so repelled by it that you won't plunge in. Embrace it. Let it be a friend. Learn from it. Then you'll have the freedom to think analytically without fear."

She shook her head. "I hate the way failure makes me feel."

Kevin stood. "It's getting hot. Let's go."

They both walked out of the cell to the steps.

"Failure doesn't make you feel any particular way," he called from behind her. "You choose to feel the way you do. Stop the self-criticism, the self-loathing. Feel free to fail."

Ten minutes later, they were back in CiliCold prison space.

"Well," Emma said, looking back at Kevin smiling at her, "there's no electric chair after—"

She cocked her head up.

"I think I smell—"

Olivia turned around, holding a squirming bundle of—

"Dog!" Emma exclaimed. "I smelled dog. I love them. That yours?"

"Nope," Kevin said, as Olivia handed the puppy over to Emma. The black-and-white pup gave a baby yelp then snuggled in Emma's cradled arms.

"That tail's going to come clean off, it's wagging so hard," Olivia said, beaming.

"It's really mine?"

"If you want it. Thought it was time you had a lifelong companion."

Emma began to cry. "I had no idea. Thank you. Both. But I don't know what to name her."

"Him," Kevin corrected then shrugged. "I'd start with Sparky."

# DEVILED EGG

"You've been mad enough to chew concrete today."

*And whose fault do you think that is?* Jasper thought, squeezing the iPhone so hard that he thought he was crushing it.

"You promised me that you were going to figure this partial-antibody thing out, yet months have gone by and you've done nothing, Stennis. What the hell is going on with you and your people?" Spit flew out of his mouth.

"It's like I told you," the head of infectious diseases said. "We just can't make the damn chemistry work. I have five PhDs w—"

"Then you need ten. I don't care—"

"What we need is time w—"

"Which you have had in abundance. Now you're out of it."

"No, you're—"

"You need to have your ass fired."

Jasper hung up, his head pounding. He smashed his hand onto the wooden desk.

Once.

Again.

Sure, Meredith had pissed the executive committee off and was ripe to fall, but he needed a victory. He was looking to Stennis to help, and Stennis's group was just incompetent. *It wasn't like they didn't have the solution.* It had been handed to them on a silver platter. *Meredith gave it to me—to him—for pity's sake.*

And his leg was killing him.

Leaving all parts below the knee numb, his right leg pain shot tendrils up throughout his thigh. He felt like the muscles were being separated one hot, painful slice at a time.

It hurt so much he could only grip the desktop ledge hard, seeing only white until the pain episode passed.

And there was nothing anybody could do for him.

He resorted to the wheelchair as a last resort, but that was no damn good either.

"Come in!" he shouted, responding to the new knocking on his office door.

Denise Cowars, executive VP marketing North America, walked in. She also looked like her day was from hell: Squinting eyes. Flat mouth. *That was a blessing*, he thought. *Her teeth were yellow.* Hair done up high in tresses of white-and-yellow coloring. *Looks like she's wearing a deviled egg on her head.*

"What can I do for you, Denise?"

"What can you do for me? Throw Doucette down an elevator shaft."

Giles grunted. "Frankly, you're putting yourself in danger even just talking with me about it."

"I don't really care anymore," she said, falling into one of the two brown chairs on the other side of the desk. "Have you seen the informed consent her team has drafted for our new ASD drug?"

Jasper shook his head.

Her phone was in her hand, and she jabbed its flat screen like her finger was a knife and she was killing it. "Well, let me just describe its contents. It says that the child patient may experience irreparable damage to their nervous system.

"That they may die from a disease no one has heard of before and that we don't know how to treat."

She dropped her arm so hard the phone fell to the floor. "Who's going to sign a consent like that, Jasper?"

Jasper shook his head. *I don't have time for this.* "Maybe somebody who is desperate to have their child avoid autism?"

The exec VP snorted, jumping up. "Sounds like a lethal injection. A consent like this will frighten anybody. Who wants to run the risk of killing their child in order to prevent a disease they may not get? This whole thing is just crazy. Maybe—"

"Denise, maybe you need to sit down."

She flicked her hand at him. "Don't tell me what I need to do. Plus, she wants every family that consents to having their child in our ASD study to be videotaped as they sign the informed consent."

The executive VP sat back down, this time in the other seat. "I'm leaving SSS."

*Good*, the attorney thought. She was a blowhard who offered no original thinking. Like a wind that you heard but didn't feel. But he needed her support in the fight that was coming, so he held his tongue. His right leg was screaming at him, and he started to sweat.

"Denise. There are many steps that we need to take before you think about that one. You are far too valuable here."

She sat and brushed one of the deviled egg curls out of her eye. "Jasper, we can't market what the FDA won't approve. And Doucette's choices, her decisions, her actions, regarding this drug are going to kill it. You know that, and I know that."

"Well, not if we can help it."

"What are you going to do to stop this?" she almost shouted. "Are you going to go to the board? That's the only thing that would make a difference."

"That's exactly what I'm planning to do. I just need to have all the ammunition I can muster."

"Well, here's a good piece of it for you." Cowars leaned across the table. "She's going to fine any doctor who doesn't consent to patients in this format $10,000. Jasper, these are our own investigators that she wants to penalize."

Jasper blinked. "What does the FDA say?"

"The FDA doesn't know about it!" Cowars shouted.

She closed her eyes and took a breath.

Then another.

"Jasper," she said, taking a breath. "Every week we delay the trial, we ultimately delay the marketing of the drug. Delaying the marketing of the drug by a week costs us several million dollars. Millions. That's how much this drug is worth. And Doucette is deliberately slowing the approval process down. At this point, the FDA may decide that they don't want to approve the drug, after all. If we have no confidence in it, why should they?"

Jasper was now getting angry. He saw his future going right down the same hole that the VP described. "Denise, thanks for coming by, but . . ."

He leaned across the desk toward her, eyes narrowing, enjoying her involuntary move back away from him.

"I need to know that I have your complete support when I make my move."

"Well, if you don't know that now, then there's nothing I can do to convince you." She got up, knocking her chair over as she walked out of the office. Jasper's stomach turned over. *The very id*—

Phone ringing.

Stennis.

"What do you want now?"

"We found them."

Right leg better.

He reveled.

# SPOCK WAS WRONG

Two days later, Emma watched Jon pace back and forth in front of her outside in the prison courtyard. She had never seen him quite so worked up. *He lives for his ideas,* she thought.

He whirled. "Got it. Do you remember the second *Star Trek* movie?"

Star Trek *movie?* She screwed her face up. Then she realized.

"Oh, 'The Search for Spock,'" she said with a huge smile.

"Nope," Luiz said, closing the door behind him. "'The Wrath of Khan.'"

"He's the expert," Jon said, pointing at Luiz. "Anyway, toward the end of the movie, Spock turned to Kirk in the heat of battle and said that Kirk's adversary, Khan, was engaging in 'two-dimensional thinking.'"

"Oooookkkkaaayyy," Emma said. "What's that g—"

"Actually, Spock was wrong. Khan just turned the ship around and came back hard at the *Enterprise.* That's really one—"

"Thank you very much, Luiz. No wonder you're in Starfleet." Jon turned again to Emma. "Anyway," he said, shrugging, "that's the same mistake we're making. We need to change the dimension of the attack."

Emma looked at Luiz who simply shrugged. "This ain't the planet Genesis, man. Where are you going with this?"

Jon sat on the ground, folding his feet under him. "Em, you are doing great work on the wrong substrate. Maybe you shouldn't design a new antibody based on what nature has given you. That one is shaped like a Y, right?"

"Yep," she said, crouching in her jeans. "You know the drill. The $F_c$ chain is the stem of the Y, and the two $F_{ab}$ chains branch off at the top of the $F_c$. It's the $F_{ab}$ chains where the action is."

"But that's what nature gave us. Let's do something related but different."

"Such as?"

"Why not add another $F_{ab}$ chain?"

"What?" Luiz said, standing.

"We have two $F_{ab}$ chains synthetically assembled, each of which plays a role in gripping part of the viral surface. And that's not working."

"Right." Em heard Luiz say it with her.

"Not a tight enough grip. Why not add another?"

"Anoth—"

"$F_{ab}$. Why not a third $F_{ab}$ chain?"

"To tighten the grip."

"Something like that, yeah," Jon said, looking up at them both.

"Jon, it will be a hell of a thing to manufacture," Luiz said. His arms were waving. "How will that even be stable? I mean, the chemistry is very delicate. The Y is not held together by magic, but chemistry."

"Disulfide bonding."

"Right. We'd have to stick in another disulfide bond to attach the third $F_{ab}$. The whole molecule could fly apart. Listen—"

Emma, stunned by this idea, ignored Luiz's complaint list. The concept of a third $F_{ab}$ hadn't been considered by anybody. *Anybody.*

Not her.

No other scientists.

Her heart raced. *So much work to do.* Still.

"Hey."

Both men looked over at her.

"What we're doing is not working. Maybe Jon's won't work either, but it's worth a try."

"It means—"

"Yeah. I'll have to work out a new set of subroutines to come up with the strongest affinity for the three $F_{ab}$ sequence. That will take some time and several million comp iterations."

"Well," Luiz said, "if you want to go along, then I'll play. Let me have your first configuration"—Luiz rubbed his hands together—"and I'll work on assembling it in the extracellular fluid. That's where it has to work, and that's where it needs to be stable." He turned, heading back to his lab at the back of the prison's first floor.

"One second, Luiz," Jon called out. "What's the official designation of the Starship *Reliant*?"

"NCC-1864," he called back without turning around. "Miranda class."

Emma looked at Jon who was shaking his head and said, "My man."

# ROOTED OUT

"Coolidge, Arizona."

"Well, how did you do it?" Giles demanded. To him, Stennis looked like a preening turkey.

"Patent application."

"Those idiots never had a patent."

The VP infectologist smiled.

"Not for what we've been given. For something new."

*Something new?* Giles's mouth gaped.

"I bet you didn't know that," Stennis said.

"Well, what the hell is it?"

"How do I know? I just know that it was registered in Coolidge, Arizona."

But w—"

"Then I asked around here and found somebody who worked for AT&T and one at Verizon. I assumed those CiliCold nitwits used cell phones out there."

"And?"

"And I asked them to find the cell phone numbers of these people."

"That's illegal, Doctor."

"What the hell do you care, Jasper? You want to find these folks or not?"

Giles had not seen the infectious disease director so focused. Engaged. Giles shrugged.

"I just simply asked them to ping until they found the towers that were using these numbers. Took weeks to coordinate, especially since it was done on the QT and across two companies. All seven had a common foci—southeast Arizona."

"But what the heck is in Coolidge?"

"Nothing," Stennis said, raising his thin arms. "That's the beauty of it. We'd never think to look in a desert agricultural community. The question, Jasper is what are you going to do now?"

"Take the damn company," he said, rolling himself back behind the desk, swirling around to face Stennis.

"Well, here's a factoid for you. They won't give it up."

Jasper smiled. After all these weeks, the thriving flower was in his hand, waiting for the death squeeze.

"When I'm done, they'll beg me to take it."

# ALWAYS THE DUCKETS

J on hated this.

"Hey Emma," he called out as they both walked into what they all called "the prison laboratory." Five contiguous cells with the bars gone.

"Where's Sparky?"

"I think Cassie's got play duty today."

Ever since he gave her permission to bring her new dog to jail, Cassie, Breanna, Olivia, Kevin, Luiz, Rayiko, all became its buds. *Sparky's gang*, he thought. They all played with him, letting him follow along, and Sparky, neglected most of his young life, loved it all.

But his effect on everyone was nothing when compared to Emma. Before, she kept to herself. Not sullen. Just quiet. *The ultimate scientific loner*, Jon thought. Now she was outgoing, laughing with them all about themselves and herself. Housing stories. Arizona stories.

Home stories.

*Everybody needs a dog*, he thought, *whether they know it or not*.

Plus, Emma had been making very good progress from his conversations with both him and Luiz. The multiple $F_{ab}$ chains amplified the viral affinity and hence its killing power.

"It's remarkable to me, Emma, that this math process of yours works."

"Well, not without your idea," she said, play punching him in the right shoulder.

"As much as math plays a role in this, it's more the chemistry," she continued, sitting on one of the desk chairs. "Luiz's map of the viral surface lays out the viral topography—the irregularities and outcroppings on the viral surface. Those contours are created by protons and electrons that are part of the viral surface amino acids. I have to find the sequence of amino acids that will form the tightest bond to them."

"To fit them."

"Trying random sequences would take way too long," she said, rubbing her face with both of her hands.

"If we wanted to map a sequence ten amino acids long, we would have twenty billion combinations to plow through. So instead, we look at the forces that are in play. Matching London forces. Counteracting van der Waals. Looking at the strength of those forces and their location along the ten amino acid chain is all the mathematics needed to find the amino acid chain that would complement those forces. Cut down from looking at billions to a few hundred strands."

"That's where the simulation comes in."

"And the time savings."

"So what did you drag me back here to tell me?" he said, smiling. "Or did you just want to boast some?"

"That I think I can have this fully developed in about eight weeks." She paused, looking up at him, eyes bright and blazing, "Maybe six."

*Better do it now.* He sighed, beckoning her to join him on a prison bed in an adjacent cell.

"Emma," Jon said, lowering his voice. "I'm . . . I'm not sure we can finish the project."

She pulled back. "What, Jon? I just told you that we are almost there."

"And you've done something incredible, but we don't have the money anymore."

"But—"

"Breanna's accounting and Rayiko's tight-fisted management of supplies have gotten us this far, but we're going to run out of money in about a month."

She paused, running her left hand up and down the bars. "How're you gonna manage this?"

"I'm going to have to let people go."

"Who?"

He hesitated. "Everybody."

"Jon, they just moved here a few months ago."

He nodded.

She shook her head. "Always the duckets." After a moment, she asked, "Can't you just go to the bank?"

"Well, there are several banks here in town, but remember, we're trying to steer clear of people's radar. That means their financial radar as well."

"I can't believe, Jon, we've come this far."

"How far?"

Jon turned to see Kevin and Olivia.

"What's up?" Olivia asked.

"Well, I guess I might as well just tell everybody. Let's get together about nine this morning."

"OK."

As Kevin turned away, Jon caught his shoulder.

"My friend, the future looks brutal."

Kevin look at him. "Always does until you face it squarely."

●

Forty minutes later, Jon told everyone what he had explained to Emma.

"We're all affected," he said, rubbing his hands together, "but, Emma, I think is the most disappointed because she's made such great progress with her science."

"Way to go, Emma," Cassie said. Jon watched Emma give a thumbs-up in return.

"You used to raise money," Rayiko said.

"I sure did. In frigid northern Indiana. I'd be out publicly talking about our project. Thing is, anybody who's sniffing around will find out what we're doing here. And then our cover'll be blown. Plus . . ." Jon shrugged. "I really only raised peanuts."

"In winter?" Luiz asked. "I thought peanuts w—"

"Sorry, I meant only a little money."

"How much money do we need?" Olivia asked, shifting in her seat.

"Well," Kevin said. "I'm no accountant, but I'd say, trying not to focus on my girlfriend's pretty face for a moment, that we need north of $750,000 to finish off 2017."

"Really?"

"That much?"

"Yep," Rayiko said, crossing her legs. "Figure half of that is salaries. The other half is supplies that Luiz needs." She nodded his way. "Plus, we have a huge electric bill, now that Emma is driving her servers hard. She's not doing all this math in her head, you know."

"You said it." Luiz nodded. "I mean, these mathematics are pretty complicated. They need fuel."

Everybody was silent for a minute. Jon could feel the enthusiasm in the room wane as the seriousness of the matter seeped into everyone. Cassie coughed.

"And the banks aren't an option?"

Jon explained again why they couldn't go to the banks.

"Well, short of going to gangsters and loan sharks, I'm kind of out of ideas."

"Why not go to a loan company?" Breanna asked.

"Isn't that the same as a bank?"

"No," Cassie said, arm stretched out toward Kevin. "Actually, they're quite different." To Jon in the fluorescent light, her skin looked a little yellow.

"The reporting lines for a bank are very different and much more stringent than from a loan company. And I don't think we'll have any problem raising collateral here. All this equipment here is worth a lot. I don't know if it's worth $750,000, but not so far off."

"Can we look into that?"

"Sure, Breanna and I can check it out."

# IDIOT SAVANTS

Healed by Jesus.

Jasper was feeling great. Right leg pain-free and full of new energy. He almost believed that he could navigate without using the wheelchair.

Almost.

He was in this small filthy Arizona home that smelled of sweat and old food.

*Good thing I told the driver to keep the motor running.*

But even that didn't matter much today.

Ever since Stennis had zeroed in on Florence/Coolidge, the rest was easy. A little spreading-around money had located the newcomers in a prison. (*What a hoot.*) Some judicious calls to local banks dangling the possibility of investing in them revealed that the CiliCold stragglers were on the financial ropes.

*Drug companies investing in banks.* Used to be the other way around. The circle jerk was now complete.

Jasper shook his head clear.

"Are you with us on this, Gib?" Jasper asked, trying not to wrinkle his nose.

"Hey, it's going to make me money," Gibson Elster of Bluebird LLC said, shrugging.

Jasper liked Gib because coming in at six foot seven and 497 pounds, he made Jasper feel small. In fact, the president of Blue Bird, a "corporate loan company," never left his small Coolidge house anymore.

But after bringing down $1.9 million in profit last quarter, Elster didn't have to be thin.

He just bought thin people to run his business for him.

*And now*, Jasper thought. *I'm buying him.*

"I was looking to be owned by a bigger group anyway." Gib shrugged. "Just not a pharma giant."

"Well," Jasper said, wheeling his chair around to face Fat Elster in the smelly living room, "I want to keep our purchase out of the public eye."

The giant man shrugged his huge shoulders that if done in the Pacific would have caused a small tidal wave. "My company's private so that shouldn't be a big deal. I don't have shareholders, Jasper. You do."

"Yeah, yeah, yeah," Jasper said, waving his hand. "I need your Arizona residence."

"Want me to buy something in Florence?"

"No. Stay in Coolidge. I don't want this to be too obvious and too easy."

Elster belched. Jasper had to steel himself not to vomit in the face of the repugnant air.

"When do you buy us?"

"Just after you make the loan," Jasper said, going through the tortured arm movements of pulling a thick envelope out of his suit coat, itself drenched with sweat.

Gibs opened it, studying the enclosed purchase agreement.

"Seems OK to me, but why wait?"

"Because if they snoop around before signing, they will see that there are no Triple S strings. They won't know the amount of SSS's involvement until I bring the hammer down. Then it won't matter."

"But you want me to pay them before you own us?"

Jasper saw his eyes narrow.

"I'll stake you the money up front, Gib."

He watched Gib relax.

"Checko. Why don't we give them a little more than what they want?"

"They're not dummies. If we make it too easy for CiliCold, they'll start asking questions. Let them sweat a bit for their money. Then let them feel like you're doing them a favor. You could also say," the attorney finished with a shrug, "that in a year or so, they can ask for more. But that time will never come."

"Why not?"

"I'll own them before that."

Jasper pulled his phone out and listened then held it to his chest. "My guy is coming in here to wheel me to the car in a minute. Listen, it's key that you write the contract carefully."

"Checko." The big man belched. "Isn't it always?"

"I want their IP."

Gib's eyebrows shot up. "The company equipment's not going to be collateral?"

"No, we have better equipment than they have." He belched. "But what do you care. It's not your dime, Elster."

He explained in detail what he wanted to do as an alternative.

"That's strange."

"That's the way I want it. It's the only plan that will destroy these idiot savants."

"Checko. Hey, Rafael!" Jasper watched the giant man twist his fat head toward the kitchen and shout. "Are you going to get those buffalo wings out here or what?" He turned back to Jasper. "Not my place to ask you, but is your boss OK with this plan of yours?"

"Like you said"—the attorney shrugged—"not your place to ask."

"You know, Jasper, I'm trying to understand what these people mean to you."

"Let's just say they have some ideas that my company would be interested in. And I need them not just to give us their ideas. I need them to work for us."

"You can't make them work for you."

Jasper turned around. "I'm leaving."

"Checko."

# SWEET BABY, NASTY GIRL

Breanna came back to their Queen Creek home with groceries in one arm. She leaned over, placing the big grocery bag on the kitchen table, then walked back and to the left toward their bedroom.

One bag was all they needed these days. *Wasn't always like this*, she thought. When they first moved in a trip to Basha's, it required both of them to unload the car. Now . . .

Well. Something wasn't right.

She looked in.

Cassie was still asleep. That was just as well, the accountant thought. Maybe sleep could fix what was wrong. Cassie was pulling the hours, working on inventories with Rayiko and the money with Breanna, trying to nail CiliCold's worth to the penny. Plus, looking for a group to loan them almost a mil.

She just needed sleep, was all.

*Fat chance.*

Breanna turned to walk out. *Seemed like the kiddo's—*

"Hey, come on back in here."

The accountant turned. Cassie was sitting up.

"Jackie at the sitter's?"

"For another two hours."

"How're you doing?"

"Feel like a new person."

Breanna frowned.

"Not a healthy person, though, huh?"

The lovers looked at each other, an unspoken truth flowing from one to the other.

"No," Cassie said. "I'm not in the best shape."

"You're losing weight, aren't you?"

Cassie cocked her head, black hair moving to the left and falling toward the bed. "How do you know?"

"At night, I can see a little bit of your pelvic bone when you lie flat."

"You checking me out?" Cassie said with a smile. "The weight loss badge."

"Only if it's a harbinger of something bad," Breanna wanted to keep it serious, but the smell of Cassie was in the way now.

In her.

Inhabiting her.

She loved it.

Breanna reached over to stroke the attorney's thigh, moving back and forth across the pale skin, letting its softness be part of her.

She watched as Cassie sighed then lay back, spreading her legs. Breanna's heart raced, the attraction overpowering. She lifted herself up, mouth open, breath quick and shallow, tongue entering her as Cassie said, "Come be my sweet baby and my nasty girl."

●

"I'm OK," Cassie said forty minutes later, lying flat, Breanna's head on the attorney's right breast, all legs intertwined. *Like we're one being*, Breanna thought.

"I know your concern is for my health," Cassie said. "I'm worried too. But right now, we're all trying to save this company. It's desperate, and it's dire." Cassie took a breath, playing with Breanna's hair.

"And we may fail," Breanna said, closing her eyes, warmed by her lover's body.

"Then we fail. But it feels so good to be part of a process that is so . . . full. Worthwhile. Not to be doing something just because you make all the money in the world."

"Making all the money in the world's not so bad."

"It's nothing next to the feeling of you."

Anxious to hear more, Breanna was quiet. Minutes went by. Then Cassie said, "If you hate what you're doing, Bree, then you have a choice. Stay and lose yourself, or quit and lose the money."

Breanna picked her head up. "So you enjoy all the CiliCold trouble?"

"No, I enjoy working with all of you to solve it."

# POWER FAILURE

Her breaths came in deep ragged heaves.

And now she was sweating, the rivulets breaking through her makeup and running down her left cheek. Sitting perfectly still, she let the seconds pass in her VP finance's office.

"Who was this who called?" the CEO asked again.

"His name was a Gibson Elster," Nita said, glancing down at her notes. "He's running a company out of Arizona. He called to tell us that Jasper is up to something out there." She paused.

"CiliCold."

"Yes, Meredith. Where Cassie works."

The CEO closed her eyes tight. "How does Mr. Elster know that she works for them?"

"He met with her to work out the terms of the deal."

"What d—"

It broke through to her.

"He wants to break them. Jasper. He wants to destroy CiliCold and Cassie too."

"And you," Nita added, sighing. "He hates you too, but why?"

The CEO shook her head. "After a time, hate is its own ruler. Jasper just follows its orders." She was silent for a few moments. Then she said, "I'm meeting with him."

"Meredith, he's a force here. And growing."

"I'm not?" She watched her VP finance shift in her austere metal chair.

"People don't understand your ASD decision. Jasper's making headway using that."

"What I've done, I've done." Meredith's eyes were closed. "I'll deal with that. Invite Stennis as well. Let's set it for 4:00 PM today."

"But Stennis is a Jasper friend. Are you sure you want hi—"

"You be there too. Here's what I have in mind."

•

"Jasper, I'm telling you she called me in."

Giles sat back in his wheelchair. "Well, Stennis, what did she say?"

"She asked about CiliCold," the infectious disease chief said, Jasper's gray office door closing behind him.

"Why did she ask you?"

"Stop wasting time," Stennis said, pounding the office door behind him. "I'm in infectious disease. Of course, she's going to ask me about antibody production concepts."

"What did you tell her?"

"This is the CEO, Jasper. I told her the truth."

Jasper leaned over the cluttered desk. "And what was your version?"

"It is simply that we are after CiliCold to bring them in to work for Triple S." Stennis sighed.

"Seems harmless enough," the VP legal said, rocking back and forth in the seat of his overworked wheelchair.

•

4:05 PM.

Stennis and VP finance sat to the left and right of Meredith.

"No matter how bleak the weather, media discussion reminds you that the Preakness is coming this time of the year, and with it, spring," the CEO said.

Stennis shrugged. "Winter's not don—"

Jasper wheeled himself into the CEO's office.

"Why are you harassing CiliCold, Jasper?"

Meredith saw with satisfaction that he froze as everyone turned to Nita.

"Why are you asking me questio—"

"Answer her question, Jasper," Meredith said, leaning forward over her desk toward him.

"You can't force me to answer, and you won't dare move against me."

Meredith sat back, prolonging the silence. Then she said, "You're opening with your queen, Jasper."

"Well, you can't. I'm not going anywhere."

"True, true," the CEO said. "But I can take your office and give you one in the basement next to the furnace, let you work without an admin assistant, cut your bud—"

"You wouldn't da—"

*Such arrogance.* Meredith, sweating again, pulled out her iPhone. "This is the CEO. Can you put me in touch with Pers–"

"Why do you say I'm harassing them?" Jasper said, waving his hand, wheeling himself to her desk.

The CEO was tense, trying to smile. "Thank you, Jasper. This will go better if you just answer some simple questions." She pushed back from the table, keeping her eyes focused on Jasper. *What a weasel.* "Just to remind everyone here, I gave you CiliCold's product on a platter. That was what you wanted but couldn't get on your own."

"Well," Giles said, parking the wheelchair at the desk, "it turns out that the information you gave me was false."

*Liar.* Her heartbeat quickened. "How do you mean?"

"It doesn't work."

Meredith almost snorted as she looked at Nita who was shaking her head.

"That doesn't mean it's false, Jasper," Nita said, looking now at Stennis. "It just means that your team can't reproduce their chemistry."

The CEO leaned forward again. "What we gave you was exactly what they used, and their data is incontrovertibly positive. So again, why are you harassing them now?"

"I'm not," he said, smiling. "Just trying to get them to work for us." She saw that Giles was actually smiling.

"Jasper, they traveled 3,100 miles to get away from Triple S. You think they're going to just report to work here at 8:00. AM one Monday, hats in hand?"

"Not exactly. There are other ways they can satisfy."

"Such as?"

Meredith saw Jasper's eyes harden. "I have some thoughts on that."

"You want to destroy their work."

"What?" Jasper asked, smiling.

"Yes," Meredith said, staring at Giles, flipping an arm in his direction. "This was his inane plan all along. To catch the scientific breakthrough of a decade and then kill it so the common cold remains a scourge, and people keep buying our over-the-counter products, keeping us in business."

"Holding aside this nefarious idea for a second," Nita said, "how do you plan to get them in SSS?"

"By going after them financially."

"Well," Meredith said, throwing some papers across the desk, voice hot and raised. "You're not going to succeed with this agreement."

They skidded across the desk's surface, landing in Jasper's lap. Meredith watched with satisfaction as his jaw dropped while scanning the jumbled mess in his lap.

After a moment, Jasper said. "I'm just offering financial support for them."

"By hiding behind a loan company then emasculating CiliCold?" Nita said. Meredith saw her VP finance leaning forward, fully engaged.

The CEO saw Jasper glare at her, clenching his fist.

"Maybe you don't know the company that you run here, Meredith, but that is what we do sometimes," Jasper said suddenly, sitting back in his wheelchair in full persuasive voice. "We get money in here any way we can.

"I'm not saying there's no collateral damage," he said, raising his arms, "but if we are to stay in business, if we are to meet our obligations to shareholders, if we are to pay our own salaries, we have to do this.

"You might actually claim that it's your idea, Meredith," he said, smiling at her. "That would be appropriate as well and save your job."

"Not sacrifice science for the sake of shareholders, Jasper," Meredith said, raising her voice. "Not on my watch, you don't." She clenched her jaw, biting back her thoughts.

Jasper cocked his head. "What did you just say?"

"I said you won't do it while I'm working here."

"Actually, Meredith, I'm going to proceed with this. Whether you like it or not."

The CEO sat stunned in the suddenly quiet room. "Jasper, you think you have the support to do this?"

"I do." He stared back.

"You don't have the pow—" Meredith said, raising her voice.

"I most certainly do, and I exercise it," Jasper said, slamming his right fist down on the table. He paused, and the CEO saw him draw a breath.

"Meredith, look here," Giles said, sitting back in the chair, holding a hand out to her. "Face it, dear, your time is over.

"You're already in trouble with the executive committee over our autism drug. By the time I'm done with the board, they're not just going to throw you out of your position, but they're going to throw you out of the window too."

He wheeled around and rolled toward the door.

"Thanks for coming by, Jasper."

He turned, raising his left hand, giving the remaining occupants his trademark middle finger. Meredith watched as Stennis rushed out of the chair, hurrying to get the door for him.

As soon as the door closed, Meredith called Jan, her executive assistant.

"How can I help you, Ms. Doucette?"

"Please call this number for me."

When Jasmine left, the CEO showed the number to Nita, who took it, shook her head, and handed it back.

"Meredith, calling that number won't help you at all."

"Not supposed to, but it will help them."

# IN MY HAND

"Elster, you told me you had this handled?" Giles said into his phone, slamming his hand onto the elevator wall when he got on the elevator heading back to his office.

"I did. Exactly as you asked. In fact, they signed off on the agreement yesterday."

*This idiot.* Jasper's face turned red. "Doucette had the agreement, jerk. She knows all about us."

"Well, since Triple S owns us, the financial group there should know about our initiative."

"And," Giles said, "where in here does it say that they are going to give us the company if they fail on the debt?"

"That's such an unusual request for collateral. I didn't think that you really mea—"

"That's exactly the whole point of this!" Giles shouted, his leg roaring in pain. "That's how I get them in my hand."

"You're not the only lawyer," Elster said, voice suddenly raspy. "Mine had trouble with it."

"Shut up and listen, you idiot. I'm going to send you a contract amendment that's got this required change in it."

"You want them to sign a postcontract contract amendment. I tell you what. You tak—"

"Hold off on that." Jasper thought for a second.

"Did they get their money?"

"Checko. The debit just hit our account."

"Well then, let's not say anything about this contract amendment for a while."

"This is wholly unethical, Jasper. You know t—"

Giles had already hung up.

# IP

"That was a very disturbing phone call."

Olivia put the cell down on Cassie's desk. She watched Cassie close her eyes. *She seems tired.*

"Who from?"

"From your—I mean, our friends at Triple S," Olivia said, shaking her head.

"Well," Cassie said quietly, putting her pen down. "They know we're here now."

"Yes. They know."

"At least the part of all this is over. We won't be hiding anymore."

"I'd better get Kevin and Jon over here," Olivia said. Then she added, "I hated hiding anyway."

"What were you guys working on?" Olivia said when Jon and Kevin walked over.

"We were talking about developing a website," Jon said, smiling, "but with our publicity issue, this is not the time for it." He shrugged.

Olivia looked at Cassie. "That won't matter now," the attorney said.

Olivia explained what Meredith had said to her on the phone.

"How?" Jon said. Olivia saw that his face was tight. Severe.

"Hey," Cassie said softly, "it doesn't matter how they know. Only that they kn—"

"And it's worse than that," Olivia added.

"The loan we just signed," Cassie said, "that had very favorable terms for us is now serviced by Triple S."

"What?" Jon plopped into a chair. It tipped over, and he sprawled onto the floor.

"Here," Olivia said, getting up and offering him a hand. Jon stood, running his hand through his hair front to back.

Again and again. Then he said, "How did they do that?"

"They must have bought the company after they loaned us the bread," Kevin said. "That's why Cassie's due diligence didn't turn it up. Come here, boy."

Sparky ran over and jumped into Kevin's outstretched arms.

"My God," Jon said, standing. "What does he want?"

"Meredith didn't know," Olivia said. She made a tight fist, barely able to control herself. "Only that Giles wants CiliCold's work."

Jon began to pace, breathing loudly. Deeply. "Meredith and I gave it to him."

"So," Kevin said, "if we default on the loan, t—"

"Then he gets our work product?"

"That's how we think this plays out," Olivia said, looking over at Cassie. Something wasn't fitting though. She closed her eyes. *Have to think this through.*

"Jasper knew I'd look for a SSS footprint on this loan," Cassie said, shaking her head, "so he postponed buying until after the loan was complete."

"Well," Jon said, righting the chair then carefully sitting back in it, "I don't see the problem. We simply pay the loan back. Then no other terms of contract are invoked. We don't borrow from them again, and we move on."

"However, they do know where we are," Kevin said, "and that means that Jasper is now going to focus his attack on us."

Jon shook his head. "I have to give these sonsabitches credit for perseverance."

"Again with the hot pursuit?" Rayiko said, walking over.

"You heard?"

"Not everything, but enough."

Like bricks, it fell in on Olivia.

"No, based on what Meredith told me, this doesn't make sense."

"Why not?" Kevin asked, leaning forward in his chair.

"It can't be the work product. Look, you gave them everything they needed to reproduce the partial-antibody work, right?" Olivia turned to Jon. "You and Luiz."

"Sure thing," Luiz said, walking over to join the group. "A lot more than would be in a patent."

"Right. Well, Meredith said that they couldn't get it to work," Olivia said, turning to Luiz.

"What? With what we gave them, the Marx brothers could reproduce what we did."

Olivia shook her head. "Didn't help them one bit, Luiz. They don't have the talent."

"And," Cassie said, "this is Jasper. Now that he knows the SSS failure, he has a new target."

"So," Jon said, sitting again, "it's not the patent then."

"It's us," Olivia said, face flushed.

"So," Jon said, "my plan failed because they were too dumb to get the partial antibody product to—"

"So this is all about him getting control of us?"

"Yes."

"Does the contract permit him to do that?"

"It permits him to control at least our patent," Cassie said.

"That's kind of strange," Rayiko said, frowning. "He doesn't want all of our equipment?"

Her phone rang.

She looked at it, saying, "I have to take this." She walked out.

"No, they just want the patent."

"And what we're working on now?" Cassie asked.

"Emma's work?" Jon snorted. "How does he even know what that is?"

"You're missing the point, my friend," Kevin said, turning to Jon. "Giles wants what's in your head and"—he pointed a long finger Cassie's way—"to destroy our attorney here in the process."

•

When he saw she had put her phone away, Jon walked over to her. "Rayiko, are you OK?"

"No. Yes. No." She sighed. Jon thought she was going to cry. Fighting the impulse to hold her, he asked, "What can I do?"

"I have to go home now."

Jon nodded. "We can catch up tomorrow."

# MEDIEVAL LAND

"This can't be right," Rayiko said the next morning.

Jon saw her reading a note, the envelope on the floor.

'What's wrong?" Jon asked. He knew she was devastated from the midday call she received yesterday, but she was keeping it locked up.

If she wanted his help, she'd let him know.

*Not that she'd need it*, he thought. He shrugged.

Rayiko turned, showing the letter to Jon.

Jon stared then ground his teeth. He crumpled it up then stopped.

He took his Android out then stopped.

"This isn't a phone call. It's a visit."

He turned and left the prison at once, heart pounding.

From anger.

From fright.

•

Two hours later, Jon entered the prison's main door and saw his crew gathered at the center of their circle of jail "suites" staring at him.

Sparky came to greet him.

"It's the rent," he said, bending over to scratch Sparky's ears. "It's gone up."

"Well," Olivia said, leaning against Rayiko's desk, "they never go down, do they? How much?"

"They were charging us $250 per month," he said, blinking rapidly.

"Nominal," Kevin said.

"It's up four hundred fold."

"What?" Breanna said. "You mean our rent is now—"

"That's right. It's $100,000 a month."

"That's beyond outrageous."

"As of when?"

Jon let his arms fall by his sides. "As of March first."

"Fifteen days away? Way wrong."

"Wrong?" Emma said. "It's an insult."

To Jon, Emma looked like she wanted to spit.

"Fifteen days? Why not make it fifteen minutes," Luiz said.

Jon passed around the notice.

"Well, I'd say that we've worn out our welcome," Olivia said. "Too bad. The Arizona heat was growing on me."

Jon laughed despite himself. Everyone knew Olivia struggled with the dry heat more than anyone.

"But this increase is . . . egregious," Breanna said. "Why stop there? Increase it to four thousand fold, forty thousand fold. We can't pay any of it."

"They know that," Cassie said in a low voice.

"Aren't there rules out here about this kind of rent abuse?" Breanna said, on her feet now, hands balled into fists.

"This is Arizona, folks," Kevin said, leaning against a bookcase. He sighed. "Not only is there no limit on rent increases, but there's a rule on the Arizona books that prevents cities from interfering with rent increases."

"Where the hell are we? Medieval land?"

"We are under ARS § 33-1329," Cassie said. "Cities and towns are precluded from the imposition of rent control."

"And that, folks, is the 'Wild' in the 'Wild West,'" Luiz said, slouching in his chair, feet crossed.

"This feels like Jasper's hands are all over this," Cassie said. Jon heard her voice fill with disgust.

"What does this mean for our bottom line?" Emma asked, looking over at Breanna.

"This is February 15?" Breanna asked. "With this, we default the end of next month."

"Well. We need to do something to buy some time," Emma said, running her hands through her short hair. "Luiz and I are almost done with our final trials. The algorithm is tight, and the antibodies we've produced work against all viruses we've tested. We wanted to do trials in monkeys, but—"

"No time for that now," Kevin said. He leaned down to pick up Sparky, who barked twice, tail wagging, and put his front paws on Kevin's shoulders.

"Do we have a patent for her work yet?" Olivia asked.

"For most of the pieces, yes, but we wanted to be sure that it all worked together the way Emma and Luiz wanted before we patented the entire proc—"

They all jumped at the loud bang at the door.

"I'll see who this is," Jon said, walking to the thick gray door. Sparky followed him to the door, black-and-white tail wagging.

"Probably Satan, the devil, welcoming us back home," Emma said.

Jon took a thin business envelope from the FedEx driver. *What the devil is this*, he wondered. He tore it open then studied the contents.

He had never actually felt anything from his hair before without running his hands through it.

Now, while reading, it felt white-hot.

"Patent doesn't really matter," he called out.

"What do you have there, Jon?" Kevin said, standing and turning to face the president who walked back to the team, Sparky bringing up the rear.

"The end of life as we know it."

# DIRTY FOOT

"It's a contract amendment," Jon. said. "It lists what will happen if we default on the loan."

"What?" Cassie said. "We know what will happen already."

"Well, this sounds different. Have a listen."

Jon began reading, his voice tight with rage.

> In the event that CiliCold LLC (referred to herein as the *"Borrower"*) defaults on their Loan held by Triple S Pharmaceutical Company (herein referred to as the *"Lender"*), the following will take place:
>
> 1. All experiments will cease, and all results, both partial and complete, are to be turned over to Lender.
> 2. All programming code is to be turned over to Lender.
> 3. All programming code is to be fully documented (two lines of explanation for each line of code).
> 4. All servers, hard drives, and laptops are to be turned over to Lender.
> 5. Each computer and server turned over to Lender is to be accompanied by its own inventory list detailing the hard drive's contents with an explanation of each file.
> 6. All flash drives are to be turned over to Lender with an inventory list of the flash drives' contents within and an explanation for each file.
> 7. The author of the programs will work with the Lender's programmers, explaining to each of the

Lender team member's satisfaction what each code line does.

8. The Borrower's programmer will run the code both in total and, if necessary, each subroutine individually, explaining in detail how the code works.

9. Biologic experiments, their preparations, their execution, their output, and their interpretation will be reproduced by the Borrower's cell scientist in the presence of the Lender, to the Lender's cell team members' satisfaction.

10. The Borrower's president will explain in detail each of the Borrower's scientific protocols.

The terms of the contract will not be met until Lender has on their own demonstrated that they can reproduce the work of the Borrower.

This holds for all past protocols and current work of the Borrower.

Any abrogation of the above-listed items triggers the seizure of all professional and personal property of the Borrower's Officers.

"Damn it!" Luiz shouted. "We could give them all this, and those luddites still wouldn't know what we're up—"

"My code is over a million lines long," Emma shouted. "Each is to be documented?" Jon noted her ragged breathing.

"Who the hell are our 'officers'?"

"So," Rayiko said, "their dirty foot is on our neck. We might as well be working for them."

The room was quiet.

"The game's not over yet," Cassie said.

# GET THE HELL TO WORK

Jon looked at her, jaws tight. "What do you mean?"

"Let's take them to court."

"What? Us?" Breanna said. "Against the entire Triple S team?" She shook her head.

"It's not the entire team," Cassie said, scratching her forehead. A lock of her hair came off in her hand. "Meredith would never countenance this. So that means Jasper is going rogue."

"But won't this go to federal court?"

"Not if we keep both parties in Arizona."

"So we don't sue SSS?" Jon asked.

"We sue Elster."

"What's our argument?"

Jon noticed that all eyes turned to Cassie.

"Clearly this is an outrageous and unjustified rent increase. And that is occurring because a business interest located outside the state of Arizona is trying to influence Arizona state prison to change its rental rates. I think I can make a decent case out of this. I can find some precedent law. At least get a court-ordered stay to allow us to finish."

"Cassie?" Jon said.

"Yeah."

"Get the hell to work."

He looked over to Emma who nodded as lightning split the Florence sky.

# ROGUE WAVE

J on had driven the fifteen miles from Florence to San Tan Valley in the cold, driving rain. Wet tumbleweed blew across Arizona Farm Road as he reached Hunt Highway, five minutes from home.

Stopped at a traffic, he watched the water flow over and then into the desert stand. Through it. Cutting into it. Making rivulets.

*Are rivers alive?*

He shook his head. Where did that come from?

*It's a simple question, actually. Yes or no?*

Rivers were water. Rivers contained living things, but rivers were not themselves alive.

*Well, why do you think a cell is alive?*

"I think a cell is alive because the cell is able to reproduce," he said to his steering wheel.

*Rivers divide into streams, which can become their own rivers. Don't they reproduce in their own way?*

"Later."

Right now, he was soaking wet. After getting home, a hot shower, and getting into dry clothes, he called Emma.

"Emma, we need to have enough space to hold a—"

He jumped at the loud door knock.

"Can I call you back, Em?"

"Sure thing."

Putting the Android down, he walked to the door. The swollen wood caught for a moment, but on the second try, the door flew open.

There she was. Her small frame under a thin and smaller umbrella.

Shaking.

Cold and frightened.

His mouth dropped.

"Rayiko, it's a mess out there. Come in."

She didn't move.

"Please," he said, holding his hand out to her.

Without a word, she walked in.

"Here. On the couch by the fire." He took her umbrella and her yellow slicker from her. When she sat, he flicked the gas jet on, and the fire ignited. He walked out with her wet things, returning with a comforter.

"I'll fix us some tea. And a little bit of a meal if you like. After that, we can talk."

"Tea, please," she said in a soft voice.

Jon went to work in the kitchen, wondering as he always did just what she wanted from him. *There are a hundred ways to jack this up.* He sighed, releasing all of his thoughts and expectations into the warm air, and walked carefully back into the living room with two cups of tea.

There she sat, on the couch, right leg bent under the left, the left foot barely reaching the floor. She took her tea, sipping in silence. Jon sat a foot away but next to her. Twenty minutes of silence passed. Then Jon asked, "Do I need to call a car or somebody to come g—"

"Richard and my baby are gone."

Jon sat up straight. "Richard took Gary?" *I knew there was tension there, but this?* "They don't live with you anymore? They're just traveling? What d—"

She sneezed then shivered. "Richard's new LA office had a 'Take Your Child to Work Day.' We were all going to fly out tonight to . . . to make a weekend of it."

"Oooookay. So he—"

"Richard just took Gary and left me here. He didn't even tell me why he changed his mind."

"That was the phone call yesterday?"

"Yes. That was him calling me from LA saying not to worry." She just shook her head back and forth. "Like he was just going to get some inkjet parts at Best Buy or something."

He moved to her on the couch, putting his arm around her. "You are injured, sweetheart. Don't rush anything. Stay as long as you like. This—"

"They will be back tomorrow."

"—will take time to figure out. And first," he said, shifting away from her to see her face, "you have to find yourself."

"I don't know what to—"

Jon leaned back on the couch, sinking into its softness. "You can't possibly know. It's like a rogue wave has upended you. You're still reacting, stunned, spinning, twisting around. The thoughts you need will come to you in time, but you just can't hurry them out of you."

"What do I do?"

He put both arms around her.

"Sometimes this is all two people can do."

She rested her head on his neck. "I can't tell you everything. It's too embarrassing."

"Yes you can," he said, rocking her. "Just do it in Japanese."

She looked at him. "That's just dumb."

"Why? You get it to say them, get them out of you. And since I don't speak the language, your secrets are still yours."

She sobbed, caught her breath, face between his neck and right shoulder. Jon put his arms around her and held her close. And then she put the Japanese words out there. Soft then with strength and ferocity.

"私は彼をとても愛していました"
"私はまだ彼を愛しています"
"赤ちゃんを元に戻したい"
"彼に私を愛させることはできません"

Over and over to Jon. Sometimes wailing. Sometimes angry.

And he couldn't help but speak back. While she spoke to him, he said, "This is nothing you deserve. For reasons I don't know, you have to go through this. But that doesn't mean you'll be ruined. You will find your own footing. And if the only thing you can do is hold on to your heart, then you do just that and let everything else go. Let your main job be to guard your soul. Protect it, Rayiko."

Though speaking two different languages at once, Jon felt them intertwining, pouring themselves one into the other. His heart pounded as they held each other, kissed each other.

Then Rayiko said, "I need to go."

"The rain's not stopped. Just be still for a time."

She rested in his arms again, her ear so close to his mouth. He wanted to whisper more. To gently nuzzle it. Lick it.

"I have nothing to hold on to."

"Yes, you do. And you always will. Come with me."

He let her into his bedroom. "This is your room tonight." Pointing to the left, he said, "There's the bathroom. Feel free to use it. But get out of those clothes. Get in bed. And sleep."

"What about you?"

"I am not your worry tonight. Your worry is your own heart. You take care of that."

# THUNDERCLAP OF LIFE

Later, Jon looked over what he had written.

Mathematically, this approach is translated to the following: for each analysis in the set of analyses responsive to the investigator's question $q$, i.e., $\omega_i \subset A_q = \{\omega_i / q_i @q\}$ investigators identify the benefit functions $\{\mathbf{Y}(\chi_i^{(b)})\}$ and the harm functions $\{\mathbf{Y}(\chi_i^{(h)})\}$. The collection of benefit function results $\{\mathbf{Y}(\chi_i^{(b)})\}$ can now be accumulated over all of the analyses $\omega_i \subset A_q = \{\omega_i / q_i @q\}$, producing $\int_{A_q} \mathbf{Y}(\chi_i^{(b)})$.

*Close, but so many missing ingredients.* Jon thought, calm after forty-five minutes spent in the living room puzzling over rivers in a T-shirt and sweatpants. He'd need a biomachinist and, of course, somebody with better mat—

*What's that?*

Walking to her door, he heard it again. He knocked.

"Come in."

He saw that the two table lights were on next to the bed, and the bright overhead was out. Rayiko was sitting on the bed in one of his sweatshirts.

He never thought a sweatshirt of his looked so good.

Jon struggled but failed to hide his smile.

"What can I do for you?"

"Just listen to me."

Jon sat and listened. About growing problems at her home. The husband, who was more and more distracted by his business and the love of his son.

"How did I get squeezed out of his life?"

Jon shrugged then leaned back. "Why did you marry Richard?"

"He was what I wasn't—strong, ambitious, driven."

"When I was married," Jon said, hands behind his head, feet on the floor, twisting back against the headboard, "I made the same mistake. I married based on what I liked about her. I didn't marry her based on what I didn't like."

"Why is that a mistake?" She was sitting up, small arms wrapped around her legs, head resting on her small knees. He blinked and forced himself to look at the ceiling to concentrate.

"I mean, if you're going to live with somebody, it's not enough to be able to live with their strengths. That's easy to do because that's why you admire them. But you also have to be able to live with their weaknesses as well. If you can't live with their weaknesses, the relationship is doomed because you won't change them."

She pursed her lips, almost pouting. "Wives always change their men."

"No, they do not, Rayiko. How do you change someone's character?"

She laughed. "That's pretty profound coming from a scientist."

"We scientists are full of surprises."

He put his feet up on the bed, shifting to rest his back against the headboard.

"Better?"

"Much."

She tapped his leg, saying, "Open up." He spread his legs, and she plopped down between them, her back resting against his chest.

"I am comfortable like this."

"I would give up the world for your comfort." *I live for her heart's peace.*

She lifted her hands to her stomach. He placed his on hers. They both exhaled. Looking down, he saw that just under the cover, she was dressed in only—

"Is that my underwear that you're wearing?" He laughed.

"You had no women's underwear in your drawers. What was I to do?"

She turned around and kissed his neck. Jon's head was spinning.

His hand gently rubbed her stomach through the sweatshirt, his chest almost bursting with the full force of his affection for her. *I am devoted to her.* To this woman that he had admired for years. *For years.* Now nibbling her neck, he said, "I have always been for you."

She nodded and leaned forward. He ran his fingers. up under the sweatshirt and up her back. Found the bra fastener. *Never good at these things*, Jon thought. *What if*—

Snap.

As the bra fell away, he encircled her, his fingers cupping the baby-soft skin of her breasts, which, taut and firm, filled his hands. *My hands.*

He all but passed out in the ecstasy. His heart hammered as he ran his hands around them, over them, the nipples swelling in his fingers. *Oh to suckle them, to give them the pleasure that they have been denied for years.*

He wanted her, now finally knowing that she wanted him.

*Maybe this isn't the best time.*

The thunderclap of life hit him. *"Best" is part of a future that never comes.*

She shifted, pulling away from him.

"Rayiko. Just relax and let this be good for you. Right now, there's nothing else in the world for us but you and me. Let's live it, if only for tonight."

She took his hands and moved them to her belly.

Jon ran his hands from her warm, smooth belly up to her breasts and back again. He inhaled her hair, intoxicated by its clean smell. She moved her head forward, bringing her right hand behind her neck, tilting his head forward.

Kissing him.

It was the kiss that reached him, took control of him, penetrated deep inside him.

Owned him.

Tongues circling, swirling, wrapping. As he encircled her with his left arm, his right moved down to her thighs.

Tiny thighs.

Firm thighs.

Ran his hands along those thighs and back up their abdomen, back up her stomach to her breasts, and back down. Back and forth. He broke their kiss, whispering, "I am for you."

He ran his hands over and then inside her underwear, too big for her, now heated and damp. His brain exploded in light as he touched her lips, and she pushed forward against him as his fingers entered her folds.

She lifted her hips, slid the garment off, and then leaned her back into him again, right arm around his neck, turning her head around, kissing and holding.

His moistened fingers reentered her, teased her folds, moving up, up, until he found her, hard and ready.

She moaned as he played with it, stroking the tender underside, nudging it left then right, sliding over it, loving it.

"I love you so much. Cum for me, baby," he said, putting a single finger inside her.

Her hips jumped up. Kissing him with her mouth, her tongue, her teeth. Then bucking twice hard, she collapsed, then jumped again. *She's my baby. I know it, and she knows it.*

Jon kept his fingers in her until she was still, reveling in the oneness of them.

●

He woke up before the sun rose. Dressing quietly so he didn't disturb her sleeping delicate form, he tiptoed to the kitchen to get breakfast going.

The tea was ready, just as the toast sprang up from the to—

"Morning, Jon."

He turned around. There she was.

In her clothes. Shoes.

Ready to move on with her day.

"Hey, looks like you're going somewhere."

She raised her head. "Toast smells good."

They sat at the round wood table, the sun just spraying itself across the kitchen.

"Jon—"

"Rayiko, they are your family. You belong to them. They belong to you." He sighed, putting his toast down. "I don't know why they don't understand that they need you. But they do. Even I know that much. And when your feet are back under you, you'll know that much too."

"They are back under me now."

He looked at her. "I understand. Know that I am always here for you. I always have been."

"See you at work, Jon."

# LUCK OF THE IRISH

"We have a court date now," she said, starting right in. "March fifteenth."

Cassie's heart pounded as she stood in the center of a semicircle of CiliCold employees. She had given summaries of a case status hundreds of times during her career and sat through just as many.

This one was different though. She was invested in this one. Exhilarated, but dreading failure.

She took a breath, believing her commitment made her better, not worse.

"Tuesday," Rayiko said. "Two weeks from now."

"Ides of March," Emma said, sitting next to her, Sparky in her lap, lying on his back, inching to have his belly scratched.

"Well, let's hope this works out better for us than Caesar."

Cassie allowed herself a small smile. She was always fascinated at the loose informality of this group. Their corporate lives were at risk, maybe even their personal finances, but they acted like this was just another lunchtime research seminar. *Because they trust me.* Her breath caught.

"We ready?" Jon asked, sitting off to one side.

"Yes," she said, taking a step toward him, now fully immersed in her style. "But I want to answer any questions that you all have about what's coming up and the likely outcomes.

"I think this will probably take an hour, but it can go as long as you like. At the end, I want to make sure that all of your questions have been answered so that you know the situation."

"Great," Emma said. "Can you start at the beginning?"

Cassie leaned back against the desk behind her. "We had a contract for an initial loan amount whose terms we all thought were fair. The money that we would use to pay it back from, of course, would be from the money we get from the work of yours and Luiz's. However, we learned three things. First, the loan company, Elster Bluebird, was purchased by Triple S. We now owe not Elster, but SSS—"

"What kind of name is Bluebird Loans anyway?" Luiz said. "Sounds like one of those commercials that come on at two o'clock in the morning."

Cassie smiled and nodded. "Second, they are trying to amend the contract in a hideous way."

"We all read that trash," Jon said.

Cassie saw him look at Emma and then Luiz.

"What we would have to do is despicable," he finished.

"The third is the phenomenal increase in our rent. This is a transparent attempt to drive us to default and then invoke the amendment—"

"Which we didn't sign," Olivia said, stomping her foot.

Sparky jumped in Emma's arms. She soothed him.

"OK, let's hold aside for the moment the fact that this would result in an insulting and demeaning demonstration of the performance of our work. The fact is, they are trying to amend the contract without our approval," she said, hands now folded across her chest, voice rising.

"We had several choices. One choice is to go along with the amended contract."

"F that."

*They are full of energy*, she thought. *Good.* "Another option would be to negotiate for better terms. However, this is Triple S, and we understand little good will come from that."

Olivia snorted. Everyone laughed. She looked around, appearing to be surprised, then laughed and put her hands up.

"Don't hold back, honey," Kevin said. "Let us know how you feel."

Cassie laughed. *You always know what Olivia's thinking.* "The next choice is to go to Arizona Justice Court in Florence to argue against the amendment."

"Why there?"

"The justice court can hear civil cases where the financial issue at hand is less than $10 million. And," Cassie added, "since we are bringing the case, we are the plaintiffs, not the defendant."

"And that matters because?" Luiz asked.

"We are being proactive in bringing this illegal amendment to the court's attention before the amendment's provisions are invoked. This is better than being dragged into court as defendants accused of being deadbeats who don't pay their bills, got caught in default, and are now arguing why they don't have to pay. Facts matter, but appearances also count in court."

"And the outrageous rent?" Rayiko asked. "How does that fit in?"

"Good question, Rayiko," Cassie said, walking over to her. "Remember that in Arizona, increases in rent are legal with notice. The rent can be increased as much or as little as the landlord wants."

"Swell," Emma said. "Twelfth century."

"Well, they are proud of it out here. So we lose as a matter of law if we just complain about the rent. So," she said, smiling, "we keep the rent increase out of the direct line of our argument. We are not asking the court to rule on it. We are asking the courts simply to rule on the amendment. If the amendment is invalid, then Jasper gets nothing of value from us, and the whole rationale for the rent increase disappears."

"So then, what is our direct argument?"

"The contract as originally written does not include the process by which the contract terms can be modified. We will use that to our advantage.

"I will argue that this change in the contract is meant to defraud us. This, in combination with rent changes, is meant to deliberately drive us into default and then rob us of our intellectual property. This is an infringement by a New Jersey corporation on the rights of Arizona citizens.

"Also, the amendment is burdensome, representing a request that is above and beyond what is reasonable for use of collateral in a business loan. The whole idea of using IP as collateral is a relatively new one in the law. The concept that an idea created by a citizen of Arizona can be owned by someone else, prepatent, is dangerous and frightening. Especially here."

"Any idea what the jury will be like?"

Cassie shook her head. "This will be a bench trial. No jury. Only the judge will make the determination. We drew Judge Roberts. He's a state's rights judge, who is a fierce defender of Arizona citizens."

"Who'd have thought," Kevin said, "that I would be pinning my hopes on a man like that?"

"Bottom line, Cassie, will this work?"

●

"Hi, Jasper," Sid Beamer said as he walked into the suite at the Hilton in downtown Dover, Delaware. "It's been a long time since I've seen you. You get west often?"

"Nope," Jasper said, belching as he rolled himself over in his wheelchair to shake the other lawyer's hand. "Thanks for flying in from Phoenix."

"Well, what's this meeting about?" Beamer said, blowing his nose. "Cold as a witch's tit here."

"We're involved—"

"You mean Triple S?"

Jasper just stared at him. His right leg was on fire, the pain flames licking at him from just above the knee, the part below having been ground down to numbness by the years' long pain battle.

"Of course, I mean Triple S."

"Take it easy now," Beamer said, backing up a step. "I had to ask because we're not meeting at Triple S like we have before. We're meeting in a hotel. That makes me think that this meeting is off the books and that this work has . . . extralegal components."

"Well don't. It's a small issue involving an Arizona group that is about to default on a Triple S loan. We are working to revise the contract with an amendment."

Sid shrugged. Jasper thought his suit jacket would fall off the thin man's shoulders.

"Shouldn't be a problem. Amendments are added to contracts all the time. In fact, most well-written contracts have a section that discusses how amendments should be added." He walked to the table, grabbing a diet root beer.

"Has the amendment been countersigned?" Sid called from over his shoulder.

Silence.

Sid turned. "I see. You want to get this amendment accepted as part of the legal contract without their countersignature. How are you going to do that?"

"Well, that's what the courts are for." *Jesus, this leg hurts.* He rubbed the swollen mottled thigh, knowing that would do no good.

"What do you know about the Florence court?"

Jasper wheeled the chair around to face him. "Well, I know Roberts is due to take their case, but I'm interested in having McKendrick preside."

"I see," Beamer said, nodding. "McKendrick is a procorporation judge."

"Plus, he hates defaulters."

Beamer nodded, walking over for another drink. "Kudos, Jasper. You've done your homework. How much do they owe?"

Jasper waved a hand at the visiting attorney. "Doesn't matter. They'll default by end of March. I want you to go out to Florence, AZ, and lay the groundwork for the proceedings."

"If I'm going to do this, then I'm going to need to be able to see the contract."

"This is what I have in mind."

Jasper spoke for two minutes then took out a thin white envelope with his right hand.

Beamer pulled back. "I don't know how you're going to pull that off. Courts frown on those kinds of maneuvers."

Giles felt him looking down at him. He glared back.

"I would ask why," Beamer said, swallowing, "but I'm not sure I want to know the answer."

"Get back out there tonight and see to it," Jasper said, handing Beamer his retainer fee.

•

"Fifty-fifty," Cassie said. "But you remember that this is a rural county. Pinal County is under increasing financial stress. Lack of water is putting pressure on agriculture, which is the mainstay here. These folks see a corporate presence, outside the state or not, as a benefit, not a problem."

"Well, the court date is not the seventeenth, but may the luck of the Irish be with us," Kevin said.

"The hell with that," Olivia said. "We have Cassie."

# A KING HENRY THING

The Triple S CEO pushed back from the table, rubbing both eyes with the palms of her hands.

The end of the long day was here.

"I do appreciate these fine discussions about regulatory," she said, coughing. "Excuse me. But I also appreciate when they're over."

Both the CFO and chief regulatory officer looked at her and nodded. Meredith knew that neither Nita nor Monica would admit fatigue in her presence. Nita was especially stoic. Monica, VP regulatory, had been gregarious recently, but even she held her tongue today.

"Before we discuss the poll, I commissioned a 'King Henry' thing."

Monica's mouth dropped. Nita, true to form, kept her teeth together.

"I sent some of my lesser-known admin assistants to hang out in the cafeterias, what recreation area we have left, even the restrooms. I asked them to be my eyes and ears. To learn what people are saying about the company."

"And you, right? To get their reaction to you."

The CEO just nodded. "It would inform my opinion."

"What did it show?" Monica said, putting her poll numbers aside.

"They despise me," the CEO said, looking down at once. "The results, uniform across all the admin assistants, were merciless."

"They're upset about the ASD decision."

"They don't know the data."

"They know your approach. The decision points to the change in your philosophy. It's the attitude change they hate," Monica said.

"Meredith," Monica continued, leaning over the table, "I understand why you're sad. But you have to understand the point of view of the people who work here. They have seen products that we have created fail. Some projects fail in the prebiology studies. Others in animal studies. Still more in our phase one through phase three human studies.

"In any event, they fail. And all of that money invested in the compounds, those drugs, goes right down the chute. Hundreds of millions of dollars."

"The states don't pay us for that, Meredith," Nita said. "Medicare doesn't pay us back. The FDA doesn't pay. We have to pay for that ourselves."

"So," Monica continued. "Now, when it looks like we have a new blockbuster on our hands, your employees look at this as not just an opportunity to pay for the cost of developing the blockbuster, but also of recouping the cost of the other failures as well. Make hay while the sun shines."

*Nothing new here.* Meredith nodded politely.

"That's the only way we stay in business. And they see you watching the ASD profits circle the drain."

"You talk about 'circling the drain,'" Meredith said, hands up. "How about children circling the same dirty drain?"

"I understand how you feel, Meredith," Monica said. "Poll said the same thing. I'm just telling you how your employees feel. That's what you asked of me, right?"

"Yes." Meredith pushed back in the plastic chair. "Of course. By all means."

"Our progress on the autism project is very slow," Nita said. "We are not recruiting very many patients at all. This last group of five patients that we recruited still have to be followed for another three months before we can go to the FDA with any data that they h—"

"I have to ask you, Meredith," Monica said, leaning forward. "Let's say that these five patients that we recruited and followed for six months don't have any problems. No neuro whatever. In the face of that hopeful finding, are you still going to insist on cleaving to your idea of recruiting another small cohort and following them?"

"Yes," the CEO said at once.

Monica sighed. "Well then, you can't blame your people for being upset with you. They look at Triple S as flailing in the water now. They want you as their champion. Yet with life preserver in hand, you refuse to save them."

"I like the metaphor, but liking it and buying it are two different things. Triple S will survive without an ASD."

"Again, this is their view. We might survive, but we're not going to prosper."

Meredith thought for a second. She had come to this point on her own. *Time to let my Catholic cat out of the bag.*

"Maybe that's how it should be. Maybe we've been spoiled in this industry. Reverse junkies, getting rich off selling drugs, any dugs, just to make dollars."

Both Nita and Monica sat with mouths open.

"I wonder if drug making and moneymaking go hand in hand anymore," Meredith continued.

She saw Monica shift in her chair. "You give a hint of what you're thinking, and Triple S will run you over."

Nita walked over. "Meredith, don't fool yourself. You don't have monks and nuns working for you. They are neither charitable nor self-sacrificing. They are . . ."

She paused for a moment.

"Cannibals," Meredith finished, turning her chair around to watch the storm front coming in.

•

Are we going to have the bandwidth?" Jon asked. He looked at Emma who turned to Kevin. Jon saw that even Sparky, tail wagging, followed Emma's gaze and was now tracking Kevin. *He may be CiliCold's mascot. But he's Em's dog.*

Kevin nodded. "Don't worry about bandwidth. We'll send the signal. Plus, we have multiple servers. They'll stand the strain."

"You could open your own electronics shop," Emma said. "That is, when they let you out of jail."

They all laughed.

Jon ran his hair through his hair. "I wish I could think of a better way to manage this."

"Well, we all trust Cassie," Emma said. "She'll do her best, but"—she looked straight at Jon—"we're up against evil here. Commonly in these battles, evil wins."

"Not this damn time."

•

"Even Nita?" the voice said on the phone.

"Neither of them reacted well to my thoughts."

208

"You're going to have to get used to that. That is, if you keep talking."
A pause. Then . . .

"Maybe it's time for the next phase."

"You mean a—"

"Where I'm from, when you hit somebody, you knock them down so hard they can't get back up."

The pair talked for two minutes.

"I wouldn't dare," Meredith said.

"Of course you would. You told me that it's either your soul or the dollars. You can't keep both."

"I wouldn't know where to start," the CEO said, a tight grip on her phone.

"I do. Three phone calls get things in motion."

Meredith swallowed. "Let's talk some more when we're farther down the road."

"OK," Olivia said. "But we're already closer than you think."

# WORTHY

"I can't believe you came to bed early the night before," Breanna said, looking up from her book as Cassie came into the bedroom and sat on the bed.

"Yeah. I've never believed in pulling an all-nighter the night before a trial."

"Well OK, but really, this isn't such a big deal for you, right? I mean, you've spent so much time in other cases." Breanna tossed her book on the table by the silver lamp. "Multimillion dollar cases. Multidistrict litigation. Federal court." She smiled. "This is just a hearing. In front of a civil court judge. In Florence, Arizona, for heaven's sake. It doesn't involve very much money."

"What do you think CiliCold wants?"

Breanna watched Cassie turn her head around to face her. "Freedom."

Breanna rubbed Cassie's back. *How different she is from when I first met her at Perkins back in West Lafayette. Loved her then too.*

"It's not that I want to avoid a court embarrassment—"

"You mean like throwing up?"

She watched Cassie purse her lips. "Don't think that doesn't happen. These attorneys are under inhuman pressure, and they can react physically and at the worst time. Anyway, I just want to be sure that at the end of the day, I can say I did everything I could." She paused for a second. "I want to be worthy."

"Well, you convinced everybody that you take this seriously. To victory," she said, raising her right hand high.

"No, to friends. And to strength of heart."

# HOME

The roosters had long since stopped their crowing, and the streets were empty, Cassie saw, just like in those westerns when all the law abiders just knew a beatdown was coming.

Her CiliCold team was nervous. As Kevin, Olivia, Rayiko, and Jon finished walking the ten-minute walk with her to the courthouse, she realized that not one of them had spoken. Not about the air that was a crisp thirty-six degrees. Nothing about the sky that was a perfect Arizona blue at eight thirty-six in the morning.

She sneezed.

Not even about the reek of cow manure that made your eyes water.

*What did the Arizonans call that odor? Oh yeah.*

*Money.*

"Here we are," she said, and as they walked into the tall courthouse building, she couldn't help but smile. Even though she did not like much of what she had done in court for years, court had become her home.

*You've been away too long*, she thought.

"We're upstairs," she said, taking the lead. *So ornate.* The winding steps of wood and gold plate leading them to the conference rooms and courtroom shimmered in the morning sun.

Cassie smiled, walking through the heavy wooden doors into the courtroom. The message of the court, indeed of the building, was plain.

The law mattered.

*We'll see about that*, she thought, sitting at the front table to the left of where the judge would sit. Ignoring her adversary sitting on the other side of the court, she turned to the CiliCold team. "Jon, as plaintiff, can sit with me, but the rest of you should sit behind us."

Turning right, she called out, "Hi, Sid."

The attorney for the defendant walked over. "Cassie," he said, smiling. "Somehow I thought you wouldn't show up."

She smiled back with her classic smile that she had been told would melt neutronium. "But somehow you knew I would."

They both turned when the bailiff walked in. "Hi, Jed," they called out at once as he ambled over to them.

"You both working for the same team?"

"No," Sid said.

"Used to," Cassie followed. "Nice to see you again after our pretrial meets."

"Judge will be here in a minute."

As Sid and Jed walked away, Cassie returned to her table and picked up some small yellow pads.

"All good?" Jon asked, leaning forward.

"Good as can be." She waved for the CiliCold team to gather around.

"Just want to remind you that once you passed through those doors," she said, lifting her eyes to the tall doors they had just passed through, "you are now in a different world. Here, the judge rules. You stand when the judge comes in, and you stand when he leaves. In between, you keep your teeth together unless he asks you a question. And if he does, begin your answer with 'Your Honor.' Whatever he asks you, state the truth. Nothing more. Don't pretend to be respectful. Be respectful."

"You act like he's God," Olivia said, looking where the judge would sit.

"In here, he is. If you have a message for me, don't whisper. Here." She handed out the pads. "Use these. Oh, turn off your cell phones. Not silent mode, not airplane mode. All the way off." Dutifully, Cassie took hers out and turned it off while watching the others do the same.

Looking at them with steady eyes, she said, "We're all set."

Turning back around, she opened her briefcase and lifted each document out, carefully inspecting them.

The contract.

The contested amendment.

Precedents with which she hoped to persuade the court. *I hope th—*

"All rise."

Reflexively, she stood.

"The Honorable Judge Edgar McKendrick presiding."

*What is this?* she wondered. Not Rogers. Why? Death? Illness? Something else? She whirled around at the murmuring behind her.

"Shh."

She turned back around, drew in a slow breath, and emptied her lungs.

*A change but not necessarily a bad deal.*

She noticed the judge having a conversation with the bailiff then suddenly walking out.

McKendrick had a tough view on people who defaulted on contracts and was known to be procorporate. *But* we *haven't defaulted*, she remembered. In fact, we are trying not to default. He was also a fighter for the rights of Arizona citizens.

*Adjust. Sure, I can adjust my argument for that*, she decided. *Just emphasize more of the outsider-versus-Arizona aspect.*

She heard the door behind her open. Somebody from CiliCold gasped. She turned to silence them when she saw.

Jasper.

# IN A BAD WAY

Cassie froze, fighting to keep studied neutrality etched on her face. His head seemed much bigger. In fact, his entire body seemed bigger; and he was listing to the right in his wheelchair, the right leg extended and swollen, making the pants leg appear tight around the encased flesh that she knew was gross and tender.

"Who is that?" Jon whispered, leaning toward her.

"Jasper Giles, acting head of Triple S legal," she whispered back as he was wheeled to the left to join Sid.

"Oh," Jon said, waving his hand. "The devil. For the defense. Looks like he's in a bad way. Why would he come way out here?"

*That is the question*, Cassie thought.

The answer pounced on her.

To intimidate her. *Meredith was right.* In the end, he's out to destroy her and CiliCold.

And he wanted to bear witness to the process.

Her training kicked in at once. Sitting still. Eyes front, unblinking.

She knew that the court proceedings were filled with all these types of ploys.

One judge being substituted for another.

Evidence being admitted that shouldn't have been admitted.

Witnesses disappearing, new witnesses appearing without prior warning.

This was all the stuff of courtroom theatrics that took up much of the energy in the courtroom. *Without it, court would be boring, wouldn't it?* She smiled. Plus, there was nothing about Jasper's appearance that would affect what the facts were in this case. In fact, she remembered that she had pulled a lawyer substitution once and twice in her past.

The lioness in her growled.

"Folks, I'm sorry," the bailiff said. "The judge will be another minute."

This was her chance. She stood and walked across the aisle, tapping Jasper on the shoulder.

"Jasper," she asked. "How are you?"

He looked up at her, squinting with flat eyes that reflected no recognition. He greeted her, "Cassie, last time I saw you, you were screaming and crying on the floor."

*Animal.*

She shook his hand, then nodding toward his right leg, said, "Still bothering you?"

"What do you think?"

"Don't be too angry with me if I twist the damn thing off today."

"You ungrateful bit—"

"All rise."

She returned to her seat. Pulse down.

Settled.

•

Cassie saw Judge McKendrick walk in, sit, and survey the room. His hair was a little thinner than she remembered from the photograph, but his mustache was still long and curled at the ends.

*Quintessential western judge*, she thought.

*No.*

*Sheriff.*

"Are all parties here?" the judge called. Sid and Cassie stood. Jasper just raised his hand, she saw.

"Cassie Rhodes for the plaintiffs, Your Honor."

"Sid Beamer for the defendants."

"I apologize, Your Honor, for not being able to stand. But I am Jasper Giles, here for the defense as well."

"Sid, how have you been?" the judge asked.

"Thank you for asking, Your Honor. I'm tolerable."

The judge laughed; then the smile disappeared. "Mr. Giles, I don't recognize you. Are you admitted before the bar of the State of Arizona?"

"No, Your Honor," Giles said, raising his voice. "I am here simply as an interested party and as an observer. I am not planning to make any arguments before the court."

"Very well," Judge McKendrick said. "Let's keep it that way." He turned to Cassie. "Plaintiffs, you may proceed."

Cassie stood. "Your Honor, I am representing a duly certified solvent LLC located in Florence, Arizona, by the name of CiliCold. We are a small scientific organization and have been here in Florence for nine months. We have been working on our projects with the approval of the city of Florence and the Arizona State Prison Authority."

"The State Prison Authority?" the judge said, pursing his lips.

"Yes, sir."

"Why do you need their involvement? Where exactly do the employees of the LLC work?"

"We work at the Florence State Prison, Your Honor."

She saw the judge's bushy eyebrows shoot up.

"You are actually working at the prison? Why?"

Cassie drew a breath. She had to be careful. To say they were there hiding from the defendants would complicate the discussion. But she couldn't lie before the court.

"Your Honor, we are comfortable there, and we are able to conduct our work there. We have no complaints and are thankful to the prison authority for giving us the space and resources that we need after they vacated the premises."

"Well, I must say this is unique," McKendrick said. "I've never heard of any such arrangement like that before, but no matter, please continue."

Cassie laid out her case in the detail that she had anticipated. There were no interruptions. Finally, she sat down.

"Sid?"

"Judge." Beamer began. This is a very simple case. We have a signed contract with CiliCold that governs the loan that they took out from Bluebird Loans LLC here in Florence."

Cassie watched as he extended his arms.

"We fully admit that there was a mistake in the contract. This happens commonly. And we have supplied an amendment. The amendment is really straightforward, Your Honor. It involves nothing but collateral."

"I have read the contract and the amendment," Judge McKendrick said, resting his head on his right forefinger. "The amendment addresses the issue of intellectual property."

"Yes, Your Honor. That is what we decided would be collateral. In fact, we thought that would be fairer to their LLC, Your Honor. They have many different ideas, some of which I've no doubt are valuable, but many of which are not. However, surely, they could depart with those much easier than they could with the valuable equipment that they have."

"But I also note this amendment has not been countersigned by CiliCold?"

"Your Honor, that's right."

Cassie noted that Sid's voice was a little higher now.

"CiliCold has not signed this even though it is a fair arrangement," the lawyer continued. "It permits them to continue to work, and in fact, Your Honor, we would be willing to extend the period in which they can work after default."

The judge looked up from the papers. "But they have not defaulted yet. Isn't that what you have said, Ms. Rhodes?"

Sensing victory, Cassie answered simply, "Yes, Your Honor."

"Ms. Rhodes, do the plaintiffs have a comment about this new concession being offered to CiliCold?"

"Yes," Jon said, standing. "We think—"

Cassie turned and motioned with her hands that he should sit.

"Your Honor," she began, turning around to face the judge. "My apologies. My client is new to the court and is not familiar with its rules and processes. He thought you were addressing him and not his company's representative."

The judge smiled. "I understand. Scientists feel strongly."

"Yes, Your Honor. CiliCold is afraid of losing its productivity to the defendant. As we sit here now, the interaction between our LLC and Bluebird is contained within the four corners of our contract with them, duly signed and countersigned. There are no external ev—"

Kevin noticed it first.

# ONE WORD

Kevin watched Cassie who was now frozen, mouth open. His first thought was that she saw something, and he looked around whirling first left, then right. He was ready to yell "Gun!" but no threat.

He turned to see Cassie, trembling and unspeaking.

Eyes blinking. Unseeing.

"Seizure!" he cried out, leaping forward to get to the teetering attorney with Jon who had already started.

*Too late*, he thought as she crumpled, her head crashing against the unforgiving wooden floor, body stiff as a board.

"Let's get her away from the table," Jon said.

"I got her."

Jon stepped back as Kevin stood over her head and, bending down, grabbed her stiff arms, clumsily pulling her forward away from the attorneys' table.

At once, one of her hands pulled free of her grasp.

Kevin and Jon stood watching in fright and fascination as her right hand began to twitch. Regular beats. Then the arm.

Both arms.

Legs.

Neck.

All stiff, but all jerking awkwardly. Wildly.

"Uruuuouf," she cried out in a low guttural voice. "Uruuuuouf uruuuouf, uruuuouf . . ."

"You," Kevin heard the opposing attorney call out. "Cell phones on. Someone call 911."

Kevin looked down. Cassie was writhing and jerking uncontrollably, thrashing against the unyielding floor, her eyes staring blankly at the ceiling, spit running from her mouth. Kevin's eyes welled up. *No idea. No idea*, he kept thinking. "Cassie!" he heard someone scream.

Breanna was there.

"My God, Cassie. What happened?"

"Grand mal seizure," Jon said, grunting as he tried and failing to control her neck's heavy pounding against the floor.

"Keep trying, Jon," Kevin said, standing. He saw that the judge had vacated the room. He jerked off his suit coat. Then turning, he said, "You too, Olivia."

She was there in a flash, jacket off. He took both, then after wrapping them into a soft ball, put them under her head.

He turned to watch the liquid flowing from her puddle on the floor around her knees.

"Incontinent," Jon said.

"Epilepsy?" Olivia asked.

"Maybe." He looked around, saying, "Breanna, we need you."

"Yes?"

"Get down here. OK, sit on your butt, legs outstretched. Kevin, let's get Cassie's head on Breanna's thighs . . . There."

Cassie's head moved over Breanna's thighs, sometimes rubbing, sometimes thumping.

"Jon—"

"Lean over and speak to her," Jon said, hand on Breanna's back.

"She will hear?"

"Yes, just say that you are here, you love her, and it will be over soon. Don't leave her in there by herself, Breanna. Sing to her. Anything to let her know she is not alone."

Kevin, heartbroken, held Olivia sitting next to him as they helplessly watched Cassie's agony. Olivia moved to be near Cassie's head. He watched, fascinated as she whispered to her as well.

•

Her second seizure began when the ambulance team had just put her into its bay after a long transport down the steps.

"They're taking her to Casa Grande," Kevin said.

"We'll need to drive there."

"Breanna, you hitch a ride with these ambulance folks," Jon said. "The rest of us will get our cars and then drive straight to Casa Grande ED." He grabbed Kevin's arm. "Can we talk for a minute?"

"Sure." Kevin squinted for a moment.

He and Jon parted after a thirty-second discussion.

# PREJUDICE

" So we're just to wait here," Luiz said, pacing back and forth at the prison. "And why couldn't we go?"

Emma picked Sparky up, who was figure eighting around her legs, tail slapping her ankles.

"Luiz, just relax. We have the most important job of the day. Maybe of the project."

"I was hoping to see the court proceedings."

"Why? They are like other meetings. Moments of illumination surrounded by the weight of enforced drudgery."

•

Kevin bounded up to the second floor, taking the steps two and three at a time. When he arrived at the door, he took ten seconds to catch his breath then walked in.

*Jon was right.*

There was the judge addressing Beamer and Giles with no one else being present. Absolutely nobody to represent the plaintiff. *And there's nothing I can do*, he thought, *but watch this calamity unfold.*

"—as this health situation been resolved."

"We bel—" Beamer started.

"Your Honor," Giles began in a strong voice, "please forgive my impertinence, but this is such an unusual day. I have not seen anything like this. The fact is, we don't know how or where she is."

*What? Beamer was the one who called for the ambulance.* Kevin's heart jumped.

"She, in fact, may have regained consciousness. All we can say is that the court has reconvened and plaintiff's attorney is nowhere to be found in midhearing."

*These bastards were stealing the case.* Kevin's hands tightened into fists.

"Do we know if anything like this has happened before with Ms. Rhodes?" the judge asked.

"N—" Beamer tried again.

"Yes, Your Honor," Giles jumped in again. "She is an ex-colleague of mine, and I can attest to her instability."

*Giles.* Kevin tried to swallow, but his voice was too tight. *It's all him.*

"Well," the judge said, shaking his head. "I will need to take some time to consider how to proceed."

"Your Honor, we are asking you, in the face of an unexplained absence of plaintiff's attorney, that you dismiss this case and allow us to proceed with attaching the amendment to the contract."

"Yes," McKendrick said. "I may have to do that."

*No. Jesus, no.*

"And considering that she has disappeared in midhearing," Giles added, "and has not reappeared as soon as possible, we are asking that you dismiss the case with prejudice."

*What was this now?*

"She should not be permitted to refile this travesty with the court, only to disappear again."

"That's a fine point, Mr. Giles, but you are not the attorney of record. Sid?"

Kevin watched as Beamer sat and said nothing.

It seemed that a minute went by in silence as Kevin prayed to his god, to the universe, to all gods, not just for justice, but a chance at justice. *Please gi—*

"Yes, Your Honor. We ask that you dismiss with prejudice."

Anger took Kevin. Shook him. Consumed him.

"Well, I concur," the judge said. "This case is dismissed with prejudice. I will need just need thirty minutes to record my verdict." Banging his gavel, Judge McKendrick said, "Sine die," turning to leave.

Kevin's blood boiled. But now, he could act.

# SEND

Kevin dialed.

●

Both Em and Luiz watched the phone ring. Emma picked it up as Sparky jumped from her lap and pat-pat-patted on the hard floor to Luiz.

"Hello? Kevin?"

She put her hand over the mike.

"We all set to blow here, Luiz?"

"A little late to ask, but yeah. I hit return, and that's that. What's wrong?"

She moved her hand. "Kevin? Kevin?"

●

Kevin waited.

Waited until Beamer wheeled Giles toward him and the exit door.

Waited until they were next to him.

Giles looked at him, saying, "Be a good boy, would you, and open the door for us."

●

"Kevin, is that you?" Emma said. She noticed that suddenly she was covered in sweat, the enormity of what she was about to do breaking through to her. The sacrifice of everything.

"Maybe the connection's dead," Luiz said. "I have problems in this place all the time. Hang up and let him call again."

●

"Yessir," Kevin said. "Jessamoment now."

●

"OK, maybe you're right."

She fumbled with the phone, finding, then pressing on the end ke—

"Send now."

Kevin. Loud and clear over the speaker. She pointed to her colleague.

"You asked why he does this, Luiz?" she cried out in triumph.

"Yeah. Why are we—"

"Because the only way to really hurt these people is to give away what they want to sell."

"Bueno."

"Punch it, man."

# SIGNS

Kevin wheeled into the Casa Grande Emergency Department just in time to see Jon rushing through its double doors inside. Kevin screeched to a halt and hustled up to catch him.

"Just like you said," he said to Jon, catching up to him. "How did you know?"

"Just a hunch and a little push from Olivia."

"Olivia?"

"You've got quite a woman on your hands. Did you have a c—"

"Jon."

Kevin looked left and saw Rayiko, tears streaming down her face. Olivia had her arm around her shoulders.

Kevin walked up to them. "Do we know anything?"

"Not yet," Breanna said, seated next to the group.

"Let's all get off our feet," Kevin said, sitting down in a row of black chairs with silver arms.

"She seized twice more," Breanna said. "Once before the IV and a smaller one after."

"How we—"

"Hello, is anybody here that is with Cassie Rhodes?"

Kevin turned to see a white jacket, green scrub pants, and white shirt encasing a man who had to be at least six and a half feet tall including the turban.

"I am Dr. Ruyan. Are you here for Ms. Rhodes?"

"We all are," Kevin heard Jon say.

"Then you are family?" he said. Kevin suppressed a smile as the doctor looked around at one white and one Asian woman plus two black men.

"She has no family," Olivia said. "Only us." After a moment, she added, "We are her friends and all that she has."

225

"Well, I will tell you what I can," the doctor said, sitting next to Breanna. "We are very concerned about her. She had some major neurologic events, and frankly, they may not be over."

Kevin suddenly had to force himself to breathe. Breanna began to cry. The doctor put his hand on her shoulder. "Obviously a major seizure event," he said, lowering his voice. "Plus, she now has an acute small fracture at the base of her skull."

"She did fall."

"Did you all see these seizures occur?"

"Yes," Kevin started, noting the doctor as he listened patiently to each team member describe what they saw.

"And she has no history of epilepsy?"

"She had an . . . an unhealthy childhood," Breanna said, wiping her eyes with a ruined Kleenex. "But no problems as an adult. Not even a car accident."

"She ever stared into space much?"

"Not that kind of girl," Olivia said.

"Pretty focused," Jon said.

Kevin watched, pulse trip-hammering as Dr. Ruyan sat back in the chair. "This is very helpful, but confusing. I will tell you that except for some post-ictal changes, her neurologic exam is normal. So is her physical exam. However, I must tell you that we are very concerned about what we are seeing from the metabolics."

"What does that mean?" Rayiko said.

Kevin watched as Jon took his phone out. Listening, he said OK then put it back, nodding at Kevin.

"Well, I have to be very careful in what I can and cannot tell you because you are not family. But the situation is such that perhaps we can provide more effective treatment if we tell each other what we know."

"Doctor," Olivia said, "we only know that we've been working with her and she has been in relatively good health. But perhaps working a little too hard."

"Poison."

•

Kevin watched all heads turn to Jon.

"What do you mean?" Dr. Ruyan said, turning to face Jon.

"Uhm, I can't put my finger on it yet, but there have been some changes in Cassie over the past few weeks. Signs, I guess. I think she's been losing some hair. Also, her skin color is not what it typically is." Kevin watched Jon close his eyes tight, trying to remember. "She is much paler now than she was when I first met her months ago. I haven't noticed any change in her thinking. Just a sense that she was somehow off."

"I talked with her about it a few weeks ago," Breanna said. "She brushed me off."

The doctor hung his head. "Well, that fits some of this. It looks like her liver, pancreas, and kidneys are in poor shape. We are also seeing some small lesions in her brain."

"I assume you're going to be hospitalizing her?" Kevin asked.

"Yes, but now that we have this notion of toxicity, we'll be doing some additional screening on her. But based on these numbers I'm seeing and her clinical condition, she will need dialysis."

"Jesus. Permanently?"

Kevin watched the doctor shrug.

"We all care very much for her," Olivia said, wiping her eyes.

"I can tell," he said, smiling. "We'll do all that we ca—"

His phone blinked. He took it out of his shirt pocket.

"Yes. Thank you," he said.

Turning to them, he said, "She is awake now."

CiliCold stood.

Dr. Ruyan smiled. "You can't all go back, but I can give one of you a couple of minutes."

All stepped back for Breanna.

"This way please."

•

By the time she walked through another set of double doors to a series of small rooms, Breanna was sweating, heart pounding.

"This one," Dr. Ruyan said. "Remember, now, two minutes."

*Cassie.*

There she was.

In a hospital gown now. Hair swept back from her head. Makeup smeared. An IV coming out of her right arm, running up a pole from which multiple translucent bags hung.

"Cassie," Breanna said, head throbbing, rushing toward and leaning over the bed's locked sidebar. She cradled her face and kissed her hair, eyes, cheeks. At once, the headache was gone.

"I was so scared. But here you are now. I don't know how or why, but you are here and I love you so."

After a moment, Breanna pulled back a few inches. Cassie lifted her head, and as Breanna put her head over the bed rail, getting in close, Cassie coughed then whispered into her ear, "So how'd I do today?"

The lovers laughed and sobbed into the other.

•

"This is Ms. Doucette."

"Jon, Ms. Doucette. From Arizona."

She smiled. "Jon, how are—"

"Forgive my rudeness, Ms. Doucette, but there isn't much time. Cassie is very ill."

At once, Meredith saw only white. "Dear God. What happened?"

"She was in court helping us with a decision on our rent when she had a seizure. Full-blown gran mal."

*No, no, no, no, NO.*

"Is she . . . is she in the hospital?"

"Yes. The seizures are over, at least for now."

She almost collapsed back in her chair. "Tell me, Jon. Everything that happened."

Jon described what he saw. "That's what I know." After a moment, he added, "Oh, that Mr. Giles was there."

"What? He was there in Arizona?" Meredith gripped the phone tightly. "What did he want?"

"He said nothing during the proceedings."

"He's there to hurt her, to intimidate her."

"Well," Jon said, sounding nonchalant for just a moment. "If that's what he wanted, he failed. She seemed surprised by him, but remained calm Even collected. If he was the bogeyman, she wasn't scared."

For the first time in the conversation, Meredith's pulse dropped.

"I want—"

"Also, I must share with you that I think what happened today was not acute."

"Not ac—"

"Chronic."

*What does any of this mean?* Doucette shook her head. At least Cassie was alive. "Thank you, Jon. This is terrible. Let me know."

"Will try to call every few days."

Her anger was up at once. "Don't try. Do it."

"I will."

●

Three days later, Cassie was discharged home. All in CiliCold was there and cried in relief, ignoring the dialysis cannula in her arm and her occasional disorientation.

# THE WHOLE WORLD

Jasper's leg was on fire. *How stupid I was to fly out there*, he thought, half believing that the change in barometric pressure would make his leg better. In fact, it made it worse. The right thigh pulsed white-hot with pain. And even though he had good pulses (or so the doctors told him), his lower right leg was gray red and angry.

But he had to admit, rubbing his leg, that it was all too easy to dispense Arizona justice.

"Trip was good?" Stennis said, walking into his office.

"How do you think?" Giles said, grimacing as another pain wave coursed through him. "Got her done."

"And," Stennis said, "the fruits are already available for the taking."

"What do you mean?" The fire leg was really going now, the fat right thigh trembling.

"In fact, I just heard from IT that there is a serious download now available to us from the CiliCold website."

"What website?" Jasper said, looking up at him.

"Just appeared Tuesday night after the hearing. You must have really put the fear of God into them."

"Giles. Fear of Giles," the attorney said. He turned his laptop around. "Get me there," he commanded.

Stennis showed him how to manipulate his browser.

"Ah, here it is. Why don't you do the honors?"

Giles, his right leg suddenly pain-free, pulled the wheelchair around and pushed it under his desk. He stabbed the Download button. Saw a huge file appear at the bottom of his browser. "Now what?"

"Click 'open in folder.'"

There was the file. It was even titled "CiliCold Findings."

*Those pussies.* "Next?"

"Now right-click on that and extract."

230

Giles did that to see.

*Finally.* Hundreds of documents appeared. Relief poured over him.

"Look at this. Even—my God, video files."

*Triumph at last. Triumph over CiliCold and their daffy president. Triumph over Cassie and now over Meredith. That cunt won't know what hit her.*

Jasper could barely stand, the erection trying to break through his tight suit pants.

"The mother lode!" he cried out.

He clicked on one after another. Word docs. PDF files reeking of math. Graphs in Excel. Video files sho—

He stopped.

"How can I do this?"

"What?" Stennis asked.

"I didn't put a password in."

Stennis just looked at him. "Was that part of the amendment?"

"No, no, no. This is supposed to be confidential.

If I could do it, then . . . Get your son."

"Why? We don't talk much. I don't do well with Nazi wannabes."

Jasper was sweating. "Tell him he gets a thousand dollars if he downloads these files."

Five minutes later, Stennis told Jasper that his son was at a screenshot of the files already displayed on the laptop in front of him.

"This is unprotected. Anybody can get them."

"I just called a number that CiliCold has on their site. The message said that this URL was sent to the *New York Times*, the *Washington Post*, the *Washington Times*, *CNN*, and *Fox News*."

With a giant hand, Jasper swept his desk clear in a rage. Pads, pens, paper holders, laptop, phone all slammed against the wall. "This does me no good if everybody received this."

"Also, NIH, WHO, as well as the health services of the EU, Canada, Iran, China, and Russia. So the recipients were the—"

"The whole world."

Stennis's hands jumped to his ears, too late to stop the effect of Giles's roar.

Then Giles said, "That's all for now, Stennis."

Stennis left, watching Giles reach for the phone.

# MESS OF LIFE

A week later, Olivia cried out, holding Kevin's head between her legs. After a few moments, she exhaled and let him go.

"Marvelous, Kev."

He emerged. "Smells like . . ." He shook his head. "I don't know . . . like victory."

Olivia clapped her hands with delight. "I saw that movie. Robert Duvall."

"Yep."

Kevin lifted himself from between her legs and lay beside her.

"Those SSS lawyers must be con—"

Her phone rang.

"Yes."

"This is Seb Collins."

"Sebastian?"

"One and the same."

"Wonderful to hear from you."

"Ollie, I'd love to catch up with you, but I'm being pushed to clean out some old business."

"Sure."

She listened.

"OK, I'll get back to you."

"Kevin," she said, putting her phone down. "Your tablet. Look for this email."

"Sounds like work."

He sighed, getting up and walking to the table.

He snapped his S6 Tab open. "Got it. From STCollins."

"Does it contain a URL?"

She walked over to be next to him. *Look at us*, she thought. *Both naked standing over a computer screen.*

"Sure does."

"Great, click on it."

Kevin lifted his hands from the keyboard, looking back at her. "What do you mean 'click on it'? Olivia, we don't know where this URL points. This is how viruses get started."

"Kevin, if this is a virus, I'll buy you five new Galaxy tabs. Just please go ahead and open this. It's from someone I know."

"OK, but this one's on you."

He clicked on it, and they found themselves staring at a PDF.

"This is"—he checked the word count—"over fifteen hundred pages long."

"But what is it?"

He navigated the mouse around the screen. "These are SSS documents, all appended together."

"Any other files?"

"What, isn't fifteen hundred pages enough?"

"Just look, silly."

He navigated to the directory. "An ema—"

They read the three-line note and just stared.

"Who is Cristen?" Kevin asked.

●

Five minutes later, as Kevin showered, Olivia, still naked, hung the phone up.

She knew who Cristen was.

And what the email's contents represented.

It had taken a lot of convincing. She had never done anything like this in her life, but this had been a long mean year. Her heart raced.

And finally, after all the long mean years when she had held her tongue, she knew who she was.

In fact, Sebastian almost hung up on her. But she had persuaded him, and the *Times* decided to move away from the story.

And now, she knew what she must do.

After all, she thought, a cocked pistol does you no good if you don't know where to point and when to fire.

Everybody's turn had come and gone. Now, in this mess called life, it was hers. She had the pistol.

*No*, she thought. *I am the pistol.*

She would be used.

And those people would suffer as they had never suffered before.

When Kevin came out in a towel and a smile, she sat him down and explained.

The smile disappeared.

"You mailing it tomorrow?"

"Now."

"I'll go to the PO with you."

"I want to go alone," she said, getting up from the bed. "But I will be right back."

"Well," he said, sighing, looking thoughtful. "At least let me get a picture."

She smiled, sprawling back on the warm sheets. "You wicked man."

# ANTIFA ON THE MARCH

Giles dialed then heard the click.

"Edgar, you and I met a few months ago."

A thick voice, sodden with alcohol, answered, "Wheelchair, right?"

Giles paused, slowly digesting his anger. *This is a tool*, he thought *Use it.*

"That's right. Listen, I just learned of an Antifa plot in Arizona. Government won't move. You and I are patriots. Not like your dad. Can you help your country?" Jasper explained what he wanted.

"Where can I find out about these folks."

Jasper gave him the details, and they both hung up.

Two hours later, Jasper's phone rang.

"Uh, I need some time."

"You also need funding. How about $10K US?"

A pause. Then "Tell me more."

Jasper gave him the details. "This must be deep and dark. I want you to build it special. But—and this is key. You must take them out."

Jasper listened, responding to the questions, which surprised him. Focused and on point.

"For a device like that, I need special parts," Edgar said.

"Come up here and work on it. Parts will come to me, and you'll have space here to put it together. When the time is right. You drive and deliver it."

"When do I get the money?"

"When you leave here with the device."

"Devices. Fair's fair. Will be there in three days."

"Get there tomorrow. Go to BWI. United. There's a first-class ticket in your name. A rental car will be there for you. See you in forty-eight hours. Come back ready to build the things."

"All right then. How will I—"

Jasper hung up. His right leg felt so good it almost glowed.

# WORLD NEEDS A BREAK

"How can I be on the CNews anchor desk and still be getting the 'for shit' stories?" Domino "Dom" DeBecca said, rolling her chair up to the news desk.

"It's an easy story to do," her producer, Ronald, said. "Earpiece set?"

"What do you think," she said, raising her voice while slamming the flat of her hand on the desk. "Jesus." *Still getting the bimbo treatment.*

"Did you read the background material on this?"

"Yes, yes, yes," she said, checking her makeup. "It actually wasn't much."

"That's because nobody really knows what these people are up to."

"OK, OK," she said, getting her bearings in the newsroom. "Let's get on with it."

Red light on.

"We have one of the most interesting stories of the year to report to you," she began with her best anchor smile. "With us today are the members of a company named CiliCold that claim to have discovered a novel way to make vaccines, speeding the process up from months and sometimes years, to simply a matter of days. I have to confess that that is all that I understand about it, but their process of working and then getting their results out are, shall we say, unique."

"Careful," the producer's voice in her ear said.

"Before I ask you to introduce yourselves," Dom said to the televised projections, "is it true that your headquarters are located in a . . . prison?"

"Play it straight," the earpiece said.

"Thank you. I am Dr. DeLeon," one of the heads said on her monitor, "and yes, for the last six months, we have operated out of state prison in Florence, Arizona."

"Are you prisoners there?"

"Hey!" the earpiece screamed. "Cut it out."

She watched the doctor look at her for a moment who then took a deep breath. "Make fun of it all you like. We rented the space in this abandoned prison because it was spacious, safe, secure, and at least until recently, affordable."

Dom watched as the camera pulled back, panning from left to right, revealing a well-lit work area, surrounded by rows of empty cells that receded into blackness.

"Let me now introduce my team," the doctor said. "This is Luiz and Emma, who are our cell scientists and our computational biologist respectively." He pointed to his left. "To the right, we have Rayiko Snow, Breanna Vaughn, Kevin, and Olivia who are our financial, resources, and regulatory team. Cassie Rhodes, our lawyer, is also here today."

Dom noticed that Rhodes was the only one sitting, logging that observation for possible later use.

"Well, Dr. DeLeon, just what does your product do?"

"You said it best earlier, Dom. We make antiviral vaccines within forty-eight hours of receiving the virus." He looked left. "Em, can you add some detail?"

"What we do is look at the molecular structure of the surface of the virus," the tall, short-haired blonde started.

*She looks like she's right out of a Levi's commercial.*

"This is where the antibody must attach, and the fit should be exact, tight, and strong. The mathematics of organic chemistry and physics allows us to compute the exact sequence of amino acids that we need to have in order to get the tightest bond with the virus."

"So," Dom said slowly, "you do with math in days what it has taken biologists to create in months or years?"

"That's a good way to put it," the tall blonde said. "As other scientists look at our work and our computer code, no doubt they will be able to optimize it and do it even faster."

"Does it work in humans?"

"Luiz's in vitro work tells us it should," she said, "but we don't have the resources to do that type of testing."

"Not in jail, anyway."

"Dom!" the earpiece yelled.

"It's not just a question of where we work, Dom," the doctor said. "The collection of chemists, biology engineers, project managers, nurses, and doctors would be overwhelming."

"So you can't prove it works, is that right?" she said.

"Drop the attitu—" earpiece said.

*Dropping the earpiece instead*, she thought, surreptitiously placing it on the desk.

"All we can do is provide the process by which the new antibodies can be produced. We're going to leave it to other scientists who have more resources than we have to chemically produce them and then put this idea to the test."

"Now, Dr. DeLeon, you didn't publish this in a regular journal like most scientists do, correct?"

"That's right. We—"

"Why won't you allow your work to be peer-reviewed?"

She saw Dr. DeLeon tilt his head. "Why, it's being peer-reviewed by the world's audience of immunologists as you and I speak. And they each have all of our worker materials. Research protocols. Preliminary results. Not just a thirty-page summary of our work, such as in peer-reviewed papers. Over a million lines of computer code are now out there. Videos of the execution of our own in vitro testing. Over fifty graphic depictions of the three $F_{ab}$ chains alone. Research to be peer-reviewed doesn't submit that level of detail, Dom. I'm sure you know that."

She shook her head. "Seems odd, but let's move on. What if your idea for vaccine production doesn't work?"

She was astonished that he just shrugged.

"You answered your own question. If it doesn't work, then it doesn't work. But if that's the case, then there certainly is the seed here for somebody to provide the missing code to get it working.

"But—"

She noticed he smiled.

*Arrogant punk.*

"With all of our testing, we think it will. Let's all find out together. We are anxious to know what the world community of scientists has to say."

"You should know, Dr. DeLeon, that there are some eminent virologists who say this will not work. That this is junk science, maybe even fraud," she said, making the statement up, probing for weakness, "and that you are trying to get your career back after charges of intellectual property theft were leveled at you."

"What I've learned in science, ma'am, is that there are two reactions to new ideas. The first reaction to something new is that 'it won't work.'

The next reaction when it's proven to work is 'we knew it would work all along.'"

"And the charges against you? You haven't answered that question."

"Yes, there were charges in which I was accused of scientific misconduct. There was a full investigation. I was completely cleared."

"Well, what reaction have you seen from scientists so far?"

"Stupefaction. But then as people work through the information they've downloaded, they are starting to ask us lots of questions. We now have video calls on a regular basis. In fact, we spoke with a consortium of scientists from the EU and Russia yesterday about some source code details. And there's no need to protect the work since there is no copyright."

"What? You don't intend to patent it?"

"Obviously not. We've given it away."

"So who in fact has it now?"

"Everybody."

Dom was silent.

"Of course," the doctor continued, "we sent it to the National Institutes of Health here in this country, as well as the FDA, but in addition, we sent it to newspapers and international organizations for people to download. Emma's going to remind me that it's also on our website for anybody in your audience to access."

"But you sent it to other countries. Canada. The EU. Iran. Brazil. Russia. China, the World Health Organization."

"Well, if the NIH is too busy or overworked or just not interested, perhaps other countries can make progress on it."

Dom looked down at the piece of paper in front of her. "Interesting that you said 'everyone.' I don't see a drug company on this long list."

*Gotcha.*

Again, she watched the doctor inhale deeply. "Of course, now that this is widely available, the drug companies can easily get to it. All they have to do is go to our website and download it. But we didn't send it specifically to them because they are in the moneymaking business."

"You are not?"

"No."

"Don't you get paid salaries?"

"From donations."

*Liberals,* she hissed to herself.

"So," Dom said an exasperated voice, "why do all this work and give it away?"

"For us, the accomplishment is sufficient. We know what we've done."

Dom exhaled. "I need a more specific answer than that."

"Well then, two reasons," the doctor continued. "Most of my education was in public institutions. Paid for by somebody else. By many of the people who are watching your show, actually. Think of our result as a return on their investment."

She shook her head. "And the second, DeLeon?"

He looked at his team as if getting permission from each of them.

"Do you have answe—"

"This is a gift," he said. "To a world that really needs a break."

"So you are in reality socialist scientists with yet one more idea that you can't prove works."

"Well, one thing is true. We cannot rely on you to tell a straight story about the facts. Thank you for your time, Dom."

She saw the doctor nod to the team. Her mouth dropped as she watched them take their mikes off and walk away.

She cleared her voice and returned to the audience.

"We have to cut for commercial."

•

Red light off.

She saw Ron coming her way. "I had to break through them, Ron. What a load of crap." *I need a cigarette.*

"Nice job, everybody, and I mean everybody, Dom, is calling to get these scientists back on the air again and that you not do the interview."

"What—"

"The only people who want to see you are upstairs. How dare you disgrace this network," he said, standing straight.

"I'll get up to exec lev," she said, waving him away. "I have to finish my segments here first."

He leaned over the desk. "Now, Dom. Upstairs. Cynthia will finish up here."

She looked right at him, heart skipping a beat. "Wha—"

"Better take your things."

She watched him turn and leave.

"Am I being fired?"

"No," the producer said as he turned to face her. "Worse."

# TEN MILLION YEARS

"You've never taken me out in the car before," Cassie said, trying and failing to pull banter into her voice. Her heart hammered fast and furious.

It was six weeks after the CNews interview, and now, the hammer was going to fall.

*On me,* she thought.

"You know, I was told you can't teach lawyers anything," Jon said, looking over at her in the dark and smiling. "Maybe you'll prove me wrong." He moved the Cherokee into the right lane onto 60 east.

"Are you going to fire me?" she blurted out. Couldn't help it. Had to know.

"No, Cassie," he said, still looking at her. "I'm not gonna fire you. I want you to stay here at CiliCold."

*For as long as I can*, she thought.

"When did you decide to release the documents?" How did you know?" she asked, stomach in a new knot.

"I didn't. Kevin brought the idea up to me. Emma was all in."

She nodded. "Emma's a pistol."

"You bet. When her dander's up, she'll let fly."

"Glad she's on our team."

"Anyway, Kevin thought that even if you won the case, SSS would stick it to us, one way or the other."

"They wanted to confine us," she said, looking straight ahead. "To confine you."

"That's what Em saw. So she and Kevin argued for the reverse."

Cassie nodded. "Total release."

"The real trick was getting the word out before the judge signed the order."

"Of course," Cassie said, nodding with a smile. "That way, they can't charge you for violating the judge's order if you released the data before he signed it."

"Yep." He shook his head. "But what I didn't see was that by getting it around the world, the world would be so generous in return. Thousands of dollars a week from organizations. From individuals. We just got $50,000 from the Polish Ministry of Health, for heaven's sake."

She watched him smack his head. "My goodness. We have more money than we've ever had. Soon, we'll have to look for new digs."

"Too bad. I kind of liked working in jail."

They both laughed.

"Enough talk now. Now, let's relax," he said, cracking the back windows. "I want you to enjoy this ride. We don't have to talk through it. Let your guard down and let it inside you."

She was quiet, no longer wondering about this curious man, but watching the undulating brown hills begin a rapid illumination in the predawn light. Cactuses were everywhere as the car climbed the hills into dark mountains that were coming alive with light. She cranked her window, then quickly closed it.

"Still cold out there?"

"Uh-huh."

A few minutes later, they were in Superior.

She saw him flick the blinker on, drifting to the right and into a gas station.

*But the tank is full*, she noticed.

"Be right back," he said, stopping the car and opening his door. "I'll keep the motor going."

She heard him close the door as she looked around. There were twelve pumps, five of them being used. Lots of burly white, black, and Hispanic men stood around, joshing and shoving each other, spilling steaming coffee from overfilled paper cups.

She jumped as the car door opened.

"Here," he said, holding a cup in his left hand, cup in right hand extended to her. "Best hot chocolate in the state."

Smiling, she reached out, but he pulled it back from her. "Be careful, now. I had to double cup them because they're so hot."

"OK."

She took it from him and sat for a minute, holding the cup in front of her face, enjoying the rich brew's aroma.

"How much higher are we going?" she asked.

"Only about ten minu—ow."

She watched him pull the cup from his lips.

"Like you said, hot."

They both laughed, and she watched him as he craned his neck to study the sky through the closed window.

"And we'd better get going if we're going to catch it."

He pulled out and then turned right onto the highway that now climbed to the sky.

They drove in silence. She sipped her cocoa, letting both the sky and Jon into her, the mountains revealing their reds in the glowing presunrise light.

"I didn't get a chance to talk to you in much detail as we prepared for the CNews interview, but I thought you did a great job preparing and being in court."

She looked down, shaking her head.

"You couldn't control what happened, Cassie. You walked into the court, without arrogance, without anger, but controlled and disciplined. For those moments, we all saw the best professional we'd ever see representing us in court."

She noticed that he turned off the highway to the right. "You made us all proud. More than that, Cassie, you elevated us."

She looked at him, eyes wet.

"Don't look at me, girl. Look outside."

She turned just as the land awakened.

Through the gaps in the mountains, not one hundred yards away, the sun's yellow presence streamed through. Shadows appeared and moved. It seemed like the mountains were growing to catch the sun as it climbed off the horizon.

"Come on, Cassie," he said, opening the door. "Let's be part of it."

She opened the door before he finished the sentence then closed it, leaning against it as the sun shone upon her.

"This is for you, Cassie. Think of the sun as waiting for you to finally arrive on this spot to splash the young day's sunlight on you."

*What is he talking about? I mean, really.* She looked at him. "What are—"

"The light now on you was born ten million years ago."

"What?"

He pointed to the sky. "Light born in the sun tries to travel fast as it tried to leave the sun. But the sun's gravity continues to pull it back. That plus the trillions of atomic collisions a second knocking the light particle all around. It took ten million years to shake loose of it all. Then when it finally broke free, it sped 93 million miles in nine minutes just to land on you, and you alone, Cassie. The sun's light was made for you."

She closed her eyes, leaning her head back, letting the light on her face, in her nostrils and hair, mouth and eyes. Consuming her.

"Forgive yourself, Cassie. Of everything. Of anything. The time that guilt has crippled you is now over. Life begins again for you, like there is new light to land on you tomorrow. Every day."

"Yes, for as long as I—"

He put his finger on her lips.

"Hush now. Let it be your special place. You deserve one."

She loved it. Absorbed it.

"So," he said a few minutes later, turning to face her. "How long have you been using?"

# MADGE OBERHOLTZER

With nothing to hide, it spilled out of her. "Just a little, but for years. But how did you know?"

"I had some suspicions, but that's all they were. What did the docs tell you?"

Cassie's heart trip-hammered. *Can I misdirect him? No, we are up here because he cares for me. I won't li—*

"Did you ever hear of Madge Oberholtzer?" Jon asked.

She pushed the hair out of her eyes. "No. A lawyer?"

He smiled. "Nice try. An Indiana schoolteacher." He opened his jacket. "It's warmer now."

"Sunlight matters," she said.

"Let's sit here." He pointed to a large flat rock, bright red with sun. They both sat with their backs to the sunlight, letting it warm them back to front.

"She lived in the early twentieth century. Died in 1925. She was in her twenties, teaching elementary school children when she met a man named Ray Stephenson. Name ring a bell?"

She shook her head.

"Well, he always liked to be called 'Steve.' Anyway, Ray Stephenson was a very rich man, and he fell for Madge. Big-time. Maybe because most women fell all over him and Madge didn't. Anyway, he pursued her. Bought her clothes, even purchased books and learning materials for her students, many of whom were black. Plus, he was very popular in the state as was his organization."

"And that was?"

He looked at her. "The Klan."

"You're kidding. The KKK?"

"Yep. The KKK was a major political force a hundred years ago. They held major rallies and public meetings. They had an influence on many if not most local businesses."

"I remember seeing old videos of the Klan marching down the streets of DC."

"Yep. They were almost everywhere. The Klan leadership encouraged entire families to join them. Women, even children. Special outfits were made for them. And sold to them."

"How could she stand him?"

"Steve used to argue to Madge that the Klan was no longer racist. All behind them. Now, they only hated immigrants, Catholics, and Jews."

"The country was that stupid."

Jon shrugged. "Still can be. Well, over time, she decided to believe him, and her resistance crumbled. His support for her black students touched her. He was uplifting and very sweet to her, sent her all kinds of new learning material for class, gifts for her. The showering of attention was too much."

His voice had changed. Clipped. Sharp.

"You seem both angry and sad at the same time, Jon."

He shook his head, exhaling long and hard.

"One day, Steve explained to Madge that he had to go to Chicago. Business meeting or something. Anyway, he asked Madge to attend, and she agreed. She was so excited when he sent his private car to her parents' home where she lived just to take her to his private rail car."

Warning alarms went off. "I don't want to hear the rest," she said.

"I'll move this along," he said, placing a hand on hers. "After the train pulled out of Indianapolis, she was asked to go to the kitchen. There, she was forced to drink whiskey until she was sick.

"Steve's henchmen half pushed and half carried the screaming Madge to the private car where he was waiting. He banished them from the room, pulled the dress up over her shivering shoulders, threw her on the bed, and raped her repeatedly. These assaults went on for hours as the train worked its way up through northern Indiana to Chicago."

"Jesus," Cassie whispered.

"In Chicago, she begged to be let off the train to go buy some rouge at a drugstore. Instead, she bought mercuric chloride. She drank it then climbed back on the train."

"The thing about this stuff is that it doesn't just make you feel sick. You look sick."

He looked at her. "But you already know that, don't you, Cassie?"

"How did you know?"

"There aren't many cases of mercury poisoning, but my aunt drank some."

"Where is she now?"

"Dead."

Her head was down, but she felt Jon's steady gaze.

"What did they tell you in Casa Grande, Cassie?"

"The same."

He exhaled. Knew it was coming. Feared it.

"Breanna know?"

"After that courtroom episode? Absolutely. Finish up, Jon. What happened?"

She saw Jon in anguish, looking up at the sky like he feared a piece would be torn from him if he did as she asked.

"Once Stephenson saw how ill she looked, he lost interest in her."

"Of course. That was the idea."

"But rather than take her all the way back while she was sick in his car in his train, he had somebody drive her to her home in Indianapolis. They threw her out of the car onto her driveway then took off.

"The family called the doctors at once, who couldn't figure out what happened to her. Not many cases.

"They were especially confused by the lacerations, Cassie, which were everywhere. Neck. Cheeks, abdomen. Breasts, arms, inner thighs. One of the doctors actually suggested that they call a vet. The vet showed up and after an examination told everyone that they were bites, but not animal bites. They were human."

"Human bites." Cassie shuddered. "Ghastly."

"Stephenson fully expected her to die," he continued, "but in fact, she recovered enough to give a statement of what happened to her. It was called a 'deathbed confession.'"

"Cassie," Jon asked in the softest of voices. "How long have you been taking this?"

She sighed. "Years. Circumstances arise with a man that I didn't want to follow through with, and so I would just drink some. And as you say, it makes you look sick, and he would want nothing to do with me and I could leave. I did this many times."

She paused. "Once with Jasper."

Jon inhaled then exhaled rapidly. "So here we are. Yours has been chronic poisoning over the years." He shook his head. "Well beyond the reach of chelating agents."

"It's pretty much digested my liver, kidney, pancreas, and part of my brain. I decided to stop my kidney dialysis."

Jon gave her a hard look then closed his eyes. "Well," he said. "That means, what, ten days?"

"April 4, more or less."

"Monday in, what, two weeks?"

She shivered. "Shouldn't be too bad from what I've heard."

"Not for you, it won't," he said, smiling, "but you'll smell like urine."

"I'm not making any."

"Smell comes from urea in your breath. Through your skin."

He stood, and she stood with him.

"So what's left to do, Cassie Rhodes?"

*No wonder she loves him so*, she thought.

"If you'll have me, I want to work with you all. Plus, Breanna and I are good for each other."

Jon sucked his teeth. "We're glad to have you. One thing though."

He slowly pulled her head to his so they were touching.

Forehead to forehead.

"All that's very good, Cassie, but in the end, you die in your own embrace. Make it count."

She smiled. *You have no idea.*

# A JOB'S A JOB

"Ladies and gentlemen, we are on our final approach for Tucson International Airport. Please stow away all your belongings and place your tray tables and seat backs in their upright and locked positions. Thank you very much and welcome to Tucson, Arizona."

Edgar did as he was told.

He always did as he was told. That's why no lawman never paid him no attention. Even left his piece at home.

*First time to Arizona*, he reflected as he maneuvered through the secure area with his carry-on and then on to Hertz and his rental car.

Wheelchair had arranged the flight to Phoenix, but he'd changed it to Tucson. Phoenix would be too obvious a destination if somebody wanted to connect the dots. Coming into Tucson would not be expected. He could have come into El Paso, but that would have been a longer drive.

He navigated the Forerunner off the airport grounds and found his way to Route 79, the old Arizona state highway. He knew most people driving the Tucson–Phoenix run did I-10. That's what MapQuest said.

What MapQuest didn't say was that the Tucson–Phoenix stretch of I-10 was the most heavily patrolled highway section in the state. Dollars going south. Drugs and guns coming north.

He wanted nothing to do with that, so he drove the bumpy old two-lane highway because it was not well patrolled.

Plus, it went straight into Florence directly.

*Don't pass go. Don't collect $200*, as his dad would say.

He had done this kind of job before. Prodeath abortion groups. Sick collections of niggah activists getting ready to inject another Black Lives Matter "victim" into white America's bloodstream.

Easy targets, worth killin'.

Just like Antifa. Had gotten into scraps with them. That was easy too, though. The thing about them liberals is that they can't fight. They can outthink you to death, but beat up easy in a chain-and-pistol matchup.

But CiliCold? Well, he couldn't figure them.

No manifesto or slogan. A website that was all fake science, but as far as he could see, no threat.

He'd watched the CNews thing. Part of it, leastways.

Men and women. Black, white, Mexican. A real "We Are the World" group.

Made him want to throw up. But kill them? What were they going to do? Murder Aryans with math? Beat us over the head with calculators?

Somethin's missin' for sure.

"Job's a job," he muttered, reaching into his jacket for a cancer stick.

He navigated around the State Road 79 Coolidge- Florence circle and headed into Florence, parking right across the street from the Arizona State Prison.

Perfect.

A crowd of fifteen or so people milled around outside, all hoping to see the digs of their new local celebrities.

And also to drop some dough on them.

All too easy.

Five minutes later, he was through the door with the crowd.

Yep.

It was laid out just the way YouTube said.

Thick gray-green doors revealing an open area cleared of everything resembling a jail.

Nothing but computers and desks. Wheelchair told him that there were some other computers and lab work on the second floor, but he didn't really need to know about that. His idea was to take out the first floor and let the work kind of collapse on itself. He looked around.

*Easy peasy.* He'd build and place two devices, both on the inside wall, facing toward the work area, on the inside wall, next to the door. Paint them so they matched the lousy inside wall color.

The shrapnel bits would be blown at high-speed forty feet to the desk area, shredding anything they hit, be it flesh or computers.

He looked back at the door. He wanted to make sure that it was far enough away from the entryway so that the door was left open for whatever reason. The blast would not have to fight its way through the thick door in order to get to the targets.

*That was the mistake the assassins made in the botched Hitler plot.* A thick table leg blocked the blast of the briefcase bomb. Plotters were hanged from piano wire suspended from meat hooks for their mistake.

Ugh.

He looked around.

Strange. No posters. No weapons. No ammo. No oily smell anywhere. Biological weapon? Where were the protective suits?

Maybe it was somewhere else, but then why bomb here?

*Why not?* He shrugged. Wheelchair would pay, and a job's a job. He finished his walkthrough then headed out to his car and back to Tucson for the long flight back to BWI.

Two weeks to build it. Another two days to plant it. It would be Monday, April 4, 7:00 AM, Arizona time. This would be no problem.

Should be a beaut. Blowing up a prison. Sweet.

# AS IF

Cassie U-turned and headed south, back to Superior and from there to Queen Creek. April 1, but still cool in the morning, she thought.

Coming out of the red mountains into the valley with its cactus, she watched each plant and rock as it flew by, trying to memorize every single one as if.

As if.

She could already tell. She had cut back on water since she hadn't been dialyzed for ten days.

Jon and Breanna knew. The others, if they didn't sense the end, then sensed something strangely like it.

*Come on,* Cassie, she thought, focusing, losing herself in Roberta Flack's "Suzanne." She came up here every other day now, loving to sit with the sun on her face. To empty every thought in her head until there was nothing.

Just the sun and who she was.

As if.

As if nothing mattered.

At first, she had to work at this, this cosmic emptying for fifteen minutes, only to enjoy it for a few seconds before the cacophony of thoughts roared back at her.

Now she could do it for most of the hour she spent each time.

She liked it.

No, she loved it. Needed it.

Well, it was already April. Wouldn't be long now.

# AIM

Edgar arrived in April 1 to place the device. It was a clean shot. The color matched, and he walked in the door, crouching, lifting it out of the bag. He felt in his hands for the adhesive tape that wou—

"And what can I do for you?"

"Dropped my bag here," Edgar said, suddenly nervous. "Waiting here for the fiddy-cent tour."

"Well, you're the first one who showed up for a ride, so let's get started. I'm Jon DeLeon."

"Yes, I heard about you, I mean, saw you on TV."

"Oh that," the scientist said. "None of us really enjoyed it. Anyway, what we do here is . . ."

Edgar listened to Jon talk. Or partway listened. The doctor looked at him as he described CiliCold, guiding him to a whiteboard and a couple of chairs.

The two of them talked for thirty minutes. Edgar was surprised at how easy it was to ask questions.

"Well, I have to go," Edgar said.

"What's your name?"

"Cyrus."

"Great talking to you. Come back anytime."

It wasn't until Edgar was in the car heading back to Tucson when he realized what concerned him so much about the conversation with the doctor.

It was the first conversation he'd ever had with a niggah.

He didn't know what quite to make of that. Then he made up his mind, turning the car around.

# APRIL 4: QUEENS' SACRIFICE

**8:35 AM EDT**
**Jasper Giles's Office**

"Are we all set with the device?"

"Yes, we are," Edgar said, putting his suitcase down, standing across the desk from Jasper.

"What time?"

"It will detonate 10:30 AM Eastern daylight," he said, pulling a chair out.

"Don't bother sitting. You won't be here that long." Jasper checked his iPhone. "I have a meeting at 10:00 AM. Here." Jasper tossed the money on the desk.

"Your fee, plus a little something else."

Edgar shook his head. "Naw, this one's on me."

Wheelchair shrugged. "Anyway, why don't you see your dad. He'll be here any minute now."

"Nope. And for the rest of it, happy to rid the nation of that scum you introduced me to."

Edgar walked out, heading back to the eastern shores and his comrades.

Giles pushed away from the desk, mind focused on the CEO's destruction, maneuvering around the suitcase to get out and down the hall for the meeting of meetings.

•

**9:45 AM EDT**
**Triple S Headquarters, CEO's Office**

"I can't do this."

Triple S's CEO sat at her desk almost in tears. The board's 10:00 AM meeting had one agenda.

It was a menu, she thought, and Meredith Doucette was the main course.

SNW17012 was dead. One additional case of the nerve disease had occurred in an adorable two-year-old Cherokee girl from Oklahoma. Over the heads of advertising, legal, and executive officers, she had pulled the autism drug's plug. And the FDA, disappointment dripping from their emails, went along.

A $855.7 million dollar product right down the drain.

The media had savaged the company and Meredith personally.

"CEO kills blockbuster drug that treats ASD," was one of the kinder headlines.

Meredith shivered.

The board had asked for an investigation, which of course Jasper had been happy to conduct. Personnel, parents, and even the physician researchers savaged her.

"She is an 'anti-CEO.'" one SSS doctor said.

Meredith was not ready for this. And not ready for today's meeting. Her stomach rolled.

*You were wrong. You should have stayed out of it. That way, if the drug was killed, the FDA would bear the burden. You tied yourself to the tracks, and the train is coming.*

*They will eviscerate you.*

She shook.

*You will be a laughingstock. Expect a lawsuit from the shareholders. Life is over for you.*

Meredith's heart pounded hard, and she rested her head on her desk.

She sobbed, sighed, then looked at the clock.

9:50 AM.

*You know, you could resign now. Save yourself the pain, coward. Just call Jan and throw in the towel then leave the building. You never had the heart for this anyway, fool.*

She stood, reaching for the phone. *I've done with—*

The phone rang, its harsh buzzing jolting her like an electric shock.

●

**9:46 AM ET**
**Arizona**

For the third time, Cassie opened her eyes, swung her feet around, and threw up on the floor.

"I'm sorry."

"I should have thought to put a pail by the bed," Breanna said. "Next time."

Cassie lay back on the bed, pale, sweaty, and exhausted.

Yet this morning was strange. No internal struggle. The taste and smell of urea was there, but now distant, like it wasn't her. Same thing with skin color. Kind of like hers, but not hers. And she had no dark thoughts. Like some weighty decision had been made overnight and—

Cassie knew.

"Cassie?"

She looked over at Breanna who stared back then looked away.

Now, Breanna knew too.

"I don't know when," Cassie said, lying back down.

"But real soon?"

"Days?"

"Hours. You remember?"

Breanna, crying now, said, "I'll send the note."

"No," she said, now coughing. "I'll do it, but you be with me."

Breanna brought the laptop to the bed.

"Won't take too long," the attorney said, coughing.

Cassie sat up then opened the mail client, typing carefully but making mistakes. Then slowly, joints pulsating with pain, she attached the document.

She felt Breanna closer now, looking at the screen with her. "That's not to Jon?"

"Nope," she said, sending the email on its way.

●

**9:49 AM EDT**
**Triple S Headquarters**

"Yes?"

"Ms. Doucette," Jan, her administrative assistant, said over the phone. "I wanted to tell you that an email and a package have arrived."

"From whom?"

"No name on the return."

"Well then, just—"

"Both from Arizona. The email's from Ms. Rhodes."

"Bring them to me."

●

To: Meredith Doucette
From: Cassandra Rhodes
Date: April 4, 2017

Dear Meredith,

My time is up. I wanted to share this document that I have authored. It describes my actions as an attorney on behalf of Triple S.

Your heart will break as you read the things that Jasper and I have done on the Company's behalf without your knowledge. Most are not illegal, but most are immoral. Not many care about that, but I know that you do.

As for the rest, I get what you told me. With the help of new friends, I am whole.

Go get 'em.

Cassie.

●

**9:51 AM ET**
**Arizona**

"Who are you writing now?" Breanna asked, rubbing Cassie's back, wanting to hold her, to protect this sweet source of new life for her and her daughters.

"Jon."

> To: Jon DeLeon
> From: Cassandra Rhodes
> Date: April 4, 2017
>
> Jon
>
> It's time. We'll meet you at "CiliCold Prison" at the top of the hour.
>
> Cassie.

●

**9:53 AM EDT**
**Triple S Headquarters**

Meredith reread it again.

Cassie.

She was dying but sent this list of names, dates, activities.

And thumbing through it, rage surged through the CEO as she read what had occurred and was likely still occurring on her own watch. Reading parts over and over, molten anger fused her spirit. Reconnecting it.

Revitalizing her.

Powering her.

She sat still, letting this energy restore her.

Jan poked her head in. "They are waiting for you down the hall, Ms. Doucette."

"Let them. No, Jan. Wait."

She bent over the desk, briefly scripting a note then giving it to the administrative assistant.

Jan, reading it, began to wobble some.

"Jan dear," the CEO said softly, placing a gentle hand on her shoulder, "just type it up for each member, then put them all in a folder and give them to me before I walk in."

Jan left as Meredith turned her attention to the package, opening it.

It simply said, "Something you can use."

She leafed through it then put it down.

*That Olivia is something.*

"Oh, Jan," she called over the intercom, "during the meeting, please scan these pages on my desk and email to me."

She smiled, owning herself again.

"I know I'm asking a lot of you today, dear. This will be over soon."

"As you say, ma'am."

Five minutes later, the CEO, folder in hand, passed Nita's office on the short walk to the Statler boardroom.

"Coming?" Meredith said, poking her head into the CFO's office. She looked at Nita, resplendent as ever. "You're more pregnant and more beautiful every day."

"Thanks, but I'm not invited."

Meredith smiled. "I'm the CEO. You are now."

●

**9:58 AM EDT**
**CiliCold President's Office**
**Arizona**

Jon got the email addressed to him and cried. Grieving over what was coming. What he would lose. What he had to do. Then he called his team. They all agreed to be at the prison by quarter after the hour.

●

**10:05 AM EDT**
**Triple S Headquarters, Boardroom**

"Meredith, we want to make this as easy as possible," Giles started.

*Jasper,* she thought. *Leading the meeting. He loves a spotlight.* The CEO surveyed the room. All board members were there.

"Easy for who?" she asked Jasper, sitting down.

259

"I think you know why we're here," he said, She saw that he kept his eyes on her. A shark scrutinizing his kill. Meredith was surprised at her confidence. *Now that I'm not fighting for my job, I can actually do my job.*

•

**10:10 AM EDT**
**Arizona Florence State Prison**

"They're all outside," Breanna said, as she and Cassie drove up. "Do you really want to go in?"

"Yes," she said then coughed several times. "With your help." *So weak*, she thought. *Just finish the game.*

Olivia rushed up to Cassie to support her. "What are you doing here, sweetheart?"

"Wanted to see my digs once more."

Rayiko, Jon, Luiz, and Emma stood aside as Kevin held the door open, then all followed Cassie to her desk, Sparky bringing up the rear, tail wagging away.

Cassie looked around.

*Last time*, she thought.

•

**10:20 AM EDT**
**Triple S Headquarters, Boardroom**

"We all heard about the debacle with the FDA and the autism drug. Many smart people lay the blame squarely at your feet."

"Blame for what, Denise? For saving the lives of children who would never have come down with Asperger's? I'm happy to take the blame for that," Meredith said, getting seated at the board meeting.

"You know what she means," someone said.

The CEO leaned forward. "I don't know what you or she mean. Why don't you just get it out on the table for once."

"OK," Denise said, leaning forward, jabbing her index finger hard onto the wood. "This was an opportunity for us to recoup the losses of our past drug failures and make money. Finally."

"You're confused about your job," Meredith said, heart pounding.

Stella sat up straight. "I know my job."

"You do not. You simply know how to keep it. You think you're here to care for a moneymaking machine. You are here, Denise, to help preserve people's health."

"Please."

"Say 'please' to children with vitamin D deficiency in Arkansas, legs twisted by rickets, or the poor who are unvaccinated for measles in Missouri, or those struggling to restart their anticancer treatment after killer Louisiana storms have devastated their communities. You want to say 'Please'? Say it to them, dear, but you'd better shout because their deathbeds are a long way away."

"How dare you lay these problems on me and on our company."

"And how dare you not rise to the challenge, Stella," Meredith said, the blood rising hot. "I don't blame you for the inception of these issues. You didn't choose these health battlefields. But like it or not, you are in the fray now. And you choose not to fight when you have the financial weapons in your hands. The extent that you don't stand and push these problems back is the degree to which you are responsible for these health debacles."

"Meredith," someone else said, "we are here to make money for our shareholders."

"Above all else?"

"And for our big investors, the banks," someone interjected.

"They can make money coincident with our goals. Our mission to protect and preserve predominates."

"I am an investor, and I disagree," Fields said, raising his voice.

"Then sell your shares back to me."

Silence.

"You seem to think our highest goal is shoveling money to shareholders. I think it's treating customers in accordance with their high value."

"We all want to do that."

"No, you don't."

There were several gasps.

"Sure, you all say that when caught in the bright glare of the public light, but when that light is off, we fall back to a shockingly low standard. Once we reject the value of people, we disconnect ourselves from the best that our community, our civilization, offers."

"I don't need to hear this," Cowars said, standing.

"My experience," the CEO said, rising to stand in front of her, "is that people who cannot bear to hear this are precisely the ones who need to."

"Are you blocking me?"

Meredith smiled. "Only if I have to." She pointed to the chair. "Please be seated."

"So, ladies and gentlemen," the CEO said, watching Denise reseat herself, "maybe you should read the SSS mission statement because that is now our North Star."

"Meredith," Scott said in a soft voice, "you talk about weapons. Wasn't our antiautism drug one of those weapons? And you yourself pulled it."

The CEO sat back, nodding. "SNW17012 had the promise of being that drug, but it just was too dangerous a drug. I am glad that I killed it based on the latest data."

"But why didn't you leave the decision to the FDA? They may have said yes."

Meredith pursed her lips for several moments. Then she said, "That is what I was afraid of."

"What?"

"Those people sometimes approve drugs that they shouldn't. They can be weak, and I wanted a safe drug. This wasn't it."

"Enough," Jasper said, waving his hand. "Please, let's move on. Here's a letter"—he pulled a single sheet out of a manila folder—"that the board would like you to sign."

"Belay that," she said, pushing the letter away.

Jasper looked stunned.

*For a change*, she thought.

"I need you all to sign these." The CEO stood and walked around the table, handing the letters out.

"I'm flabbergasted."

"Well, fortunately, Denise, since you won't be here, you need not be upset for too much longer."

"You can't force us to resign."

"No, but I can make life hell for you," Meredith said, lowering her voice.

"We can do that to you as well."

She shrugged, sitting back down. "Please proceed. I'm used to it."

"This is a good company you are ruining," Jasper said.

She looked around the table then in a loud voice said, "Then God damn good companies."

"You shouldn't be CEO," Jasper, shaking with rage, struggled to stand and said.

"And you were born to be slaughtered."

•

**10:29 AM EDT**
**Florence State Prison, Arizona**

"This place saved me."

"You saved yourself," Luiz said, placing a hand on Cassie's yellow arm.

"And you saved us," Jon said. "The best part of you stays with us. We will grieve over you, talk about you, absorb you, letting the Cassie we love burrow in deep."

"It's time," she said, coughing.

They helped her up as she walked slowly to the door at 10:30 EDT.

Luiz turned to Kevin. "You know, we should rename thi—"

•

Some said the explosion could be heard a half mile away. Shrapnel, on its hard, blind flight, slammed into everything in its path. Shredding computers and printers, ramming through wall dividers, tearing into people. All those within a hundred feet, stunned by the blast wave, never felt the pain of thousands of sharp metal bits that lacerated flesh, eviscerating livers and lungs, brain and bone.

It was over in two seconds.

# EPILOGUE

## *"City of New Orleans"*

**11:35 EDT**
**Ten minutes out of Superior, Arizona**

By the time the two-car caravan worked its way up to Superior and then to the sun crevasse, Cassie was barely awake, leaning back against Breanna, both of her lover's arms swaddling her. Sparky left Emma to sit in Cassie's lap, hand licking and tail wagging away.

Cassie listened to the chatter, trying to laugh at the banter that surrounded them.

The fun they'd had with each other. The surprise that they'd sprung on Jon at Perkins, way back in Indiana. The whopper they'd given Triple S. CNews. The ti—

"We're here now, Cassie."

They turned right, onto the red rock.

*My spot.*

"How do you want to do this?" Kevin asked.

"I've never died before," Cassie said, coughing. "Just put me on the hood of the car."

Jon and Kevin hoisted Cassie up, gently turning her so that her legs stretched out on the warm hood, her back resting on the windshield. There she lay under a blanket that Emma brought, her face to the sun.

"I adore you," Olivia said. Kevin, squeezing both hers and Cassie's arms, cried. That was the last thing the CiliCold attorney ever saw, her eyes now finished for good. She nodded and squeezed back with a weak hand.

She heard Jon say, "It was my honor to work with you."

She felt the car rock, and then someone nestled in close.

Breanna.

"I love you so," she whispered.

Cassie tried to say, "Back at you," but her lips wouldn't move.

Then she heard Breanna, now sounding distant, clear her throat and, in perfect pitch, sing.

*Good morning America. How are you?*

Cassie smiled as the rest took up the refrain.

*Don't you know me? I'm your favorite son.*
*I'm the train they call the City of New Orleans.*
*And I'll have gone five hundred miles before the day is done.*

The CiliCold family continued, lifting Cassie's favorite song up as a warm flush surrounded and suffused her, the sun outside, life ending inside.

Disconnection from all she knew.

Mouth open, she leaned her head back.

Then before the good death, one final pure thought.

*I am alive and finally, I belon—*

In 2023, the finale . . .

# *Catching Cold Volume 3: Judgment*

Printed in the United States
by Baker & Taylor Publisher Services